Praise for
Death on a Casual Friday

"[Scotia MacKinnon] is the most believable new private eye in a half dozen years. . . . The action unfolds with wit, grace, and tension, and the climax . . . is gripping. I have a hunch that when Best First Novel Edgartime rolls around, Sharon Duncan will be at the head of the line."—Joe Gores, author of The DKA File novels and TV scriptwriter for *Columbo, Kojak,* and *Magnum P.I.*

"Duncan has fashioned the appealing and, at times, prickly Scotia into a realistic character, fully capable of supporting a new mystery series."—*South Florida Sun-Sentinel*

"Fans of female P.I.s are going to cheer the arrival of Scotia MacKinnon. Appealing and intelligent, she's a welcome addition to the ranks."—*Romantic Times*

"[Duncan] has hit a level that it takes some authors many books to achieve."—*Mystery News*

"You'll love this snappy mystery debut!"—Dorothy Cannell, author of the Ellie Haskell mystery series.

"Sharon Duncan makes her debut with an intricate and interesting novel."—BookBrowser

"A masterful debut by Sharon Duncan. Scotia MacKinnon is a strong, believable, tenacious, and lovable character who will sail into readers' hearts."—*I Love a Mystery*

Other Books in the Scotia MacKinnon Mystery series

Death on a Casual Friday

A DEEP BLUE FAREWELL

A SCOTIA MACKINNON MYSTERY

SHARON DUNCAN

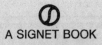

A SIGNET BOOK

SIGNET
Published by New American Library, a division of
Penguin Putnam Inc., 375 Hudson Street,
New York, New York 10014, U.S.A.
Penguin Books Ltd, 80 Strand,
London WC2R 0RL, England
Penguin Books Australia Ltd, Ringwood,
Victoria, Australia
Penguin Books Canada Ltd, 10 Alcorn Avenue,
Toronto, Ontario, Canada M4V 3B2
Penguin Books (N.Z.) Ltd, 182–190 Wairau Road,
Auckland 10, New Zealand

Penguin Books Ltd, Registered Offices:
Harmondsworth, Middlesex, England

First published by Signet, an imprint of New American Library,
a division of Penguin Putnam Inc.

First Printing, August 2002
10 9 8 7 6 5 4 3 2 1

REGISTERED TRADEMARK—MARCA REGISTRADA

Printed in the United States of America

PUBLISHER'S NOTE
This is a work of fiction. Names, characters, places, and incidents either
are the product of the author's imagination or are used fictitiously,
and any resemblance to actual persons, living or dead, business
establishments, events, or locales is entirely coincidental.

WITH SINCERE APPRECIATION TO . . .

My arbiters, experts, and critical readers: Guy Bentley, Trish Birdsell-Smith, Helen Jean Bowie, Bill Crago, Bill Cumming, Sabrina Duncan, Marion Duncan, Martin Garren, Jr., Gerri Jones, Michelle Kirsch, Ted Mattson, Mona Meeker, Steve Percer, B. Scott Sallay, Sharon Stuckey, Meridee Talbott, Louise Wells, Rudy and Bill Weissinger, Chris and Jon Zerby, and the staff of the Friday Harbor Branch of the San Juan County Library.

To Meg Ruley and Annelise Robey at the Jane Rotrosen Agency.

And to my editor, Ellen Edwards, and her assistant, Alexis Adams.

PART 1

All nature is but art, unknown to thee;
All chance, direction which thou canst
not see.

—Alexander Pope

1

The First Tuesday in May

The Second Law of Thermodynamics is that everything tends toward disorder, and chaos theorists have suggested that the flap of a butterfly's wings in Brazil might precipitate a tornado in Texas.

This may be so.

With the clarity of hindsight, I admit that the strength of the brandy served in Henley's Bar on Kodiak Island may have precipitated the recent tragic disappearance of Tina Breckenridge in the San Juan Archipelago of Washington State two decades ago.

It's not impossible.

Twenty years in law enforcement and private investigation have convinced me that life is nothing if not disorderly and chaotic.

My name is Scotia MacKinnon. I'm a private investigator in the small town of Friday Harbor on San Juan Island. Chaos theory was not foremost on my mind the first Tuesday in May as I trudged down the second-floor corridor of the old brick county courthouse a little after 9:00 A.M. I was, in fact, attempting to ignore the acrimonious complaints my body was registering over the twenty-six asanas I had just subjected it to in my Bikram yoga class.

I was also dwelling on the abrupt ending to the bucolic sailing weekend I'd spent with my significant other, Seattle maritime attorney Nicholas Anastazi. It was a weekend that had been rudely interrupted by a hysterical plea from Nick's ex-wife, who had been arrested on a DUI charge. Just as I was replaying Nick's hasty departure by float plane—leaving me to sail *DragonSpray* from Montague Harbor back to Friday Harbor in the wind and pouring rain—I collided with a body that came hurtling backward out of the county commissioners' office.

"This island is not a harlot! And it's bloody well time you pimps stopped trying to sell it to the highest bidder! Over my dead body are a bunch of jerks in Gore-Tex jumpsuits going to take over American Camp. There are eaglets in the nests and newborn kit foxes on the prairie. Are you all a bunch of *dunderheads*?"

It was the very angry figure of Abigail Leedle, her tall, sinewy body clad in faded blue denim overalls and a brown barn jacket, a thick plait of white hair hanging down her back. Abigail is a retired teacher and a wildlife photographer, an octogenarian who has spent her life among these rocky, forested islands. I clutched at the wall for support, regained my balance, and recovered my worn leather portfolio from the floor. Abigail slung a faded red rucksack over one sloping shoulder.

"Sorry, Scotia. I didn't mean to knock you over." She nodded at me with narrowed blue eyes.

"Not a problem, Abby."

"Mrs. Leedle I'm really sorry. I just can't discuss the matter with you." The tall, thin commissioner from Orcas Island stepped into the hallway. "But please do not get upset. They've promised not to disturb the foxes or the eagles."

"I don't give a rat's toenail what they've promised. What about the Indian paintbrush and the Nootka roses?" Abby stalked down the hall toward the stairway. "I'll see you in court, young man," she threw over her shoulder. "Your daddy would roll in his grave if he knew what you've agreed to." She shook her head in disgust, her sandals slapped along the corridor, and she disappeared down the wide stairway.

I made my way past a woman in a red suit and a tall, bearded man in a black leather jacket outside the county clerk's office, and reflected that Abby wasn't alone in her outrage. The commissioners' decision to allow On the Edge, a major manufacturer of upscale outdoor wear, to do a catalog photo shoot on the pristine prairies of the island's national historic park was not a popular one. Last week's Letters to the Editor in the three island weeklies bore vociferous testimony to the general belief that the decision was a capitulation to the tourism interests. I nodded to the woman in the red suit, a Friday Harbor attorney I had done an investigation for a few months ago. I'd heard she was representing On the Edge. The tall man with her moved away from the wall and extended a hand.

"Ms. MacKinnon? I'm M. J. Carlyle. We've never met. I need to talk to you as soon as possible. It's about my sister, Tina Breckenridge. Would it be possible for me to come by your office this morning?"

I returned his handshake. Tina Breckenridge was a local islander who had disappeared from her sailboat recently. No body had been found, and a memorial service had been held yesterday. I took in Carlyle's lightly tanned face and windblown hair, the thick, creamy turtleneck sweater under the elegant leather jacket. Not exactly local attire, even if he was wearing wrinkled and less-than-clean blue jeans. I mentally reviewed my morning's obligations, which included my least favorite task of report writing, followed by lunch with a friend. I was about to wind up two investigations, and no new clients were hovering on the horizon.

"I'll be back in the office by ten, if you'd like to come by. I'm upstairs in the Olde Gazette Building."

"Yes, I know," he said. "I'll see you at ten." He returned to the attorney in the red suit. I made my way to the prosecuting attorney's office, handed in my surveillance report on a child custody case. Back downstairs at the licensing office, I wrote out a check and stood in line to get the renewal license tags for *DragonSpray*, the thirty-eight-foot sloop-rigged sailboat that is my home.

Ten minutes later, the collar of my fleece jacket turned up against the cold wind blowing up off the harbor, I scurried across the courthouse parking lot. Large and ominous gray clouds scudded overhead. It was a day halfway between winter and spring. Rain was predicted for tonight. I wondered why On the Edge hadn't waited until summer for the photo shoot. I also wondered how I could help M. J. Carlyle. From what I'd read in the newspapers, Tina Breckenridge had drowned.

I have a small second-story office in the historic, brown-shingled Olde Gazette Building on Guard Street, where I do mostly routine investigations for lawyers and insurance companies. The first floor of the building is occupied by a naturopathic physician from Orcas Island and by Zelda Jones, who runs a computer graphics and consulting firm called New Millennium Communications. Zelda provides me with computer assistance in connection with my investigations, and—like many islanders who work several part-time jobs to keep bread on the table—she's recently added events arranging to her entrepreneurial endeavors.

There was a crackling fire in the tiny woodstove at New Millennium, and I was greeted by the scent of fresh coffee and an operatic aria—Puccini, I think— neither of which was unusual. M. J. Carlyle was already lounging in the upholstered chair beside Zelda's scarred walnut desk. Which was also not an unusual phenomenon. In the years that I've had an office in the building, a number of men have spent time lounging beside her desk, some handsomer than others, some more smitten than others by the pretty, zany, and unpredictable young woman whose antics border on the eccentric. Zelda was in Asian garb today: gold-and-red-embroidered Mandarin jacket, black pajama pants, red stockings, and black Mary Janes. The hair color du jour was Old Cherrywood, her hairstyle a neat bun punctuated with two black-lacquered chopsticks. I moved over to the coffee machine, noticing that the red fleece-covered futon in the corner was unoccupied. I wondered what had happened to Dakota, Zelda's black Labrador.

"Edie wants to do a crew party on Saturday," Carlyle was saying. "I know she needs help." He put his coffee cup down, reached for a Post-it pad on Zelda's desk, and scribbled a number. "Call her. She likes to do exotic parties."

I filled a yellow cup that said IF IT HAS A TRUCK AND TESTICLES, DON'T TRUST IT and moved over to Zelda's desk. It sounded like the man in the black leather jacket was two clients in one. Carlyle unfolded his six-foot-something frame from the chair and smiled at me. The smile was warm and full of charm—he looked astonishingly like a model in a recent Got Milk? ad, sans the moustache. But the face looked tired, and deep lines bracketed his mouth.

He followed me up the narrow stairs and stood while I unlocked the door that said S. J. MACKINNON INVESTIGATIONS AND RESEARCH. I switched on the overhead light, draped my jacket on the coatrack, and motioned him to one of the white wicker chairs in front of my desk. The warmth from the small radiator provided a pleasant counterpoint to the wind-tossed maple tree outside the old casement window.

Carlyle declined my offer to hang up his jacket, set his attaché case down beside his right leg, and glanced around. My office is modest in the extreme. I've never replaced the old oak desk abandoned by the last tenant, and neither the apricot-colored Art Deco lamp nor the wicker chairs would ever make their way onto the pages of *Architectural Digest*. My only floor covering is a multicolored braided rug over the old plank floor. I was chagrined to see that the leaves of the tall ficus in the corner were turning yellow. When plants do that I can never figure out if it's because of too much water or not enough water. I stole a glance at my new client's leather jacket and wished I'd worn something a little more classy than a dark green sweater over blue jeans.

I reached for a yellow lined pad and pen. "What can I do for you, Mr. Carlyle?"

"Call me M.J., please. I grew up here. It makes me feel old to be called Mister." The smile disappeared from his handsome face, and he took a deep breath. "You probably know I'm with the crew from On the Edge. We're shooting out at American Camp. But the matter I wanted to see you about is my sister. I want you to find out why she disappeared."

"I thought she had an accident with her sailboat." I opened the bottom desk drawer and removed my tape recorder. "I'd like to record our conversation."

"Sure." He reached for his attaché case, extracted two pieces of paper. He handed one of them to me, a newspaper clipping from last week's *Friday Gazette*. "It was no accident. Never mind what the official record says!"

I scanned the article, remembering that there had been an extensive air and sea search involving not only the local sheriff's department but also U.S. and Canadian Coast Guard cutters and helicopters.

Sea Search for Missing Friday Harbor Woman Abandoned

San Juan County Sheriff Nigel Bishop announced today he is abandoning the search for

Tina Breckenridge of Friday Harbor, whose thirty-eight-foot sailboat, Alcyone, *was found abandoned near Sucia Island on April 20 by a commercial fisherman.*

Tina was raised on San Juan Island and moved with her parents to the Ballard area of Seattle when she was ten. She attended Shoreline Community College and worked as a boatbuilder in Ballard and as a deckhand on crab boats in Alaska. At the time of her disappearance, she was the owner of the Roche Harbor–based Pleiades Sailing School for Women.

In addition to her husband, Paul Breckenridge, Tina is survived by her son, Stephan, of Friday Harbor; a brother, Michael James Carlyle, of Seattle; and an aunt, Patsy Malone of Seattle. A memorial service will be held at the Congregational Church in Friday Harbor on Monday, April 30.

"Why do you think it wasn't an accident?" I asked.

"Because she knew boats inside and out. We both grew up on a sailboat. She's built boats, she's raced boats, and she did the single-handed Trans-Pac twice. There wasn't even a storm the night she disappeared."

"She could have had an accident," I said. "She could have slipped and hit her head and was unconscious when she went overboard. Even if she was conscious, she would have drowned very quickly in these waters."

"Yeah, forty-six degrees or something like that. But it still doesn't compute. Tina always wore a life jacket and made her crew do the same. She was a complete nag about it."

"If she didn't fall overboard, what do you think happened to her?"

By way of reply, he handed me another piece of paper. It was an E-mail message from pleiades@bluewater.net to carlyle@ontheedge.com dated April

18, two days before the *Alcyone* had been found drifting near Sucia.

Big Brother: Could we get together when you come up for the hearing? My little problem has become a big problem. Love, T.

"Do you know what she meant by her 'little problem'?"

"When I was up here in January, she was depressed. She said it was stuff with Stephan. That they were seeing a counselor and she'd work it out."

I glanced at the *Gazette* article. "Stephan is her son."

"He's fifteen, a freshman. He started getting into trouble last year." He frowned. "The truth is, I was so preoccupied with my personal problems and the politics of getting our permit for the shoot here, I didn't push to find out what was going on."

"You didn't talk to her after you got the e-mail?"

"No," he said ruefully. "I got here on Sunday, after they found the boat."

"Where were Stephan and"—I consulted the newspaper article again—"Paul, Tina's husband, when she disappeared?"

"Stephan was staying with a friend, and Paul was over in Sedro Wooley with his mother. She's in bad health. He was in the process of moving her over here."

"To live with them?" Tina wouldn't be the first wife to have bailed out when her mother-in-law moved in.

"That's what he intended, but after Tina disappeared, he decided it would have to be to the new assisted-living center."

"Did Tina and your brother-in-law have any marital problems?"

"Not that they ever shared with me." He hesitated. "Paul's a fisherman. He's not the most communicative guy in the world. And very hardheaded about a lot of things. He's usually gone four or five months a year up in Alaska." He hesitated. "Tina did say she was frustrated and burned out from trying to be both mother and father to a teenager."

I could relate to Tina's burnout. I'd struggled through two intervals of single parenting: for three years after Melissa's father decamped when she was four until I married Pete Santana, a fellow cop, and another four years after Pete was killed until I married Albert.

"The *Gazette* article says your sister fished in Alaska. Was that on Paul's boat?"

"No. Tina and I went to school with Paul here before our parents moved to Seattle. When Tina was twenty-two, she and a friend went off to Alaska to look for jobs on a crab boat. Just before they spent their last five dollars, they ran into Paul. He helped them get jobs on a crab boat out of Dutch Harbor. Up in the Aleutians. Her friend did the cooking, Tina worked the deck. In the Bering Sea, in the winter." He shuddered. "She was out of her frigging mind. But the king crab market was exploding and she made a lot of money. So did Paul."

Crab fishing off the coast of Alaska—either in the Gulf of Alaska or in the Bering Sea—is easily one of the most dangerous occupations on the planet. Between 1976 and 1984, for reasons still unidentified, the king crab population was prolific. Last January I had accepted the assignment of tracking down a divorced father who was five years in arrears on child support. My search led me first to the port of Dutch Harbor in the Aleutian Islands and then to Kodiak on Kodiak Island. It was in Kodiak, at Solly's Bar, that I'd finally found my quarry. And learned that in the bonanza days of the seventies and eighties a berth as a crewman had been worth a thousand dollars a week, and a good skipper of a high-line crab boat could easily have made a million dollars a season. But I'd heard of only two other women with the courage and strength to manhandle a crab pot that weighed seven hundred and fifty pounds—when it's empty.

"When did Tina and Paul get married?"

"Right after Tina's first year in Alaska."

"Does Paul have a crab fishing boat?"

He shook his head. "No. The one Tina worked on belonged to a guy from Seattle. After the crab fishery diminished back in the eighties, Paul bought his own boat and switched to gillnetting. Salmon and cod out of Bristol Bay."

"Sounds like Tina's made of really tough stuff."

"She is. That's why I don't buy it that she fell overboard."

I had to agree with him. Any woman who could survive the brutal cold and forty-hour, around-the-clock shifts on an ice-covered deck of a king crab boat in the Bering Sea probably hadn't come to grief on the inland waters of the Strait of Georgia.

"Your sister is missing, M.J. When an adult goes missing and there's no evidence of foul play, that person is usually not around because he or she made the decision not to be around. If your sister didn't fall overboard or have a boating accident, then either she made a conscious decision to leave Friday Harbor and go elsewhere or she's been the victim of foul play."

"She would never just go off and leave Stephan. She adores him."

"So that leaves foul play."

"Yeah," he said slowly, sighing. "That's the conclusion I've come to. And it makes me sick."

"Aside from her last e-mail, did Tina ever mention any trouble with anyone on the island?"

He shook his head.

"Any enemies that you know of?"

"Like *who*? This is San Juan Island, not New York City. My God, all she did was take care of Paul and Stephan and do her gardening and teach sailing. Who would be her enemy?"

It was true that my question would have been more appropriate in an urban environment. On San Juan Island, an "enemy" was likely to be a neighbor whose horses annoyed your cattle or who was jealous that your homemade apricot chutney got a bigger prize than hers did at the county fair. Not exactly motives for homicide.

"What other family do you and Tina have? Any more brothers and sisters?"

"There's just the two of us. My mother died two years ago. My father, well . . . I'm not sure."

I looked at him questioningly.

"My parents got divorced," he said softly. "That's why Tina and I and my mother moved down to Seattle. A while later our father . . . just disappeared. As far as I know, we never heard from him again."

"And Tina never kept in touch with him?"

"I think she hated him. She never forgave him for going away."

"Aunts, uncles, cousins?"

"Just Aunt Patsy, my mother's sister. She never married. She lives in Seattle. I saw her at the memorial service. She was very upset."

"Best friends?"

He shrugged. "I don't know."

"I assume Tina had a car. Where was it found?"

"At Roche Harbor. Paul said it was in the marina parking lot. The sheriff went over it. It's out at his place now."

"What about a purse or any personal effects? Anything missing?"

"I don't know. Maybe Paul has them."

"What exactly do you want me to do for you?"

"Nobody seems to know what Tina did or where she was the night before the boat was found off Sucia. I met a friend of yours at the memorial service. Jared Saperstein. He said you might be able to help find out what happened to her. Will you?"

Jared Saperstein was a retired international free-lance journalist, now the editor and publisher of the *Friday Gazette* and one of my best friends on the island.

I hesitated and glanced at the newspaper article. "The sheriff may be right, you know. Your sister could have fallen overboard and drowned. I'll see what I can find out, but you may be spending money for nothing."

"It's okay. I need to know what happened." Carlyle pulled a checkbook and what looked like an address book out of the attaché case. He wrote out a check and handed it to me. "Your assistant told me what your fee is. This is a retainer."

The check was for five thousand dollars, written on an account at a Seattle bank. I folded it, put it in the top desk drawer, and pulled out a copy of my Contract for Investigative Services form. Carlyle scanned it, signed it, and returned it to me. I handed him my business card.

"Does Paul know you were going to talk to me?"

"I told him last night. He wasn't very happy about it, but he said you could call him."

"Do you happen to know Tina's Social Security number?"

"Actually, I do." He leafed through the address book and supplied it.

"Her address and date of birth?"

"November 8, 1967. Their address is 189 Hyacinth Lane."

"Was there an insurance policy or a will?"

"Paul says no."

"Did Tina have any employees or partners in the sailing school?"

"One employee, a woman instructor. Her name is Katy Quince. I think she lives out near Roche Harbor with her husband. She's in the phone book."

"A canvas maker?" A woman named Quince had

made a new mainsail cover for *DragonSpray* a few years ago.

"I think so."

"Where can I reach you?"

"I'm at the Topsail Inn." He pulled a business card from the pocket of the leather jacket, wrote a number on it. "My cell phone. Call me anytime if you have anything." He stood up. "Tina's all the family I've got left. To be honest, I feel guilty. Like I was just too busy to listen to her."

He picked up the attaché case, shook my hand, and left.

2

I stared at the closed door, thinking about Tina Breckenridge. Remembering the icy winds and dark, soul-searing winter loneliness of the port of Kodiak. Had she survived fifty-knot winds and driving sleet in the Bering Sea only to perish in the far more benign waters of President's Channel or the Strait of Georgia?

I transcribed the high points of my audiotaped conversation with Carlyle and reread the two sheets of paper he'd left on my desk, pondering the assignment I had accepted: find out what happened to Tina Breckenridge, sister of M.J., wife of Paul, mother of Stephan. Missing since April 19 or 20, presumed drowned.

Like most private investigators, I don't usually spend my professional hours in pursuit of serial murderers, adulterous husbands, or kidnap victims. With the exception of the Montenegro case last fall, my time is ordinarily taken up with small, routine research tasks for attorneys—numerous insurance claims, occasional contentious child custody cases and personal injury matters, process serving. And, more recently, background checks on suitors of single women, particularly those met on the Internet.

If Tina Breckenridge had been a man, her Alaska fishing experience to the contrary, falling overboard would not have been outside the realm of possibility. Many a sailing man has gotten up in the night to answer the call of nature, not bothered to put on a life vest, and been found drowned with his zipper down. Few men, single-handers included, will don a harness or life vest unless they're offshore. But Tina Breckenridge was not a man. She was a wife and mother and now she was gone.

Disappeared.

Contrary to popular belief, most adults who disappear are not kidnapped or murdered. They disappear because they want to escape some unpleasant reality: financial problems, legal problems, psychological problems, business failure, incompatibility with a mate, unrequited love. Adults who disappear involuntarily—victims of a kidnapping—are rare in the United States.

I pulled a slightly used manila file folder from the box in the credenza behind my desk, wrote "Breckenridge" on a new file label, and placed the news clipping, the E-mail message, and my notes inside. I would have Zelda immediately initiate a background search through DataTech. DataTech is, in a manner of speaking, a Web detective agency that I resort to whenever Zelda lacks the time or the inclination to do my background searches or when we have very little in the way of information to start with, such as a Social Security number or date of birth. Between Zelda and Data-Tech, I've been able to uncover the innermost details of just about anybody. Details like who they called on the phone, how much money they kept in a checking or asset account, who they had been married to or lived with and for how long. And much, much more that's available to the right professional for just a few taps on a keyboard.

I found a listing for Paul Breckenridge in the San Juan Islands phone directory. An automated voice told me Paul and Stephan were not available and invited me to leave a message, which I did. I also called

Katy Quince, Tina's sailing instructor, and left a message for her as well. I wrote the personal information Carlyle had provided on a sheet of yellow lined paper, filed the Breckenridge folder in my desk drawer, and headed downstairs for a coffee refill and my mail.

Zelda was on the phone. My mail cubby yielded up one manila envelope, four catalogs, and three pink message slips.

"What a hunk, eh, boss?"

I looked up from my mail. I hadn't the slightest doubt who she was referring to.

"M. J. Carlyle?"

"Yes, indeedy. You ever see such eyes? The color of warm molasses. Not to mention that bod." She shivered. "Gave me goose bumps. What did he want?"

I stared at the side of her face. "What do you mean, what did he want? You ever hear the term 'privileged conversation'?"

She laughed. "Boss, probably no less than five people saw the creative director of On the Edge come through that front door, and at least ten people at lunch will ask me what he was here for. I'll bet my last birth control pill Mr. Gorgeous doesn't believe his sister fell overboard any more than half the town does."

I knew "half the town" referred to the lunch regulars at George's Tavern. "What does half the town think happened to Tina?" I asked, opening the manila envelope and pulling out a legal document relating to Harrison Petrovsky, a missing heir I'd been unsuccessfully attempting to locate for over a year. I hoped I'd have better luck with Tina Breckenridge.

Zelda twisted a long lock of hair that had escaped from her chignon. "That she finally had it with being a fishing widow and took off."

"And the other half of the town?"

"The jury is still out, but rumor has it that after her son started getting into trouble, Tina started taking antidepressants. Maybe she did something stupid and fell overboard."

"What kind of trouble did her son get into?"

"Vandalism, minor in possession. The usual Friday Harbor stuff."

"Minor in possession of what?"

"Marijuana. Probably B. C. Bud."

B. C. Bud is a very high-priced marijuana grown in British Columbia. It's been described in virtually every U.S. periodical from the *Wall Street Journal* to *High Times*. According to my daughter, Melissa, a political science major at St. Mary's College in California, British Columbia leads the Western world in marijuana use. And Vancouver, Canada's third-largest city, is now world-renowned for its marijuana production, much of it accomplished hydroponically. That is, the plants are grown in water instead of soil, which facilitates the indoor operations preferred by illicit growers.

There are few legal repercussions for possession of less than twenty plants in Canada, and B. C. Bud is flooding into Washington State in every imaginable conveyance—tossed across the border in footballs, floated down the Strait of Georgia in hollow logs guided by global positioning satellite, toted across the Canadian border at Blaine on foot in hockey bags. Regardless of how it arrives, it has become the scourge of U.S. Customs officials.

"Did you know Tina?" I asked.

"No, but Lily MacGregor, our new Corona, was her best friend. You know, she owns the Secret Garden out on Schoolhouse Road."

The Coronas are a group of island women of intense feminist and environmentalist persuasions. Zelda and Abigail Leedle were the founding members.

"What does the Lily MacGregor theory say about Tina's disappearance?" I asked.

"Lily is psychic. She says Tina's essence is still here."

While I do not disparage psychic phenomena, I'm more of a "just the facts, ma'am" sort of investigator. I wondered if "Tina's essence" was synonymous with "Tina's body."

"I need a background check ASAP." I handed her the paper with Tina's Social Security number, date of birth, and address.

"I'll do it right now, before I get involved with my new celebrity client." She waved the business card M.J. had given her. "A Saturday night crew party for *On the Edge*." She grinned, twirled back to face her computer, clicked on an icon on the bottom of her screen. Almost immediately DataTech's Web site appeared.

I stuffed the Petrovsky documents back into the manila envelope, returned to my office, and turned my attention to the three telephone messages: one from Nick saying he would call back—hopefully to report that his ex had left town. One from my bohemian mother, Jewel Moon, who lives down in Mendocino on the California coast with her longtime partner, Giovanni, asking me to call. And one from Melissa: "Please call me tonight. I need to talk to you." The phone number on Melissa's message slip was my mother's number. Why was Melissa in Mendocino instead of finishing her junior year at St. Mary's College? I heard the phone ring downstairs, followed by what sounded like a chair falling over and quick footsteps on the stairs. It was Zelda.

"Dakota's gone!"

"Gone where?"

"I left him with Rafie at the gallery this morning so I could go work out at the health club at lunchtime. While Rafie was on the Internet, Sophia got the back door open and they both took off. He can't find them anywhere."

Sophia was a large, supercilious white poodle that belonged to Zelda's friend Rafie Dominguez. Zelda was currently utilizing her significant computer expertise to help Rafie, a recent immigrant from Mexico, become computer-literate. "Does either of them have an ID collar on?"

"They both do, with phone numbers. God, I hope nobody shoots them. Wish me luck." She clattered down the stairs. The entry door opened and closed.

Despite its reputation as a Northwest tourist hot spot, San Juan Island has many working farms, and it is perfectly legal for a sheep farmer or a llama farmer to shoot wandering dogs. I hoped the seductive Sophia had more on her poodle mind than pillaging spring lambs.

The wind was still blowing the newly leafed branches of the maple tree against the dirty window, and now a light rain had started. I dialed my mother's number and got the answering machine. After leaving a message, I stared out the window, trying to ignore the foreboding thought that all was not right with my daughter.

My ancient wall clock began its inharmonious chiming of the midday hour. I gathered up my canvas carryall and headed to the Book Nook Café for my lunch date with Jared Saperstein. Before settling in Friday Harbor, Jared worked for the *New York Times* and then NBC, primarily in their foreign bureaus. For several years, our socializing consisted of a drink after work at George's once a week, sometimes followed by dinner if Nick was not on the island. Jared was intelligent, witty, and congenial, and it was an arrangement that worked well, even though I knew that he would have liked more than friendship from me. A few months ago, he had begun dating a sensational-looking blond real estate agent. Now our socializing was relegated to lunchtime—which wasn't quite the same.

3

I scanned the café for a fifty-something, balding, bespectacled, slightly rotund man. Jared was seated at the back of the used-book store, where the owners had wedged in a counter and half a dozen small bistro tables. He was intent on a book in a maroon leather binding propped against his coffee cup. He looked up with a smile as I approached, pulled out a chair, and leaned over to give me a peck on the cheek.

"The special today is white clam chowder. Shall I order two?"

"Sounds fantastic. And a ginger ale with ice." I watched him extricate his chunky body from the table and amble up to the counter. He returned with two glasses and two cans of ginger ale.

"How was your weekend cruise?"

I sighed and rolled my eyes. "Great sailing. We left Friday morning and went up to Montague Harbor on Galiano Island. Then on Monday morning Nick had a domestic crisis. Pure soap opera. You don't want to know about it. What's new at the *Gazette*?"

Jared poured the ginger ale and gave me a long, steady look, then began to sip the fizzy amber beverage. "I had a call from a friend of mine up in Desolation Sound this morning." He frowned. "You ever sail that far north?"

Desolation Sound encompasses an area of the Inside Passage of British Columbia north of Cape Mudge and south of Yuculta Rapids. It is a wilderness of rapidly changing weather, extreme tidal ranges, whales and eagles and great blue herons. And some of the most beautiful fjords and glacier-cut valleys on the planet.

"I've only sailed as far north as Powell River on the B.C. mainland. Desolation Sound is north of there and pretty remote. What does your friend do?"

"Ian's a caretaker at a little place called Santiago Island. I visited him once. Quite an adventure. Even once you get over to Vancouver Island, it's two more ferry rides to a place called Whaletown and a wet trip in a dinghy to Santiago."

"Did your friend choose this exile voluntarily?"

"Ian has a rather colorful history. I met him back in the sixties in New York. He was a wild-eyed journalist who violently disagreed with our government's policy in Vietnam, and we spent a lot of time drinking beer and pounding our fists on bars and declaring our politicians fit for an insane asylum. Ultimately, he headed north and spent the duration of the war in Toronto. After the war he married a woman from Vancouver and became a Canadian citizen."

"And now they're living on Santiago Island?"

A twenty-something waitress clad in tight hip-hugging blue jeans and a black stretchy tank top that exposed four inches or so of her chubby midriff delivered a flowered soup tureen to the table. She reached across the table to serve the chowder, and I could see that Jared was making a valiant attempt not to stare at the reptile tattoo that encircled her waist.

"It's not quite that tidy," he said. "Ian worked his way into a good position at the *Sun* and then had a midlife crisis. He had a fling with a winsome young reporter half his age, and his wife found out about it. She divorced him and took the house in West Vancouver. His two kids refused to talk to him. He married the sweet young reporter and five years later *she* divorced him, taking half of what was left of his net worth and ninety percent of his sanity. And he went downhill from there." Jared dunked a piece of bread in his chowder and chewed thoughtfully.

"How much further down could he go?"

"He got into the booze pretty heavy and lost his job at the *Sun*. Bailed out and went up to Campbell River to dry out, ended up working for an aquaculture enterprise somewhere up in the sound. Oysters or scallops or something. A couple of years ago, he started writing a novel about international drug smuggling and finagled a job caretaking a big house on Santiago Bay. The owners come up only a few weeks a year. When they do, Ian and his dog move out and set up housekeeping in a little abandoned shack across the bay." Jared finished the chowder, pushed his chair back, and folded his hands over his paunch. "The reason he called me was to say that he's sold the novel and gotten a sizable advance." Jared rubbed his face and frowned. "At least that's why he *said* he called. I had the distinct feeling he wanted to tell me something else but didn't." He smiled, checked his watch and glanced toward the front of the café. "Anyway, I saw the creative director from On the Edge coming out of your building this morning. New client?"

"He wants me to check into his sister Tina's disappearance. As you well know."

Jared grinned. "M.J. exchanged sharp words with Nigel Bishop after the memorial service and made no bones about the fact that he didn't buy the 'accidental death' bit."

"What did the sheriff have to say?" I dunked a piece of bread in the chowder and managed to transport it to my mouth without dribbling on my shirt.

"That Mrs. Breckenridge wasn't the first body to have disappeared into the swift currents of the Strait of Georgia. That there was no evidence found on the boat to suggest anything other than an accident. That the case was closed as far as he was concerned. You have any theories yet?"

Before I could respond, Jared's gaze shifted and I turned to see a willowy, blond, suntanned female in a black silk raincoat over a camel-colored wool suit approaching our table.

The willowy blonde was Allison Fisher.

According to my best friend, Angela, who plays weekly bridge with Allison, the stunning newcomer from Napa Valley was in the throes of a messy divorce from a California vintner whose pricey labels were to be found at the local liquor store. I studied the tailored red suit and black stiletto heels and wondered if she'd ever heard of the when-in-Rome adage. I also speculated that the stiletto heels wouldn't make it down Spring Street in the rain.

"I'm so glad I found you, darling," she said. "I'm showing a house out on Afterglow Drive at five o'clock, so I'll be a little late for dinner." Jared smiled broadly, slipped his hand under the black raincoat, and patted her a few degrees north of her shapely tush. "Not a problem. Just come by the office when you're done."

Allison planted a kiss on the top of Jared's bald head. Her lipstick was a perfect match to her long crimson fingernails. "You're such a dear. I should be finished about six. Toodle-oo." She tucked her mane of blond hair behind one ear and aimed a smile in my direction. "Nice to see you, Scotia."

I nodded. Toodle-oo, indeed.

I watched her wobble to the front of the café and out the double doors, reflecting on the cozy supper Jared had fixed for me last November when Nick was incommunicado in Mexico. I wondered if he was going to prepare lemongrass soup for Allison. Jared's cell phone chirped, and he pulled the miniature piece of high technology from inside his jacket, unfolded it, and pressed one of the minuscule buttons.

"Saperstein." A pause. "Yeah, okay, I'm on my way." He pressed the End button, folded the tiny receiver, and put it back in his coat. "Sorry, Scotia, gotta run. There's just been a big drug bust at Roche Harbor." He stood up and tossed some bills on the table.

A drug bust at Roche Harbor and the attendant publicity would not be pleasing to Sheriff Nigel Bishop, who had campaigned on a "Clean Up Crime" platform. So far, Nigel's modus operandi for cleaning up crime had been to deny its existence—the "not on my watch" approach.

I gathered up my jacket and followed Jared out the door. He gave me a quick wave and headed uphill in the rain. I stood for a minute, thinking that there were several other things I'd wanted to chat with him about and wondering what a nice guy like Jared saw in an airhead like Allison Fisher.

Zelda was still absent when I returned to the office, and the old building was silent. I poured a cup of the less-than-fresh coffee and wondered how the search for the missing canines was progressing. The rain was falling steadily now, and the wind was blowing it against the windows. Not a great day for dog hunting.

I found a new message from Nick on the answering machine: "Scotia, it's Nick. Sorry to have deserted you on Monday. It wasn't the way I wanted to end the weekend. But I know a terrific sailor like you didn't have any trouble getting *DragonSpray* home. Unfortunately, Cathy's DUI is more serious than I thought. Way too much to drink and then she got lost and did some really dumb things. But I think I've got it under control. I've got symphony tickets for Saturday night. They're doing Mozart. Can you come down? I'll be working on a brief this afternoon, but I'll be home this evening. Give me a call if you have time."

I hit the Erase button and leaned back in my chair. Staring out the window at the blowing rain, I thought about the tall, brown-eyed Seattle maritime attorney who had so completely stolen my heart back when I was with H & W Security in San Francisco and we'd worked together on an arson case. I could remember with all its nuances the day Nick had walked into the conference room at H&W. In a nanosecond I knew this was a man I wanted to spend the rest of my life with. There was no logic and a lot of chemistry behind the attraction. Chemistry in the pure sense of the word, which went beyond the fact that he was a George Clooney look-alike, had an easy, engaging smile, and brown eyes that turned my legs to rubber. Chemistry that took my breath away. Chemistry that made me euphoric.

Just like that.

The chemistry was clearly mutual, but Nick was very unavailable then, married with two kids. After we spent a couple of flirtatious business lunches at Waterfront Wanda's Bar, the arsonist was identified, the case closed, and we drifted apart. But nothing is forever, it seems. Nick's wife fell in love with her financial advisor and after a long drawn-out divorce and property settlement, Nick moved to Seattle, passed the Washington bar exam and opened an office with two former associates from the Bay Area. Several years later, when my daughter, Melissa, went off to college, I discovered the San Juans. I sold the house in St. Francis Wood that I'd inherited when Albert, my third husband, was lost at sea, and moved to Friday Harbor. After six months in a rented condo, I found *DragonSpray*, a thirty-eight-foot replica of the vessel the intrepid Captain Joshua Slocum single-handed around the world more than a hundred

years ago. And I've lived aboard at the Port of Friday
Harbor ever since.

Except for a quirk of fate, years might have passed
without my discovering that Nick was only a short
plane ride away. Nick's new firm in Seattle had retained my former boss at H&W, and Nick asked about
me. A month later, we began a romance that quickly
rose to the boiling point, and continued on from there.
One of Nick's partners had a small plane and an old
family summer house here on the island. After a few
visits, Nick bought a house up on Mount Dallas, a San
Juan Island pastoral subdivision of ten-acre lots and
breathtaking ocean views.

A fairy tale come true, right? Well, almost. The
problem was that Nick had never become what I
would call available. There was always family stuff
tugging at him. Son Art needed a loan to get through
law school. Daughter Nicole was still sulking over
Mummy and Daddy's divorce. And now ex-wife Cathy
had appeared out of nowhere, the classic damsel in
distress. It seemed as if there was nothing left over
for me but the crumbs. And that made me feel childish
and guilty.

But despite the fact that it sounded like a B-movie
plot, there was no one I'd rather be with than Nick.
I'd call him tonight. I'd better get my work done so I
could leave on Friday.

In addition to moving as quickly as possible on the
Breckenridge case, I wanted to finish a report on a
disability claim for my insurance broker client. I also
had to make yet one more attempt to locate the elusive Harrison Petrovsky, son of the wealthy, deceased
Anastasia Petrovsky, whose estate was being handled
by Friday Harbor attorney Carolyn Smith.

I started with the Breckenridge case and created
what therapists and their ilk call a sociogram, which
is a fancy name for a relationship chart. It's a helpful
exercise for people like me who are visually oriented.

In the center of the big white board I have on the wall, I drew a circle and wrote in Tina's name. Off from that circle I began to add lines and circles with the names of everybody Tina had recently been in contact with.

Husband Paul. Son Stephan. Brother M.J. Employee Katy Quince. Friend Lily MacGregor.

In the event of foul play, any of the above might be a suspect. Any of the above might be able to add information that could lead to other information that, in turn, could lead me to solving the mystery of Tina's disappearance. I stared at what I knew so far. In addition to being connected to Tina, Stephan, Paul, and M.J. were connected to each other. Katy and Lily had no other connection than to Tina. As far as I knew.

There would be more names. More friends or acquaintances or possibly enemies. People in most communities have six degrees of separation between them. On San Juan Island, it's closer to two. The Tina Breckenridge case would have a lot of interconnected circles.

I called Paul Breckenridge again. He answered on the first ring, a slow-speaking man with a pleasant voice. He sounded neither surprised nor pleased by my call, but was able to supply Tina's driver's license and credit card numbers. More reluctantly, he gave me his own Social Security number and agreed to meet with me the next morning. He suggested the Netshed, a restaurant a mile southeast of town, at eight o'clock. I would have preferred a less public venue for the interview, but some people don't want to be seen entering the office of a private investigator.

I checked the phone book, found a listing for the Secret Garden. Lily MacGregor did not answer her phone, so I left a call-back message. I also called my daughter's cell phone and got her voice message: "Hi, thanks for calling Melissa. Leave a number and she'll call you soon." As I left my message, I wondered when my daughter had begun referring to herself in the third person.

It was five-thirty. I decided to leave the Petrovsky case and the insurance matter for tomorrow. I checked my E-mail and found one from my friend, Rebecca, who was cruising off the west coast of Mexico with her boyfriend, en route to New Zealand. They had meandered down the coast of California on *Gypsy Wanderer*, spent several months in La Paz and Cabo San Lucas, and had recently arrived in Puerto Vallarta. They had had problems with the fuel filter, she reported, their water maker was broken, and their alternator had burned out. Aside from that, they were having a great time.

I heard a loud thud from outside the building. Probably an unlatched door somewhere. I re-read Rebecca's message and stared out the window, wishing I were someplace where it was warm. The rain had dwindled to a fine drizzle, but the wind had picked up and the overcast sky had produced an early twilight. I switched on my desk lamp and typed a reply to Rebecca, wishing them luck with the repairs. A new message came in from Angela Petersen, the San Juan County sheriff's dispatcher and my best friend from our days with the San Diego Police Department: *A farmer out on San Juan Valley Road just reported a black Lab chasing his cows. Could this be Dakota? Does Zelda know where he is? I'm going to the health club for a swim tomorrow after work. Wanna join me?*

I penciled in Angela's name on my calendar for Wednesday and clicked on Reply to Sender. *It was probably Dakota. Zelda is scouring the countryside. Any reported sightings of a large white poodle? See you at the health club around five tomorrow.*

The unlatched door thumped again, harder this time. I typed out a note to Zelda, gave her Tina's driver's license and credit card numbers, and asked her to expand the background search. I left the note on her desk, locked up my office and New Millennium and decided to stop by the Wildlife Gallery on my way down to the port, maybe get an update on Dakota and his abductress from Rafie Dominguez.

4

The Wildlife Gallery in Friday Harbor is owned by David Kean, an environmentalist, town council member, and past president of Save Our Islands. The gallery sits high on the hill above the harbor and is a visual delight of paintings and photographs and sculptures of wildlife in the islands. Bronzes of eagles and orca whales. Black-and-white photographs of large arachnids reposing on dew-laden webs in a field of meadow grass. A sonnet of trumpeter swans in an afternoon confab on the lake at Blazing Sky Ranch. Abby's magnificent color photography of the little foxes of American Camp.

"Oh, Scotia, it is you. I not hear you come in. Do you hear from Zelda?"

I tore my gaze away from the photos of the bushy-tailed critters that had provided the impetus for Abigail's attack on the hapless crew from On the Edge and greeted Rafie Dominguez.

Rafie was tall for a Mexican, probably close to six feet. His long, lustrous black hair brushed his shoulders. Today it was confined with an ornate silver barrette. His eyes were somewhere between brown and black, his skin and his eyelashes the envy of every woman on the island. Two small diamond studs decorated his right earlobe; a delicate gold chain adorned the open neckline of the red silk shirt that was neatly tucked into the narrow waistline of the very tailored black pants. Rafie's lovely black eyebrows were furrowed with concern.

"Hi, Rafie. No, I haven't, but I did hear from Angela Petersen at the sheriff's office that a farmer reported a black Lab chasing his cows."

"Jesús María! It is probably Dakota! I feel terrible. It is all my fault. I never thought Sophia to open the door. What a minx."

I silently admired Rafie's grasp of English vocabulary after only a year in the States. David Kean had met Rafie on an eco-vacation in Mexico and it had been love at first sight. At least according to Zelda, who had more or less adopted Rafie when he arrived in Friday Harbor and was now tutoring him in the intricacies of computer literacy. Rafie was David's Man Friday, caring for David's house at Roche Harbor, crewing on David's sailboat, and working in the gallery. Sophia, the white poodle, had been David's Valentine's Day gift to Rafie.

"Has Sophia done this before?"

He rolled his eyes and nodded. "She escaped last week, but she was alone. And she come back soon."

"Well, let's not worry until we have to." I extracted my cell phone from the carryall and punched in Zelda's number. After two rings, I got her voice recording, which was a good indication that she was somewhere in San Juan Valley where the cell reception was virtually nonexistent. I passed on the Dakota sighting Angela had sent, asked her to call Rafie, and reminded her that I needed the background on the Breckenridges the next morning.

Rafie's emotional distress was increasing. "I do not know what to do. I need to go home and begin to prepare dinner. But Sophia may come back here."

It was certainly a dilemma. I was saved from having to respond by the arrival of the other member of the partnership.

"Hello, Scotia. Rafie, you're still here! I thought you'd be at home by now. Did you forget we're doing cocktails for Forest and Jethro tonight before the theater?" David Kean, tall, blond, and elegant in a brown leather blazer and brown cords, began to turn off the lights in the gallery, which I took as a reasonable cue for my departure.

"Oh, God, David, I forget." Rafie's voice was forlorn.

" 'Bye, guys. Have a good evening."

David waved and opened the cash register. "That's the second time this week you've—"

I didn't want to hear what it was Rafie had forgotten or why. I closed the door firmly behind me, tucked my head into the upturned collar of my jacket, and headed downhill. At the Corner Grocery Store I purchased a Seattle paper and a baguette of Seattle sourdough—not to be confused with San Francisco sourdough.

The wind was blowing harder as I made my way across Spring Street and along the park above the Port of Friday Harbor. *DragonSpray* is moored on G dock, slip 73. There was no sign of Henry, my dockmate, who lives aboard a thirty-two-foot motor vessel named *Pumpkin Seed.* Henry got divorced last year and attempted to alleviate the post-divorce depression with a number of winsome females. Last week he announced his engagement to Lindsey, the most comely of the group, a redheaded barmaid at George's Tavern. As of yesterday, Henry appeared to be a few degrees less depressed, and I was feeling guilty for expressing shock at his announcement of the planned nuptials. I had probably ruined his day by asking why he thought it was necessary to get married again. And so soon.

It was not a neighborly comment, and as soon as I'd uttered it I realized it was simply my cynicism speaking, the skepticism that comes from being a veteran of three marriages.

Calico, the affectionate tabby that Henry and I share, was curled under the canvas dodger on *Dragon-Spray,* trying unsuccessfully to stay dry. She complained loudly as I unlocked the boat, then leaped from the cockpit through the open hatchway into the cabin below. I apologized profusely for my tardiness and her discomfort, followed her below, and turned on the heat.

The red light on the answering machine was blinking. I pressed the button, shed my jacket, and reached into the storage locker over the stove for a can of Fancy Feast. The shelf was bare. I'd forgotten to replenish kitty's larder when I was at the Corner Grocery and now I would have to improvise.

In the fridge I found the remains of the cooked prawns that Nick and I had feasted on over the weekend. I laid three of the giant crustaceans in Calico's bowl. Her purrs of gratitude were a nice antidote to my mother's voice on the machine inquiring in an aggrieved tone why I never returned her calls. I thought "never" was a bit of an exaggeration; she'd only called last night. Or was it Saturday?

I clicked the On button for the TV remote and learned from CNN's raven-haired, carmine-lipped anchorwoman that the Dow had fallen 135 points and that rumors in Washington were that the feds would be cutting the prime interest rate by a quarter of a point next week. It was unlikely that either event would affect me. The proceeds from the sale of the house in St. Francis Wood had amounted to a tidy nest egg that, thrifty Scotswoman that I am, I'd promptly put into several conservative mutual funds that continued to perform well. Not well enough to make financial headlines, or well enough for me to become the female of leisure I would prefer. But well

enough that I could tell the ravening wolf—that shadowy specter that prowls about my bed at four a.m.,
reminding me of all that could go awry in my life—
to take a hike.

The anchorwoman moved on to the flooding along
the Mississippi River, and I made a cup of Red Zinger
tea, found the portable phone behind the sofa cushions in the main salon, and dialed Nick's number at
the condo. Calico leaped into my lap and curled into
a ball. I stroked her silky head, anticipating the warm
tones of Nick's voice, letting my mind travel forward
in time to the upcoming weekend. He answered on
the first ring.

"Hi, it's Scotia."

"Scottie, how's it going?" His voice was brusque,
and my mental skit of weekend delights faded to
black. I asked about his day.

"Nothing but complaints from clients."

"How are things with Cathy? You get the DUI
taken care of?"

There was a pause, then a long sigh. "Don't I wish.
It's worse than I expected. Alcohol level of point-two-
zero. More than twice the legal limit. She hit a parking
meter and managed to dent one car and take the
bumper off another."

"Oh, my. Where was she—where is she—is she—
uh, is she going to be in Seattle long?"

"God only knows. She flew into SEATAC, rented
a car, met an old girlfriend down at Pike Street Market, where she says she had only two glasses of wine,
then got lost on the way to Nicole's apartment. I suppose it'll all get sorted out eventually. At the moment,
I don't want to talk about it." He sighed and I heard
the tinkle of ice cubes in a glass. "Anyway, Scottie,
can you come down this weekend? The symphony is
doing an all-Mozart concert at Benaroyal Hall. Should
be excellent."

"I'd love to, Nick. Are the float plane tickets still good?"

Last winter Nick had successfully defended the owner of Puget Sound Air in a negligence suit, and part of his fee had been an envelope full of tickets.

"Yeah, just call and make your reservations. And let's talk on Thursday." I heard the buzz of his doorbell. "Gotta get that, Scottie. Talk to you later."

The phone in my hand was buzzing with the dial tone, and I replaced it in the cradle and wondered idly, as a women will do, who was at Nick's door. Before my idle wondering had wandered down any undesirable passages, the phone rang. It was Melissa.

"Hi, Mom." There was a distinct lack of lilt in her voice.

"Hi, sweetie. What's new?"

"Uh, Mom? You're so not going to like this." I crossed four fingers on my right hand and prayed she wasn't pregnant or in jail.

"I'm sitting down, so let's have it." I tried to keep my voice light.

"I'm in Mendocino."

"I see," I said in a neutral voice. I wasn't aware of any school holiday the first week in May.

"Don't just say, '*I see*'! Do you want to know *why* I'm in Mendocino?"

"Tell me why you're in Mendocino, Melissa." This was not going to be a pleasant conversation.

"Because all this time that jerk of a Gilberto had a girlfriend in Brazil that he never told me about. And not just a girlfriend, but a *fiancée*." Her voice had become a wail.

Melissa had met Gilberto, a Brazilian soccer player, last fall. He'd invited her to go to Brazil over holiday break and had even been willing to supply the plane fare. Fortunately—or unfortunately—she'd gotten mononucleosis in early December and hadn't been able to accept the invitation. The relationship had resumed in late January when Gilberto returned to school, and I was beginning to resign myself to the possibility that my only daughter might be going to live in a faraway country.

"Oh, Melissa, I'm so sorry."

"Mom, all these *months*, he never told me. I had to hear it from his sister. In an e-mail. And she thought I knew. They've been engaged for, like, years. How stupid did he think I *was*?"

"It was dishonorable of him not to have told you, Melissa."

The only response was the sound of her sobs.

"How can I help, sweetie?"

There was a hiccup. "I can't stay in school anymore. Everybody will *know*. It's so *embarrassing*. That's why I came up to Mendocino to be with Grandma."

"Is Grandma there now?"

"She and Giovanni went to a book signing for one of their friends."

"Why don't you get a good night's sleep and we'll talk about it in the morning?"

"What's to *talk* about? I'm *not* going back to school. Grandma says I can live here. And Giovanni is going to help me find a job."

"This is your junior year, Melissa," I said in a calm voice. "You can't just walk out of school two weeks before the end of spring term. Take the rest of the week off, I'll call the dean, and then you can go back."

"God, Mother! You *never* listen to me. I'm *not* going back and I hope that stupid Gilberto rots in hell."

The phone went dead.

Merde! Merde a la puissante treize!

I stared helplessly at the phone, replaced it in the cradle ruefully, and contemplated the mixed joys of having your child become an adult. There was no way I could force Melissa to go back to school. And enlisting my mother's help was unlikely. Many decades ago, Jewel Moon dropped out of college in Vermont and ran off to St. Ann's Bay on Cape Breton Island, where she met my father. I was born a year later, and when I was five, Jewel Moon decided she'd had her fill of a small fishing village and the simple life of a fisherman's wife. She left me with my grandmother Jessica, and for the next nine years all I received was an occasional postcard. I knew Jewel Moon believed that life experiences were of equal importance with college degrees. Melissa wasn't going to get much nudging from her grandmother to complete the academic year.

I glared at the TV screen, learned that wind and rain were predicted for the weekend for the Pacific Northwest, and hit the Off button on the remote. In the silent cabin I thought about the day's events and my new investigative assignment to find out what had happened to Tina Breckenridge.

I reached for a sheet of paper and made a list of the information I needed from Paul Breckenridge. I also wanted to check out Tina's boats and take some photos. And I hoped to talk to Katy Quince, who may have been the last person to see her boss alive.

I pulled my canvas carryall out of the aft cabin, dumped the contents on the bunk, and reflected that my San Juan Island investigative equipment was far simpler than stuff I'd utilized in the past, which included a fingerprint kit, bugs, sweepers, long-distance and parabolic microphones, ski masks, and a host of state-of-the-art high-tech devices that far exceeded my ability to operate them. Which was why it was with some misgivings that I retrieved my new digital camera from the locker under the settee in the main cabin. It was a much more complicated piece of photographic equipment than I would have preferred, and it devoured batteries as if they were going out of style. However, it had the advantage of having a tiny memory card that could be used to transfer images directly into my computer, from which I could E-mail them if necessary. And I could always just give it to Zelda and let her print out the photos on her high-resolution printer.

I stared at the stack of equipment, decided that it had become too bulky to transport in the carryall, and went in search of my sturdy black rucksack, which was made of some indestructible space-age material. Rucksack parked beside the companionway, I brushed my teeth, donned my plaid flannel pj's, and crawled into bed with *The Scarlet Ruse*. Travis McGee was better than no one. In fact, better than most.

5

Wednesday

The Netshed restaurant sits out over the water on a winding shoreline road a mile or so out of Friday Harbor. It's a weathered two-story frame structure with flaking red paint and a rickety float in front. True to its name, the building was once used to store the nets of San Juan Island commercial fishermen. It is these fishermen, some still fishing, some retired, along with a few intrepid newcomers, who make up the majority of the patrons.

Peg O'Reilly, the sharp-tongued, gray-haired widow of a local fisherman, was the sole proprietor, cook, and waitress of the establishment. Her only employee was an emaciated dishwasher-cum-cleanup man.

The Netshed is open for business six days a week from 5:00 A.M. till noon. You don't go there unless you want one of the two items on the menu. Number One consists of freshly squeezed orange juice, fried eggs, a rasher of bacon, home fries, and white toast with homemade strawberry preserves. If you're eating light, then it's Number Two, the eight-inch-diameter, still-warm-from-the-oven cinnamon bun drenched in melted butter. Both are served with a huge cup of strong coffee and real dairy cream from San Juan Valley farms. There's nothing decaf, nonfat, sugar-free, or nonsmoking about the Netshed.

I paused inside the door, greeted by the early-morning smell of bacon and frying potatoes. Cigarette smoke drifted upward toward the old rafters of the high-ceilinged room. To my right and left, six ancient padded booths were occupied by large, hairy men who looked like they spent a lot of time outdoors. From some invisible jukebox, Dolly Parton belted out an old Kris Kristofferson ballad.

A man in overalls was seated at the far end of the long counter on one of the padded counter stools of 1940s vintage. Behind the counter, two swinging doors led to the kitchen. As I stood there, hesitating, Peg O'Reilly made her way through the doors, into the dining room, and set the huge platter of breakfast Number One on the Formica countertop with a small crash. I continued scanning the room, noting an auspicious lack of Gore-Tex, high-tech running shoes, and synthetic fabrics. I was glad I'd worn my oldest, most faded blue jeans with a nondescript brown sweater under my peacoat. Hoping I would recognize Paul Breckenridge, I tentatively approached the counter.

"Scotia?" A clean-shaven man with longish blond hair going gray detached himself from a booth full of men toward the back of the room. "I'm Paul Breckenridge."

Paul's eyes were a startling blue under pale blond lashes, and his handshake was warm and firm. I glanced around the crowded restaurant, wondering where we might have some privacy.

"We can sit in the back," he said. "Kenny and Al are leaving."

I followed his squarish, five-foot-ten frame to the back booth, waited as Kenny and Al nodded to me and made their departure. I slid into the wide, cracked vinyl seat across from Paul and eased out of my peacoat. Immediately, a large white mug of black coffee was placed in front of me, and Paul's cup was refilled.

"Number One or Number Two?" I looked up into the uncompromising green gaze of Peg O'Reilly, eyes set deep beneath thick graying eyebrows. Her lined face bore testimony to either a very hard life or a lot of hard drinking. Peg was not a woman who spent any time on eye shadow or lip gloss. Her gray-white hair was curly and uncombed.

I knew I'd never make it through the Number One breakfast. And if I couldn't eat my way through the cinnamon roll, it would do for a midafternoon snack.

"Number Two, and hold the butter, please."

She stared at me for a second, raised her eyebrows, silently gathered up the two overflowing ashtrays on our table, and stalked toward the kitchen.

Paul reached for the small metal pitcher of cream, added a stream to his steaming cup, and slid the pitcher my way. I considered the probable butterfat content, shrugged, and lightened my own cupful. There was a momentary silence in the room as Dolly retired, quickly replaced by the twang of a Nashville guitar and the plaintive tones of Merle Haggard wondering if we'd make it through December. As I wondered how to begin an interview with the gentle-faced, blue-eyed man whose wife had disappeared without a trace he began to speak.

"When M.J. told me he wanted to hire a private detective, I thought it was a bad idea. Seemed like it would just open everything up again. Particularly for Stephan." He paused and took a sip of coffee.

I reached into the black rucksack and extracted the small micro recorder I like to use for interviews.

"May I record our conversation, Paul?"

He nodded and waited until I had pressed the Record button, then continued. "But I've been thinking more about it, and I know M.J.'s right. Tina can't have drowned. That female could cling to an icy deck and move a stack of crab pots like you wouldn't believe."

Paul's opinion of his wife's seamanship seemed consistent with that of my client as well as the regulars at George's Tavern.

"You and Tina met in Alaska?"

He shook his head. "I've known Tina since she was in kindergarten. M.J. was four years older, and him and me were in the same grade. Then their family moved down to Ballard—I think it was when we finished eighth grade here. I never saw them again till Tina and her friend Joy Johnson turned up at a waterfront bar in Kodiak. Down to their last five bucks and looking for a job on a crab boat."

"One cinnamon bun, no butter." Peg slid the white plate with the gigantic pastry toward me.

"Thank you, ma'am." I gave her my best smile of gratitude, which was not reciprocated.

"And they found jobs?"

"Kodiak's a rough port. I found them a place to lay their heads and a week later, when the captain fired a deckhand for drinking on the job and his cook quit without notice, they both got jobs on the *Ice Queen*."

"Crab fishing?" I attacked the huge pastry with knife and fork.

He nodded. "King crab in the fall and tanner crab in the winter and spring." He smiled into his coffee. "Most people would probably wonder how anybody on a crab boat working seventy and eighty hours a week could find time for romance. But from the moment I laid eyes on that feisty female at Solly's Bar I wanted to marry her. We met in November, worked on the *Ice Queen* all winter, and when we finished in the spring, she and her friend Joy came to Friday Harbor to visit her friend Lily. I called her for a date the next day. It was what you call a whirlwind courtship. We got married a month later. Tina planned to go back to Alaska with me, but she got pregnant right away." He shook his head. "Kinda too bad. There's very few women who have what it takes for crab fishing. Tina was one of them."

"What happened to her friend Joy?"

"Joy split right after we got married. Went back to Alaska and found another boat. The *Alaska Dawn*. She married the skipper, but the *Alaska Dawn* went down in a terrible storm off Cape Chiniak on Kodiak Island. Skipper and crew were never found. Joy just happened to be in Seattle because her father was sick. Fate," he finished wryly. He drained his coffee cup, looked toward the kitchen. Behind the counter, Peg met his gaze, lifted the carafe from the warmer, and headed toward our table. I wondered if the service was always this good or if Peg wanted to find out what I was talking to Paul about.

"Joy got married again," he continued. "To a guy from Port Townsend. He died of a heart attack about three years ago."

It sounded like Tina's best friend was as unlucky with husbands as I was. "Is that when she came down here?"

He nodded. "Her and Tina always stayed in touch. After her husband died, Joy got a job cooking at the restaurant out at Roche Harbor." I mentally added another line and a circle to the sociogram I had drawn on the white board in my office.

"She still works there?"

"Yeah, I saw her last night. I told her I was going to talk to you." Paul added cream to the refilled cup, stirred it, and was quiet for several seconds.

"Tell me about your son," I said.

The jukebox was silent and the Netshed was emptying out. A tall man with a thin, poetically handsome face and long, dishwater-blond hair passed our booth and glanced at Paul. He was accompanied by a large woman with a mop of curly Titian-colored hair. Both were dressed in blue jeans, motorcycle boots, and black leather jackets. The woman nodded to both of us and followed the man out the door. It was Katy Quince, Tina Breckenridge's sailing school instructor. I didn't know the man she was with. I wondered if she planned to return the message I'd left yesterday. Paul stared after her thoughtfully, then answered my question.

"Stephan's fifteen. He's a freshman."

"How did he get on with his mother?"

"Everything was fine with Stephan until he was twelve." He sighed deeply and stared into his cup.

"What happened then?"

"Tina home-schooled him until then. When he started middle school here, all hell broke loose."

"You mean he's not doing well?"

"You might say that. Tina wanted to send him to a private school off-island, but I said no way."

"Why not?" I asked.

"Why not? I wasn't going to have any son of mine going to some damned pansy boarding school, that's why not!"

"I see." I finished the last bite of cinnamon roll and took a sip of coffee. "So what exactly is going on with Stephan?"

"For starters, he got thrown out of a school dance for rowdiness. Then him and two of his friends got caught vandalizing mailboxes. I thought doing community service and cleaning up roadkill would slow him down."

"It didn't?"

"Last fall him and his friend Sean and two girls got picked up by the park ranger for smoking marijuana out at Brown Sugar Beach."

"How did Tina deal with all of this?"

"At the beginning, she said it was just boys being boys. We got in a big fight about it. I told her both her brother and me managed to get through school without vandalizing other people's property or using drugs. She said things were different now. There's nothing for kids to do in Friday Harbor. She wanted Stephan to see a shrink."

"If Stephan was arrested on a minor-in-possession charge, wasn't counseling mandatory?"

Paul nodded and a muscle in his jaw contracted. "Yup. Outpatient drug rehab."

"Was your wife depressed about Stephan getting into trouble?"

"Hell, yes. She said half of it was my fault, being away so much, and none of it would have happened if he'd gotten off the island."

"Do you still work the crab fishery?"

"Not anymore. There's just so many years you can fight the wind and snow and ice. I slipped one night in sixty-knot winds and thirty-foot seas, almost went overboard. Scared me shitless. Soon as the season was over, I decided I'd had enough and bought my own boat. A gillnetter. I do the salmon fishery in Bristol Bay."

"Does that mean you spend more time here on the island?"

He stared into his coffee cup. "Not really. Every year it's harder to make the same amount of money. I leave in April, come back in the fall, usually September. Which, according to Tina, makes me just slightly more than a half-time father."

"What's going to happen to Stephan now that Tina's gone?"

"You mean when I head north? Well, he can either come with me or hold the fort here by himself."

"At fifteen?"

"Hell, yes! I was fishing with my dad full-time when I was his age. And given his sorry record at school, he'd be better off in Bristol Bay."

"I'd like to talk to Stephan. Would it be possible for him to come to my office?"

He started to say something, then changed his mind. "Sure. I'll have him call you."

"I'd also like to take a look at Tina's personal things. Do you have any idea if anything of her is missing?"

He shrugged and swallowed. "I couldn't . . . I can't . . ."

"I know how hard it is for you, Paul," I said softly. "Perhaps we could go through her things together, look at her business records, see if anything seems out of order."

He wiped his eyes on the sleeve of his jacket and nodded. "Sorry. I still can't believe she's not coming back."

A change of subject seemed appropriate. "When did Tina start the sailing school?"

"Five years ago. She never worked while Stephan was growing up. I didn't want her to. I made enough money. At least I used to. Then she said she wanted something to do to keep her busy while I was away." His expression hardened.

Something about the Pleiades Sailing School had not pleased Paul. I watched the shifting emotions on his face as he recounted how Tina's mother had died and left Tina a little inheritance and she went out and bought a sailboat, the *Alcyone*.

"Who were Tina's clients? Local women?"

"Only one or two. Most of our local women couldn't afford what Tina was charging."

"How did she get clients?"

"She did presentations at a bunch of yacht clubs. Got a booth at the Seattle and San Francisco boat shows. Even did the Vancouver show one year. And she put up a Web site. Targeted women who'd been sailing with their husbands on fancy sailboats and didn't enjoy it. She said it wasn't necessary to yell on a sailboat. Seemed to be magic words."

He paused, took a sip of coffee. "A year ago she took some of the profits and bought a second boat and hired Katy Quince. Katy did the four- or five-day cruises, and Tina did the one-day classes. That way she didn't have to leave Stephan overnight." He smiled ruefully. "Which I didn't think was a problem, but she did."

"Did the arrangement with Katy work out okay?"

"Far as I know."

"What's going to happen to Tina's two boats?"

"The *Alcyone* is for sale. Katy bought the *Electra*."

"Is Katy continuing the sailing school?"

"No. But I hear she's doing weekend charters. Los Angeles rockers. Old friends of her husband's."

I prayed Abigail hadn't heard about Katy's new endeavor. "What do you know about Katy's husband?"

"He's a musician. Plays the guitar. Heavy metal, I think. And he's got a yacht brokerage. It's called Inside Passage Yacht Sales. Don't know how he makes any money with three other yacht brokers in town." He nodded toward the door. "That's who was with her just now."

"What's his name?"

"Dave or Dan. Maybe Danny. Yeah, Danny Quince."

"When did you last see your wife?"

He took a deep breath. "That morning, Thursday, the day she disappeared. I left the house about five o'clock to get the red-eye to the mainland. She was asleep when I left."

"When did you return to Friday Harbor?"

"Not till Sunday afternoon."

"Did you talk to your wife anytime after you left the house on Thursday morning?"

"No. We had . . . a little argument the night before. I thought she'd have time to cool down by the time I got back."

"Would you mind telling me where you spent the weekend?"

"Yeah, sure. I'd gone over to Sedro Wooley to see my mom. She's got a little apartment there, but her

arthritis is getting bad and I wanted to convince her
to move in with us."

"How did Tina feel about that?"

"We had a couple of fights about it."

"How did you resolve it?"

He sighed. "We didn't. Every time I tried to talk
to her, she'd get mad. She said I should put Mom
into an assisted-living facility. I didn't think I could
afford it."

I had an eerie sense of the trap Tina must have felt
closing around her: no money to get her son into a
private school even if Paul would have allowed it, a
part-time husband, and the expectation that she would
become a caretaker for her mother-in-law.

"Paul, if Tina didn't fall overboard," I said gently,
"is it possible she just decided she'd had enough and
cut out? Problems with Stephan, you being away so
much, having your mother move in?"

He shook his head without answering. His blue eyes
glittered with tears.

"I don't know. I always did the best I could for
her." His voice was ragged. "And Mom had no place
else to go. What was I going to do?" He stood up
suddenly, threw some money on the table, grabbed his
jacket from the seat, and was gone.

I stared after him and absently put the micro recorder back in the carryall.

"You ever hear about sleeping dogs?"

I looked up at the angry green eyes of Peg O'Reilly.
"Excuse me?"

"Sometimes it's best to just let them lie."

I stared at her without answering, then reached into
my wallet and extracted a bill.

"I hear Tina's brother hired you to find out what
happened to her," she said. "Now you got Paul all
upset again."

I laid the bill on top of the check and slid out of

the booth. "What do *you* think happened to Tina, Mrs. O'Reilly?"

"I know nothing you do is gonna bring her back and all you're gonna do is make that man suffer more'n he already has." She picked up the money and the check and stalked back through the swinging doors to the kitchen.

Subject closed.

6

It was ten-thirty when I got to the office and the solemn tones of a dying tenor greeted me. It was the death scene from the last act of *The Masked Ball*. I recognized it because Zelda had played it for an entire day after she ended her relationship with Boris, the former Russian KGB agent from Vancouver who wanted a more traditional woman.

Zelda was seated in front of her computer and did not turn around when I closed the door. Since Zelda usually chose an operatic opus to complement her state of mind, I wondered what grim event had befallen her. Except for Sheldon, her ever-faithful, long-suffering, well-paid ship's pilot, she was currently between romances.

I pulled my mail from the cubby and glanced at the empty red futon in the corner of the office.

"Dakota's not back?"

She shook her head. Her printer made appropriate whirring sounds and began to produce a colored photo. She spun around and I gasped.

Death warmed over didn't begin to describe the pale face devoid of makeup or the lank mop of hennaed hair hanging around her face. Her couture was anything but haute: chunky black sweater decorated with lint, wrinkled blue jeans, muddy hiking boots.

"I called Rafie when I got your message yesterday,"

she said, "and we searched for them until dark. English Camp and American Camp, San Juan Valley, Trout Lake. Several people have seen one or the other of them, but always at a distance. I know they're going to get shot. I didn't tell Rafie, but it's all Sophia's fault. Dakota would *never* go off on his own. And please don't tell me how awful I look."

"Do you, uh . . . feel okay?"

"I have the world's most terrible hangover."

"But you don't drink."

"Exactly. What happened was when Rafie told David he was going out to look for Sophia, they had a slight . . . disagreement. David said if he'd known Rafie was going to be so obsessive about the stupid dog, he wouldn't have gotten it for him. I guess they were going to the theater or something last night. By the time we gave up looking for the dogs, David had left, so we went to George's for burgers. And a margarita."

"One margarita?"

"Shit, I lost count after the third one. We closed the place up. But we did have ringside seats for the little altercation."

"An altercation at George's on a weeknight?"

"Yep. Some of the crew from On the Edge have discovered George's burgers. Including your divine new client."

"M.J. Carlyle?"

"Yeah. It also just so happened that Mac MacGregor and some of his buddies were having a night on the town. I think they had a poker game at the Hunting Club, then moved the hijinks to George's."

"Who'd Mac pick on *last* night?" The Hunting Club had some serious drinkers, and Mac was known for his hair-trigger temper.

"M.J."

"M.J.?! What on earth for?"

"Scuttlebutt has it that M.J. and Lily MacGregor

were an item, way back when. And maybe now, as well."

I mentally reviewed my recently acquired info on the chronology of the Carlyle family. "You mean when they were in *middle* school? Before the Carlyles moved down to Seattle? That was at least twenty years ago!"

"All I know is what Lindsey told me. And Lindsey's mother knows everything that's ever happened in Friday Harbor. And it's no secret that Mac's insanely jealous of Lily. A couple of years ago, he and his cronies threatened to beat up the guy who delivers their propane." She paused and took a long gulp of water from the bottle on her desk. "M.J. was with a sexy-looking woman, one of the crew from On the Edge, I think. She looked Jamaican or maybe Brazilian. Anyway, they were just minding their own business, when Mac came over to the bar and said something to the effect that pretty boy should keep his hands off the wife. He was a lot more than three sheets to the wind, I can tell you. M.J. ignored him, so Mac grabbed M.J.'s shoulder, spun him around, and knocked him off the barstool. Then this big red-haired guy—I think he's the photographer with On the Edge—decided to get his licks in. It went downhill from there, and Lindsey called the sheriff."

"Is M.J. okay?"

She smiled. "Except for the first punch he took, your client's probably fine. He seemed to be familiar with the martial arts. I would say it's more likely Mac who's in need of physical therapy today." She burst out laughing. "It'll be a long time before I forget the look on Mac's face when he found himself flying through the air and landing in the corner. And it didn't help a bit that some of his cronies started laughing."

"Was that the end of it?"

"Mac grabbed a mug of beer, threw it at M.J.,

missed him by a mile, screamed that if he didn't stay the fuck away from Lily, he'd be more than sorry, or pithy words to that effect. And then he went staggering out of the bar. I'm sure glad *I* wasn't waiting up at home for him."

"Did David and Rafie make up?"

"Rafie bunked in with me last night. He forgot to take his key, and he didn't want to listen to one of David's lectures on responsibility and commitment."

"Is Rafie having second thoughts about leaving Mexico?"

"Who knows? Friday Harbor's got to be better than being a tour guide for ugly Americans in Mexico City. Rafie's had a horrible life," she said sadly.

"In what way?"

"In every way. He was born in Puerto Vallarta, and he was three years old when John Houston made *Night of the Iguana* there. Rafie's mother went to work for the movie crew, cooking and cleaning, I guess, and when the movie was done, she took Rafie and ran off with the bartender to Mexico City. After six months the bartender threw them out on the street. His mother died when he was ten."

"Did Rafie have a father?"

"He was a fisherman in P.V. Rafie never saw him again. He doesn't even know if he's still alive. Even if he was, Rafie says his dad would probably throw him out if he knew he was gay."

"That really is sad," I said, trying not to think about Melissa's father abandoning us when she was four to become a dive instructor in the Seychelles. "I hope David and Rafie resolve their problems." I opened the manila envelope I'd taken from the cubby. It contained the background report on the Breckenridges.

Zelda had turned back to her computer. "Let me know if you need any more checks on anybody. I talked to Edie—she's the owner of On the Edge. She must be richer than God. So I have to get cracking

on the big Saturday party. My first celebrity event!
Lily's in charge of flowers, Moody Rhythms is doing
the music, and all I have to do is line up a caterer
and get the banquet license for the booze."

Events arranging was a recent addition to New Millennium's services. Zelda's early training included a
stint at art school, followed by a brief interlude as a
DJ at a classical music station in Portland, several
years working at Microsoft, and almost a decade working at a computer security firm in Seattle. According
to her version of the story, she landed in Friday Harbor on the last ferry on Midsummer Night's Eve with
her underwear and a toothbrush in one bag and a
state-of-the-art computer in the other. A year later,
New Millennium Communications was born. Shortly
after that, I moved into the office upstairs and began
utilizing her on-line expertise, which was far more extensive than mine.

I headed for the stairs. "Since your state of mind
seems to be improving, could we have something
lighter in the music department?"

"Sure thing." She stood up. "I have a new Dvorak
CD. It has a great cut of Romance in F minor, opus
11, with the Budapest Strings."

I smiled at her selection. It had been three months
since the demise of Zelda's romance with Boris. Must
be about time for a new lover to enter stage right.

I stared at my calendar for Wednesday, which had
nothing on it except a notation on my daily Bikram
yoga class, which, of course, I had missed because of
my appointment with Paul. I was disappointed that
neither Katy Quince nor Lily MacGregor had returned my call. There had been nothing in Katy's cool
nod at the Netshed this morning to indicate whether
she'd received the message. I hoped Paul would remember to have Stephan call.

I settled down to read the Breckenridge background

reports. Culled from public records available on-line and probably a number of sources accessible only through professional investigative data banks like Data-Tech, the printout told me that Tina Breckenridge was born in Bellingham, Washington, was a thirty-five-year-old Caucasian female married to Paul Brecken-ridge, age thirty-nine, of Friday Harbor. Tina had no criminal record, no military record, no traffic viola-tions for the past three years, and did not owe any money to the Internal Revenue Service. One auto, a late-model Ford Windstar van, was registered to her name. Her driver's license expired in July of this year. She had a joint checking account with her husband at one of the local banks, with a balance of $1,530.75. She had another checking account in the name of Plei-ades SSW at the same bank, with a balance of $24,702.00. No life insurance policy was mentioned.

Page two of the report tracked Tina's credit card usage for the past six months. I scanned the payees, which all seemed to be business-related. West Marine. Northwest Shipyards. Safeway. Costco. Tom's Taxi. The last charge was made at the local auto repair shop on April 19, the day she disappeared. Three airline charges for clients were listed, but no other airline, cruise ship, railroad, gasoline, or rental car charges. If Tina Breckenridge was still alive, she was either living a cash existence or had created a new identity for herself in another name. Or was being held some-where against her will.

The sheet on Paul Breckenridge was equally brief, and contained no surprising information. No criminal record, no moving violations, no military record. There were Washington registrations for a ten-year-old Dodge pickup and for the F/V *Pacific Mist*, a 1966 forty-eight-foot wooden gillnetter. There was a savings account in his and Stephan's names with a balance of $2,790.90. A perusal of the last six months' charges on the credit card in Paul's name contained various chandlery and other boat-related charges and family kinds of purchases: Payless Drugs, Sears, the Gap, a local shoe store, the local pharmacy, gas station, and supermarket.

I turned to the last page of the report and smiled. Zelda had provided horoscopes on the Breckenridges and her own pithy astrological comment: *Libra + Cancer = a 4 vibration. Lots of conflict here!*

I filed the background report and updated the white board:

Tina connected to Joy Johnson, Tina's friend from her Alaska adventure.

M.J. connected to Ms. X, his exotic date at George's.

M.J. connected to Lily MacGregor.

Stephan Breckenridge connected to Sean Mac-Gregor, Lily's son.

The associations were growing. I checked the phone book, couldn't find a listing for Joy Johnson, so I called the restaurant at Roche Harbor. She was expected in about an hour; they would give her my message.

Melissa's E-mail message from yesterday was still clipped to my calendar, and I thought about our unpleasant exchange last night. I dialed my mother's number in Mendocino. Giovanni answered.

"Jewel Moon took Melissa to the Purple Unicorn for a reading," he informed me.

"A reading? What for?"

"She needs to have her aura cleansed."

I took a deep breath. "She needs to get her fanny back to school!"

There was silence on Giovanni's end of the line.

"Would you please tell my mother I returned her call?"

He agreed to give her the message and I hung up. My exchanges with Giovanni were always a tad terse. A lot of unresolved issues from my teenage years, you might call it, when my grandmother died and I went

to live with Jewel Moon and Giovanni and the rest of
their artistic little band in the dilapidated Victorian in
San Francisco's Haight Ashbury district. It hadn't
been the best of times for any of us.

I stared at the phone, then dialed Katy Quince's
home number. No answer, no answering machine. Was
she avoiding me?

I checked for E-mail and found a message from
Angela.

*You must have heard about the brawl at George's
last night. In case you were wondering, M. J. Carlyle
declined to press charges. See you this afternoon.*

I deleted Angela's message, leaned back in my executive chair, and put my feet on the desk. I stared at
the white board and searched vainly for some insight
into the disappearance of Tina Breckenridge. After
talking with Paul, I thought it seemed more than possible that she simply got tired of being a fishing widow,
tired of arguing about childrearing, tired of dealing
with an acting-out teenager, tired of being both
mother and father, and took off for a while. Or maybe
permanently. If so, I wondered how she'd arranged to
get *Alcyone* over to Sucia before she left and then
back to an island with ferry service.

A lilting soprano voice drifted up the stairs. Something from *Carmen* accompanied the unmistakable fra-
grance of fresh popcorn. Zelda's hangover must have
abated.

Downstairs I filled a large bowl with buttery white
kernels and leaned against the counter. Staring at Zelda's back hunched over her keyboard, where she was
challenging every law of ergonomics ever discovered,
I pondered the reports on the Breckenridges.

"No credit card activity for Tina outside the state
since she disappeared," I said.

"The only thing Travels Unlimited booked for Tina
in the past six months was three round-trips for her
clients. I could get a copy of the bookings if you like."

"What about Compass Rose Travel Agency?"

She scowled. "I called them. The owner said you'd need a legal document or something to get that information. The problem is, Dakota chased their Siamese cat last week and they came unglued." She continued scowling at her monitor, and I considered dropping in on Katy Quince unannounced. Paul had said Katy bought the boat named *Electra* and was doing charters out of Roche Harbor. *Alcyone* was still for sale. I wondered if it was moored at Roche Harbor. The phone rang. I glanced at Zelda's phone, which has lines for her, for me, and for Soraya, the naturopath. Mine was blinking. Zelda answered it.

"Yeah, she's right here." She handed the phone to me and went back to glowering at her monitor.

It was Katy Quince. Wondering if I was becoming telepathic, I explained I was investigating Tina's disappearance and I would like to meet with her. Could she come to my office or meet me somewhere?

"I've got a pretty full schedule this week. Is this something we could discuss now? Over the phone?"

Unless there's an emergency or a great geographical distance involved, I prefer to conduct interviews in person. It's far easier for me to interpret responses when I can see the physical gestures and facial expressions of the person I'm interviewing. I also prefer to meet in my office or a neutral environment, but something in Katy's voice told me that wasn't about to happen and I didn't want to alienate her. I told her I was going out to Roche Harbor and offered to drop by her shop.

There was a moment of silence, then she suggested that I come by around noon. Would that work?

It would. It was eleven-fifteen, and I'd have time to get some new batteries for the digital camera before I left. And after I talked to Katy I could run by Roche Harbor and take some photos of *Alcyone* and *Electra*.

1

My gray Volvo wagon was parked in the lot above the Port of Friday Harbor's administration building. It had 227,000 miles on the odometer, but still chugged its way along the island roads. A couple of years ago, when the island was struck by a rare storm that left six feet of late-December snow, followed by freezing January rain, I'd considered trading the wagon in for a snappy SUV or a sexy little sports car. But the market was down and my mutual fund was depressed, so I'd decided to keep it. Besides, only in the movies do PIs drive eye-catching, fire-engine-red sports cars; the Volvo wagon was far more helpful in maintaining my low profile.

As I drove up Guard Street past the Olde Gazette Building, a tall, slender woman with soft brown hair and a long skirt was going into Zelda's office. It was Lily MacGregor, wife of the trouble-making Mac MacGregor.

I turned onto Roche Harbor Road, which wound past the mobile home park and the road to the solid waste recycling center. The sun had broken through the morning layer of clouds, and the open, rolling meadows displayed a carpet of yellow buttercups. Stalks of purple larkspur bloomed along the roadside. Last year Angela had dragged me on a wildflower walk, and the botanist had explained that the flow-

ering meadows of the San Juan Islands are a result of
glaciers that deposited thin layers of silt and sand over
gravel and rocks. I'd also learned about the rosy flowers of Hooker's Onion and Indian Paintbrush and the
rare Chocolate Lily that bloom on Yellow Island and
at Iceberg Point on Lopez Island, and how to identify
the abundant stands of yarrow throughout the islands.

Eight miles or so from town, I turned right on Rouleau Road, then left on the appropriately named
Meadow Road. Three cream-colored horses grazed in
a field of marguerites alongside four black-and-white
Holstein cows. The one-lane road was bordered with
tall green grasses. At the end, a carved wooden sign
on a post announced CANVAS BY QUINCE and pointed
with a black arrow toward a big gray building. To the
right of the building stood a double-wide mobile home
with a canary-yellow motorcycle parked in front. It
was a late-model Ducati, which I happen to know
would have cost at least ten thousand dollars. On a
rise behind the building a large house was under construction. Two men with baseball caps and plaid wool
shirts who were putting on siding stopped, watched
while I got out of the Volvo, nodded, and went back
to work. The gravelly voice of Willie Nelson grieving
for lost loves drifted out of the dusty black boom box
on the ground beside them.

I moved around the metallic teal-green F-150 Ford
pickup parked in front of the gray building and pushed
open the door. The hinges squeaked. Katy looked up
from the gigantic piece of indigo canvas she was cutting on a long worktable that filled a large portion of
the room. The chords of a Celtic harp drifted from
speakers on the high table behind her. From the dirty
ashtray on the cutting table, a small stream of cigarette
smoke wafted to the ceiling.

"Hi, Scotia. Come on in. How've you been?" She
gave me a small smile. "Let me finish this piece and

we can talk. Help yourself to some coffee." She motioned toward the Mr. Coffee machine in the back of the room.

"Take your time," I said. I filled a green cup with coffee and wandered around the warehouse-like space. Bolts of colored canvas filled the shelves behind the worktable. To one side stood an industrial sewing machine. Several see-through plastic bags filled with cushions were stacked near the door. I pulled a stool up to the table, sat down, and watched Katy. Her mop of curly coppery hair almost dwarfed her face as it fell to her shoulders. She glanced at a pencil sketch with printed measurements and frowned in concentration. Katy was a big woman, probably five-ten, at least 190 pounds. She had wide shoulders, large breasts, ample hips. A perfect Rubens model. A *zaftig* woman, my articulate Armenian friend from college would have called her. Tugging a faded blue denim work shirt down over her gray sweats, she squinted through tortoiseshell glasses at the sketch, made a measurement with a long metal ruler, finished the cut across the wide piece of fabric, and separated the two pieces.

"You're building a house?" I asked.

"Yep. Fifteen years in a mobile home is enough. And it might even be finished in another year or so." She folded the blue fabric into neat squares. "Those two clowns out there promised to work last weekend while we were off-island. Of course they didn't show. We can't get any of the licensed contractors on the island because they're all building million-dollar houses."

I'd heard it before.

"How did you learn to sew canvas?" I asked.

She shrugged. "From my father, who learned from his father in a small town on the coast of Maine. My mother made all our clothes. I was the only girl in a family of six, so I learned to sew. And since I was a dummy at math, I took home ec in high school instead of trig. So it was just a hop, skip, and jump to helping my daddy make sails and sail covers."

I smiled, remembering my grandmother Jessica, seated squarely in a wooden chair in front of her Singer, squinting through her bifocals as she fabricated my sensible cotton shirtwaists and corduroy jumpers.

"And sewing canvas is easier than making button-holes on pinafores or welted pockets on jackets," I said softly.

"You, too, huh?" She smiled at me, rummaged around on the worktable, found a pack of Virginia Slims. "When I bought this business three years ago, it was a long shot. I didn't know if I would make any money or if it was just somebody's tax write-off." She extracted a cigarette, pulled a small book of matches from her shirt pocket, and lit the cigarette.

I wondered where the money for the new house was coming from. "And have you figured it out?"

"It's somewhere in between. The business is great from April through August. Everybody and their brother-in-law wants a new sail cover or new cockpit cushions or whatever. Then by September the season is over. Nobody seems to care about replacing any-thing for the winter. How the hell are you supposed to live up here from October to April?" She pulled up a tall stool next to me. "Never mind. I'm just whining."

"Is that when you came to the island? Three years ago?"

She took a long drag on the cigarette and shook her head. "Actually, Danny and I moved here five years ago. From Seattle."

I laid the microcassette recorder on the worktable between us. "Okay if I record our conversation, Katy?"

She gave the recorder a sideways glance and shrugged. "Sure."

"I've been hired to investigate Tina Breckenridge's disappearance. I'm trying to reconstruct her where-abouts the day before she disappeared. Since you were working for her, I thought you might be able to help me."

"Disappearance?" She frowned. "I thought the sheriff said Tina drowned."

"That's true. But her family doesn't believe it."

She stared at me without speaking.

"Tina disappeared on April 19 or 20," I said. "I understand you taught a sailing class that day."

She nodded. "Heavy-weather sailing. A three-day class."

"Where did you sail on those three days?"

"I took them up to Sucia on Tuesday. We had rea-sonable weather, about ten knots of wind. We dropped the anchor in Echo Bay. On Wednesday morning I did a lecture on sail balance and control, then we went ashore for a picnic and hike. In the afternoon we did a sail and concentrated on reefing and heavy-weather tactics." She paused, took another drag off the cigarette, and stubbed it out. "Wednesday night the weather started deteriorating."

"You spent Wednesday night anchored out?"

"Yeah, in Echo Bay again. Thursday morning we headed back, and everybody got a chance to practice their new reefing skills. It was blowing twenty-five knots by the time we got to Waldron. Perfect for a heavy-weather sailing course, but we had plenty of white knuckles." She gave me a grin. "The wind kept building, so I ducked in behind Johns Island and we took a lunch break in Reid Harbor. It calmed every-body down."

"How many did you have on board?"

"Four. They'd all had Tina's basic course. We got back to the dock about four-thirty. Everybody was ready to leave by five-fifteen or so."

"Were all the students from off-island?"

She lit another cigarette and squinted into the cigarette smoke. I could feel my sinuses filling up. "Yeah. I think two were from Seattle, one from Boise, Idaho." She shrugged. "The other one I don't remember. Some place on the East Coast, I think."

"Everybody happy with the class?"

She gave a small laugh and rolled her eyes. "There's always one complainer in every class. The woman from out East complained that what I was teaching her was contradictory to what Tina had taught her in the introductory class. That we were supposed to reef the mainsail *before* we left the dock. I told her Tina was a worrywart and that I was teaching this class."

"Did you tell Tina about her?"

"Yeah, I think I mentioned it. She always came down at the end of classes. Debriefing, she called it. Sort of a PR thing with her. Wanted to make sure all the clients were happy. Then she had this arrangement with Tom's Taxi. He took them back to the airport or the ferry, or wherever they wanted to go. It was a part of the package."

"What did Tina do after the students left?"

"She was late that day. Didn't get there until after they left. We discussed how the class went. She checked the boat over, then we locked up and walked up to the store. She said she needed some groceries. That's the last I saw of her."

"What time would that have been?"

"Probably about six o'clock."

"Did she mention any plans for the evening?"

She shook her head.

"How did *you* spend the evening of April 19?"

"You sound like the sheriff." She smiled. "But that's okay. I drove straight to the ferry, where I met Danny. We drove to Seattle and then flew to L.A. to see Danny's sister." She stood, pulled out a file drawer behind her. "Here's the itinerary. I just paid the credit card yesterday."

She reached in a folder and handed me a sheet of paper. It was an Alaska Airlines trip itinerary for Katy and Daniel Quince. On April 19 they were scheduled to fly from SEATAC airport to Los Angeles International. On April 26 they were scheduled to return from Los Angeles to Seattle. I handed her the paper without mentioning that an itinerary was no guarantee that the passengers had actually been on the flights.

"Coming back on Sunday was a shock, I can tell you." She pursed her lips, crushed out the cigarette and stood up.

"Paul said you bought *Electra*," I said. "Are you doing sailing classes?"

"I thought about it, but I'm not organized or ambitious enough to work the boat shows. I thought maybe I could do occasional charters with some people I know from California. Enough to pay for the moorage, which would let me do some sailing on my own."

"How was Tina to work for?" I asked.

She considered my question. "We had a few disagreements. My brand of East Coast sailing was a little different from her West Coast style."

"You learned to sail in Maine?"

She nodded. "I learned to sail before I learned to walk. Five older brothers with a sailing dinghy, and I was always tagging along."

"What sort of disagreements did you have with Tina?"

"Just sniveling little stuff." She took another drag on her cigarette, crushed it out in the ashtray, and turned to face me. "She didn't want anyone smoking on the boat. Another time the inflatable got a leak and she said I'd let the students drag it over rocks, which wasn't true." She shrugged. "One time she got her knickers in a twist over one of the students not wearing a life jacket." She rolled her eyes. "Sometimes Tina just overreacted, so I took it all with a grain of salt."

I glanced around the shop. "How did you juggle your canvas making with sailing instruction? Wasn't it all in the same season?"

"Like all the other worker bees, I work twenty-four/seven for six months and starve the rest of the year."

"Your husband's a yacht broker?"

She seemed surprised by my question. "Yeah . . . yeah, he just started last year, but business is pretty good. Hopefully, that'll pay off the construction loan on the new house."

"How would you describe Tina's state of mind the last time you saw her?"

She lit another cigarette, laid it in the ashtray and folded her hands on the table. "Well, it was no secret she was having problems with Stephan. Her son." She glanced at her watch. "But she never discussed it with me."

"Do you think Tina fell overboard?"

She looked at me sharply, her brown eyes probing mine. She combed her hair with her fingers, took another drag on the cigarette, stubbed it out. "Tina was in a funny mood that night, kind of jumpy. But she put up barriers, you know. You just didn't ask her personal questions." She stared at me. "Look, it was no secret Tina was drinking too much. I don't know why she would have taken *Alcyone* out, but if she did, she could have done something dumb and fallen overboard. That's the only explanation I can think of." Her voice was abrupt. Either Katy Quince didn't know anything about Tina's disappearance or she wasn't about to share what she knew with me.

The silence in the room was broken by the squeaking of the door hinges. Three large brown cushions slid into the shop, followed by a tall, white-haired man with a big belly.

"Hey, Chet." Katy walked around the worktable, reached for the cushions and put them on a bench behind the table. "Have a little project for me?"

"Sure do. My wife says if we're leaving for Alaska in June, I'm already three months behind."

She glanced at me and pursed her lips. "Be right with you," she said.

I turned off the recorder and pulled on my foul-weather jacket. She followed me to the door. I thanked her for her time and gave her one of my business cards. "Give me a call if you think of anything relevant."

"Will do." She smiled and closed the door.

Across the driveway the two carpenters were leaning against the unfinished house, drinking from thermos cups. Willie Nelson had been replaced by Patsy Cline. I glanced back at the closed shop door. Except for the information that Tina was meticulous about seamanship, and that she might have an alcohol problem, the interview had produced zip. If I was going to find out what had happened to Tina Breckenridge, I'd have to do a lot better than I had so far at following her footsteps on Thursday evening, April 19.

I pulled the Polaroid camera from the carryall. The carpenters watched curiously as I began to snap photos of the surroundings, then they suddenly disappeared inside the unfinished structure. I stowed the camera, drove out the potholed driveway, back down Meadow Road, and headed for Roche Harbor.

8

I left the Volvo behind the old Hotel De Haro at Roche Harbor, in front of the sign that said RESTAURANT PARKING ONLY. I checked my notebook and dialed Paul Breckenridge's number. He answered on the first ring and supplied the slip number on H dock for the *Alcyone*. He didn't know which slip Katy was keeping the *Electra* in. I thanked him and called the office. Zelda reported that my mother and Nick had phoned; both would call back. I asked her to run a background check on Katy and Danny Quince with what information she could put together. She said neither of the wandering canines had been found.

I made my way down the hill past the hotel and the still-closed ice cream stand and espresso booth. May 15 was the official seasonal opening date for the resort, and within a month the place would be filling up with cruisers from Victoria, Vancouver, Seattle, and points south. I stopped at the corner grocery, bought a newspaper, and introduced myself to the short, plump blond woman with pretty blue eyes at the checkout stand. Her name tag identified her as Leslie. I told her I was investigating Tina Breckenridge's disappearance on April 19.

Her smile disappeared and her eyes grew serious. "Oh, that was so terrible."

"Leslie, Tina may have stopped in here the afternoon or evening she disappeared. Did you see her? It was a Thursday."

She pondered my question and slowly shook her head. "I'm sorry. I worked every Thursday in April, but I really can't remember. You know, I saw her around here a couple times a week, but late afternoon is a really busy time." She looked like she was about to cry. "I'm sorry, really I am. I just don't remember."

"It's okay, Leslie." I handed her my card. "Give me a call if you remember anything."

I left her staring sorrowfully at my card and headed down past the café above the old marina. The smell of grilling burgers reminded me it had been a long time since I had consumed that cinnamon roll at the Netshed. With a bowl of chowder and a wedge of warm sourdough in hand, I found an empty table by the window and watched the gardener filling the flower bed above the fuel dock with red geraniums. Two small black-and-tan dogs romped on the manicured lawn. Across the marina a few weak rays of sun lit up the white chapel on the hillside, but a solid layering of stratus clouds promised more rain and probably wind. I spooned up the last of the chowder and headed down the long ramp to the main dock. The bookkeeper at the harbormaster's office advised that the *Electra* was moored on F dock, slip 21.

A sloop-rigged vessel with a white hull and a blue mainsail cover, *Electra* was moored next to a classic wooden yacht of an Edward Monk design. A gray inflatable was stored upside down on the foredeck. A small outboard engine, neatly covered by a blue canvas cover, was padlocked to the stern pulpit next to a yellow bag with man-overboard equipment. Three white fenders protected the hull. The mooring lines were all appropriately attached to the vessel and to the dock. The varnished hatch boards in the companionway were in place and secured with a padlock. By all appearances, *Electra* was being well cared for; I didn't spot anything that would have made her meticulous former owner unhappy.

Alcyone, the vessel that had been found drifting and abandoned near Sucia Island, was moored on H dock. As I approached the slip number Paul had given me, I spied the tall, lean, blue-jean-clad figure of Rafie Dominguez standing on the foredeck of *MacNamara's Lace,* the black-hulled sailboat on the other side of the dock. Rafie's long black hair hung loose, partially covering his face. He was polishing the stainless-steel bow pulpit with a small white cloth, his back to me. I stood watching him, reminded that the *DragonSpray* needed a thorough spring cleanup. My six-hour single-handed slog in the rain and wind from Montague Harbor on Monday—after Sir Galahad had abandoned me to fly off to rescue Guinevere—had left me too exhausted and dispirited to do any cleanup.

"When you finish that, Rafie, I could keep you busy on *DragonSpray* for about a month," I said.

He dipped the white cloth in the container of metal polish, turned and smiled, his teeth very white in his brown face.

"Hello, Scotia. I am trying to clean her so we can go to Victoria this weekend. I think it make sunshine on Friday."

"Rafie, I devoutly hope it makes sunshine on Friday." I pulled the camera from the rucksack, pressed the minuscule power button and set the exposure lever to Auto. "Zelda says you still haven't found the dogs."

Rafie's smile disappeared. "It makes two days now. I think someone shoot them, no?" He motioned toward the *Alcyone.* "You are making an investigation about Doña Tina?"

"Yes, I am. Has *Alcyone* always been in this slip next to you and David?" I asked, snapping some side shots of the boat. It was an older C&C, probably thirty-six feet, with at least six large self-tailing winches.

"As long as I am here."

Rafie's name did not appear on my idiosyncratic sociogram of suspects and informants, but connections oftentimes emerged in unexpected places. "Did you happen to be around the Thursday Tina disappeared?"

He dipped the cloth into the polish one more time and applied the gray paste to the port side stanchion. He frowned and squinted his eyes. "I was getting this boat ready to go to Deer Harbor with our friends. I saw *Alcyone*," he said, "when the . . . the *pelirroja*, how do you say? . . . when she come back."

"The redhead? Katy Quince?"

He nodded, moving along the deck, squatting near the cabin top.

"Can you tell me what happened after they got back that afternoon?"

"The boat come in about four o'clock, I think. I tried to help them tie the lines, but Katy say, 'No, the womans have to do it.' " He shrugged.

"Then what happened?"

He moved further aft, sat on one of the seats in the cockpit, and began polishing the binnacle. "They clean the boat, and everybody have their, their *equipaje* on the dock, and then they bringed a cart to the dock and everybody go away."

"Before Tina came to the boat?"

"She came later."

"Did you hear her talking to Katy?"

He considered the question. "No, I am inside."

"What time did they leave?"

"I do not know. I do not see them leave."

"How late were you here that day, Rafie?"

"David come to the boat, we finish the work and drink a beer, and then we go to the restaurant."

"What time do you think that was?"

"Maybe seven o'clock." He stood up and stretched. "Do you want to see inside?" he asked, motioning toward the boat.

"Of *Alcyone*? I would, but I forgot to ask Paul for the key."

"No problem."

He smiled and swung nimbly down from the deck of David's boat, walked across the dock, and stepped onto *Alcyone*. From under the crisp blue binnacle cover, he pulled out a red plastic float with two dangling keys. I followed him into the cockpit and wondered how many other people knew where the keys were hidden. He unlocked the padlock on the companionway and gestured for me to descend into the cabin. I photographed the galley, the main salon, the two small cabins and the head.

"The police check it out," Rafie offered. "They bringed the dogs that sniff for drugs and take out many things." He motioned to the cabins and the settees in the main salon.

So the possibility of drugs had been eliminated. Or at least they hadn't been mentioned in anything I'd seen or heard so far. I photographed the exterior of the navigation table, one side of which was covered with a thick stack of charts, and also the interior, where I found the usual sailing paraphernalia: a logbook, a set of dividers and parallel rules, a yellow lined pad, several sharpened pencils, a knife in a sheath, some tiny spare lightbulbs and fuses. I leafed through the logbook, found the entries for April 17, 18, and 19. According to the entry for April 19, *Alcyone* had departed from Echo Bay on Sucia Island at 0900 hours. The wind was sixteen knots out of the southeast. Subsequent entries described putting first one reef and then two reefs in the mainsail, the rising wind, and the entry into Reid Harbor on Stuart Island to drop anchor and take a lunch break. *Alcyone* had arrived back at Roche Harbor at 1615 hours. Four-fifteen P.M. There were no further entries in the log. If Tina had taken *Alcyone* out that Thursday night, she hadn't made any entry regarding time of departure or her destination.

The lockers above the settee in the main salon contained plastic dinnerware and utensils. A cupboard on the port side held cruising guides, a Clive Cussler novel, and a collection of Emily Dickinson poetry. I opened the storage lockers under the settee cushions around the table and found six PFD's, the Coast Guard regulation life vests that Tina had been so conscientious about using. There were no empty wine bottles or bottles of Cuervo Gold. If there had ever been any clues on *Alcyone* that would have pointed to Tina's actions on the night she disappeared, they were long gone.

I stared around me. Had Tina Breckenridge spent her last night on this boat, perhaps in an attempt to escape from domestic problems? Or was the drifting boat simply a ruse and she had made other arrangements to disappear? However the boat got out of the slip, it had to have happened after Rafie and David left for dinner.

I followed Rafie topside and photographed the cockpit. He returned the cabin key to its hiding place under the binnacle cover, and we stepped down onto the dock. "When did you and David leave for Deer Harbor that weekend?" I asked.

"The next day, on Friday."

"In the morning?"

"Yes, we come here at nine o'clock, but our friends they are late."

"*Alcyone* was gone when you got here?"

He nodded, staring at the boat. "Is a mystery, no?"

"It is a mystery, indeed."

I gave him one of my cards and asked him to call me if he recalled anything strange or unusual about the day Tina disappeared.

His black, thickly lashed eyes met mine for a fraction of a second. He blinked, took the card, pocketed it.

"Sorry to have interrupted your work, Rafie."

" 'Bye, Scotia."

I made a note of the other boat names and registration numbers in the slips on both sides of *Alcyone* and across the dock on either side of *MacNamara's Lace*. Back at the harbormaster's office I identified myself, and the assistant harbormaster readily supplied the names of the boat owners I was interested in. One of the slips next to David Kean's boat was currently empty.

"Do you have phone numbers for them?"

She looked up from the book of records. "I do, but I can't give them out. Security and all that, you know." She smiled, but her voice was firm.

"Can you tell me if any of them are local?"

"Numbers 32 and 36 are local."

"What about Number 35, next to *MacNamara's Lace*?"

"The moorage contract is in the name of Elizabeth McCurdy." She glanced up. "Not a local. She's got a B.C. address. In Campbell River."

I thanked her and proceeded back along the main dock and up the steeply canted ramp below the café. It was a long shot, but if any of the people from the neighboring boats had been on the docks that Thursday night, somebody might have seen something.

It was after two o'clock by the time I got back to town. My parking place in the port lot had been taken, and I circled twice around before a battered blue VW van pulled out. I darted into the spot and sat for several minutes in the car, sorting out my thoughts, staring at the harbor. The sun I had glimpsed on the west side of the island had disappeared, and now a solid ceiling of dark gray clouds hovered over the town.

What I had learned from Katy Quince was that she and Tina had small differences about seamanship and safety, and that she thought Tina drank too much, that she had last seen Tina headed for the grocery store. Rafie Dominguez had seen Tina come down to the boat, but hadn't seen her leave. After two days, I was no closer to answering the big question: where had Tina Breckenridge gone when she left Roche Harbor that Thursday afternoon? If, indeed, she had ever left.

I locked the Volvo and headed for the stairway that connects the parking lot with First Street, a stairway that has seventy-eight steps. I puffed my way up them, considering the need to improve my cardiovascular health and remembering that I was meeting Angela for a swim at the health club that afternoon. As sheriff's dispatcher, she can sometimes access information that a private citizen such as myself can't. Since our friendship dates back to my early days with the San Diego Police Department—when I was fresh out of the police academy and she was the young medical examiner—it was within the realm of possibility that I could pick her brain for more details on the alleged Breckenridge drowning.

Breathing hard, I paused at the top of the stairs, then gasped my way across First Street toward the courthouse and the Olde Gazette Building.

"Those steps do separate the girls from the women, don't they?"

Jared Saperstein stood on the corner of First and Court, a thick manila portfolio under one arm. He was attired in a soft brown sweater under a tan rain-coat, brown cords, and a brown fedora. Formal dress for a Friday Harbor newspaper publisher on a Wednesday afternoon. And especially formal for one whose usual look was blue jeans and a flannel shirt. I wondered what the occasion was.

I took a deep breath. "You've got that right."

"I'm headed to George's for a late lunch," he said. "Want to join me for a sandwich and a beer?"

After the huge bowl of chowder I'd consumed at Roche Harbor, food was not foremost on my mind, but a beer sounded good. "Sure." I glanced at the file under his arm. "Any new scandals mongering about?"

"Just came from a long and heated meeting of the whale watch operators," Jared said.

We walked down the hill past the new upscale women's clothing store and architect's office. "Anything get solved?"

"Not really. But the county is being pushed hard to do something to control or monitor the operators." He opened the side door to the tavern, and we headed toward the bar. The three other customers were bent over the billiard table, their heads faintly visible in the cloud of cigarette smoke.

"Hi, guys. What'll it be?" Lindsey Lowell, Henry's comely fiancée, folded her arms across her chest and smiled at us. She was tall, trim, and green-eyed and it wasn't difficult to figure out what Henry saw in her. It was the reverse I couldn't figure out.

"Mushroom burger medium, no onions, and a pale ale," Jared replied. He plopped the portfolio on the bar and put his hat on top of it.

Lindsey glanced at me and raised her eyebrows. "Scotia?"

"Just a pale ale," I said.

I tapped the file in front of Jared. "Homework?"

He nodded. "Bunch of stuff on orca whale research about what might be causing the decrease in the population. Chemical pollution, PCB's, noise pollution. There are so many strident voices and so many personal agendas, it's hard to know exactly what the problem is. To say nothing of trying to solve it."

The waters surrounding the San Juan Islands—in particular the ten-mile stretch of Haro Strait from Cat-

tle Pass at the south end of San Juan Island up to
Speiden Channel on the north, are home to three pods
of resident orca whales: J-, and K-, and L-pods. It is,
in fact, these huge black-and-white cetaceans that are
the prime lure for the thousands of tourists that over-
whelm the island each summer. So popular are the
creatures that it is not unusual on a July Sunday for
fifty or sixty boats—both commercial whale watch operators and private vessels—to accompany the whales
as they forage for salmon in the waters of the strait.
Over the past five years, however, the number of resident whales has dropped from ninety-nine to seventy-
eight. Recently a coalition of conservation groups has
petitioned the National Marine Fisheries Service to
list the San Juan orcas as an endangered species, and
the whole issue has become a political hot potato.

The ale was cool and tasted slightly of lemon.

Lindsey put a basket of burger and french fries on
the counter. Jared reached for the catsup.

"Any news on the photo shoot at American
Camp?" I asked.

"You mean other than Abby making a horse's ass
of herself? She was parading around out there with
posters at the crack of dawn this morning and harass-
ing anybody who tried to come in and out. Nigel's
furious."

"He's the sheriff. He could always arrest her." I
watched Jared munch his burger and wished I'd ordered one.

"Abby was Nigel's biology teacher," Jared muttered
between bites. "Apparently he cut class once in the
ninth grade, and she made him copy the entire U.S.
Constitution before she'd let him back in."

"Must have made an impression on him."

"It's not for general distribution, and it's only my
opinion, but I think the sheriff had a minor heart attack this morning."

I stared at him. "Nigel Bishop?"

"He's not in the hospital," Jared continued, "but I went by to check this week's sheriff's log and the EMS people were there. They had Nigel on a cot for about an hour. He insisted it was just a touch of the flu and refused to listen to anyone. He was still there this afternoon. White as a sheet. And his wife is off-island."

We sat in silence. I knew that Jared was considering the same thought I was: if the ultraconservative Nigel Bishop were forced to retire for reasons of health, there would be much celebrating on the island.

Someone put some money in the jukebox and the mellow voice of Johnny Mathis filled the room.

"How are you progressing with the Breckenridge case?" Jared asked.

I sighed. "I've talked to Tina's husband and to Katy Quince and to Rafie Dominguez. Paul agreed with brother M.J. that Tina would never have fallen overboard. Or, if she had, she wouldn't have drowned. She was an excellent swimmer and a fanatic about life vests. Katy Quince suggested rather broadly that Tina drank too much and could have, as she put it, 'done something dumb and fallen overboard.'" I filched a french fry from Jared's basket. "There are, of course, many possibilities: an accident, as Katy suggested, by falling overboard after drinking alcohol and drowning because she got swept away in the currents. Although if she'd been wearing her PFD, it's more likely that the body would have been found by now. Or an accident where she somehow hit her head when she went overboard, and *didn't* have her PFD on. And ruling out an accident, there's homicide, either planned or spontaneous." I savored the perfectly cooked fry.

"As well as being kidnapped or disappearing of her own volition," Jared said. "How is Rafie Dominguez connected?"

"He's not, really. I just ran into him on the dock at Roche. Since David Kean's boat is just across the dock from the *Alcyone*, I thought he might have seen something."

"And?"

"He saw the class come in and saw Tina come down after the class left, but he didn't see Tina or Katy leave."

"Any intuitive theories yet?"

"None. According to the background checks, Tina's lily white. There's no body, no suspects, no motives. My mind is mostly a blank, I'm embarrassed to admit."

Jared chewed on a french fry. "An absolutely blank mind is always an advantage. Simply observe and draw inferences." He turned to me and smiled. "Sir Arthur Conan Doyle. *The Adventure of the Cardboard Box*."

"Nothing from dear Edgar today?" I asked. Jared was an insatiable collector of Arthur Conan Doyle and Edgar Allen Poe first editions, and he had memorized the most trivial details of the two authors' cases and tales.

"I seem to recall something similar involving a lady's disappearance. I'll do some research tonight. Meanwhile, I would imagine you've got your indefatigable assistant hard at work doing background checks on all and sundry?"

I nodded and finished the last sip of ale. "If she can drag herself away from haute cuisine, floral arrangements, rock bands, and God knows what else."

"The big party for On the Edge this weekend?"

I nodded.

"Considering some of the media crew are from Southern California, she might want to add cocaine to the 'God knows what else,'" he said, glancing at his watch and reaching for the check.

"I'll pass it on. Abigail's never going to forgive her for consorting with the enemy. I hope the Coronas survive this one."

Jared laid a ten and a five on the check, waved away my offer of a contribution, and helped me with my jacket. It was three-thirty. Outside, the wind had risen, and a few drops of rain were falling. He smiled and patted my arm. "Remember, dear lady, if Tina didn't disappear voluntarily and there was foul play, it is highly unlikely that your criminal has wings. As long as he or she remains on two legs, there must be some indentation, some abrasion, some trifling displacement that can be detected by the scientific researcher. Of which you are the best." He shifted the file to his left arm and pulled a pipe from his coat pocket.

"Thank you, Dr. Watson." I turned up the collar of my jacket, checked for traffic, and cut diagonally across Second Street. For some reason, as I climbed the hill, I glanced back at Jared.

He was no longer alone. Allison Fisher, resplendent in a camel-colored wool suit and elegant brown boots, stood next to him. As I watched, she took his arm and gave him a kiss. They crossed the street and headed toward the movie theater. Jared paused in front of the ticket window, purchased the tickets, and the two of them disappeared inside.

A matinee on a Wednesday afternoon.

I couldn't remember the last time Nick and I had gone to a movie, even in the evening. Or done anything that wasn't scheduled around his work or his daughter, Nicole. Now Madame-X (ex-wife Cathy) had been added to the soap opera. And Jared Saperstein, my romantic insurance policy, had been snapped up by a sexier and apparently wiser female than me. I continued on up the hill past the courthouse. Just as I got to the top, my cell phone chirped. It was Lily MacGregor.

"I'm sorry for not calling back sooner, Scotia. I haven't . . . I haven't been feeling well. I've got some free time this afternoon. Do you want to come over and talk about Tina?"

"I can be there in twenty minutes."

9

"I've known Tina since kindergarten," Lily said, leaning slightly to one side in the old wooden chair behind the antique desk at the Secret Garden. "The Carlyles lived in the old rental house at the end of our lane. Tina and M.J. and I rode the school bus together every day. And played softball together and did 4-H. Then one day, when I was eleven, Tina came shrieking down the driveway and told me they were moving to Ballard." She smiled and sipped from the pale yellow cup of herbal tea.

Ballard is a colorful neighborhood in North Seattle tucked up next to Shilshole Marina on Elliot Bay. Formerly home to commercial fishermen and boatbuilders, it is now being invaded by trendy boutiques and Sunday excursions of boomers and yuppies and generation X-ers.

"Neither of us knew exactly where Ballard was," she continued, "but we both knew what it meant. I begged my mother to ask Mrs. Carlyle if Tina could move in with us. When that didn't work, we ran away. We made sandwiches and put them in our book bags along with our pj's and sneaked M.J.'s pup tent out of the attic and hitchhiked out to American Camp. I think we thought Tina's parents would be so worried about us that they wouldn't make her move. But when it got dark and all the little critters came out, I started crying and the whole adventure was over. We hitch-hiked back to town and got grounded for a month."

"Moving is harder on children than parents realize."

Lily smiled and glanced down at my tape recorder, which she'd said I could use. Her blue eyes stared into the air over my head. "There was something I never told Tina."

I waited and the silence grew. "Which was?"

"That what I was most upset about was that M.J. was moving away."

"More than Tina?"

She nodded. "I'd had a crush on him since I was six." She tilted her head back and ran her hands through her long, silky, pale brown hair. Her slight, small-breasted body pushed against the white cotton fabric of her dress. I noticed the purple bruise on her left cheekbone and recalled Zelda's comment about Mac MacGregor's fits of jealousy. And that Lily had said on the phone she "hadn't been feeling well."

"M.J. and Tina left the island more than twenty years ago. Did you and M.J. stay in touch all that time?"

"Tina and I wrote to each other all through high school. For a while we spent summer vacations to-gether, here on the island or down in Ballard, which I thought was a totally cool place. Then we both got summer jobs and we graduated and everything changed. For all of us." She touched the small porce-lain figure of a red fox on the desk and enumerated the changes: M.J. had received a scholarship to UCLA, gotten into fashion photography, moved back to Seattle. Tina had worked for a boatbuilder in Bal-lard and taken classes at a community college. And she, Lily, had married Mac MacGregor. "Then one day I got a postcard from Kodiak. Tina and her friend Joy Johnson were in Alaska." She sighed. "And here I was, married to Mac and six months pregnant and we were living with my parents. I was green with envy." She stared into space, lost in reminiscence.

"And then Tina came back to the island and married Paul," I prompted.

She nodded. "She and Joy came back and stayed with us. They were going back to Alaska in the fall, but it didn't work out like that."

"What happened?"

"For starters, my mom didn't like Joy. She thought she was kind of . . . *rough*, I guess you'd say. She used a lot of vulgar language and she smoked in the house even though Mom asked her not to. She'd go off and drink beer with the local guys and stay out all night. Then Tina started dating Paul and they ran off and got married. It was really fast. Tina moved into Paul's little house out in the valley, and Joy split and went back to Alaska. Tina got pregnant, and in November Paul went back to Alaska."

Again her gaze went far away. "It was a little like the old days, but not really. Tina hated Mac and didn't care who knew it, so I sort of walked a tightrope between them. We both home-schooled our kids. Mac's business took off, and Paul came and went. My dad died, and then my mother."

"What was going on with M.J.?"

"He got married. I think she had a lot of money. But it didn't last and they got divorced. Then he married Edie and he started working with On the Edge. I think she's got a lot of money. After we got computers for the boys, Tina and I and M.J. got into a three-way e-mail kind of thing." She tilted her head and smiled. "Nothing heavy, just silly stuff, like three little kids catching up from where we all left off."

"And Mac found out?" I was guessing.

She nodded. "I'd been showing him how to send E-mail and do his construction estimates and billings on the computer. A few months ago, he got into my e-mail and found a message from M.J. He picked up the computer and threw it out the window," she said ruefully. "When he found out M.J. was back on the island for the photo shoot, he went ballistic." She shook her head. "It was so stupid. I hadn't even *seen* M.J. for years."

"What was in the e-mail from M.J.?"

"Just casual stuff. What he was doing, how he was looking forward to coming back to the island for the photo shoot. How was Sean doing. Could he and I and Tina get together when he was up here?"

"Do Sean and Stephan still hang out together?"

"Yeah. Though not as much as before. Stephan's a lot smarter than Sean." She hesitated. "Stephan's gotten mixed up with some boys Sean doesn't like. I told Tina about it. After they were caught smoking pot at Brown Sugar Beach, Sean's been staying away from Stephan."

"When was the last time you saw Tina?"

She hesitated, glanced at the spiral-bound calendar on the desk, and leafed back a couple of pages. She scanned the sheet for April. "It would have been about a week before she disappeared. The tennis team had a game off-island, and we had a burger at George's while we were waiting for the boys to get back on the ferry."

"How would you describe her state of mind that day?"

She stared at me. "She was upset with Stephan. We talked about it a lot. He just couldn't make the adjustment from home-schooling to public school. His grades were in the basement, and he picked the worst troublemakers in school to hang out with. A bunch of them got arrested for vandalism out at the airport. The only things he cared about were tennis and computers."

"Was Tina depressed?"

She considered the question. "Not exactly *depressed.*

But jumpy. Like something was on her mind. It was hard to talk to her. It seemed like her mind was a million miles away."

"Did Tina have a drinking problem?"

She looked at me in surprise. "No. Not that I knew about. I never saw her have any more than one or two glasses of wine."

"Any marital problems with Paul she ever told you about?"

"They've been fighting for a couple years. When Stephan was ten, he tested out as gifted and she wanted him to go away to private school. Paul refused. He worships the ground Tina walks on, but he dug his heels in on that one. That's when she started the sailing school."

"Where'd she get the money for Pleiades?"

"I think she and M.J. inherited some money when their mother died."

"Paul was away in Alaska a lot," I said. "Did Tina ever get involved with anyone else?"

She frowned and her eyes searched my face. "A couple of years ago, she mentioned she'd met an old friend," she said slowly. "She seemed excited about it. But she never mentioned it again and I forgot about it. Paul's not like Mac, but I don't think he would have put up with Tina playing around."

"Did Tina ever talk about leaving Paul?"

She hesitated, then shook her head.

"She ever share any problems with the sailing school? Problems with clients or people who worked for her?"

She pursed her mouth, considered the question and frowned, then shook her head. I thought she was about to say more when the phone rang. She answered it and reached for a pencil and paper.

I stood, stretched, and wandered toward the big cooler in the back of the shop. I stared at the elegant bouquets waiting for a recipient. Red roses, freesia, larkspur, and snapdragons. Tiny purple iris and tall apricot gladiolas and three pale gardenias. Across the room from the cooler four ceramic vases in a spectrum of earth colors reposed on a tall étagère. A rectangular wrought-iron table held greeting cards and small gift cards and bolts of ribbon. Behind me, Lily's soft voice confirmed a date for a wedding and made an appointment to discuss the details. I gazed through the tall windows that overlooked a fenced garden where a slight female figure bent over a row of new plants. A large white cubical package was open on the ground beside her. Peat moss or some other soil amendment, I imagined.

Lily hung up the phone and stared at her calendar. I was out of questions. Whatever Tina's "big problem" was, it didn't appear that she'd confided it to Lily. I gave her my card, asked her to call me if she thought of any information that would help my investigation, and let myself out. I drove slowly through the woods and came to a stop at the intersection, mulling over my conversation with Lily and remembering that out of all of Tina's family and friends, only Lily had referred to her in the present tense. I turned right onto Schoolhouse Road and was wondering whether there was any more sleuthing I might accomplish before returning to the office when my cell phone chirped. It was Lily.

"I just remembered something, Scotia. Tina called me the afternoon before her boat was found. Thursday afternoon. She was looking for Stephan, and she wanted to get together later for a drink. She was calling from her cell phone. She said she had a problem with a client she wanted to talk to me about. I couldn't meet her because Mac and I were just leaving to go to his mother's for dinner."

A problem with a client. "Did she mention the client's name?"

"No, but she was really upset."

"What time was that?"

"It must have been about five thirty. Mac's mother always wants us there by six."

I thanked Lily and drove into town. Tina's cell phone would have a log of incoming calls. I wanted to get my hands on the cell phone, and I wanted to talk to the client with the problem.

I took the steps behind the Grange two at a time and panted my way up the hill to the office. Zelda was on the phone. I grabbed the two pink message slips from my cubby, dropped the little data card from my camera on Zelda's desk, and raced upstairs. Still breathless, I clicked up my E-mail and pounded out a message to Angela, hoping she hadn't left for the health club yet. *Was a cell phone found on the* Alcyone? *Does Paul have it? Need to know ASAP.*

If neither the sheriff nor Paul had the cell phone, then Tina had it with her, wherever that might be. The latter was the most likely, since she'd used it to call Lily just a few hours before she disappeared. I stared impatiently at the computer, noticed the pink message slips I'd grabbed on the way up, and called my mother. There was no answer and I didn't leave a message. Nick's message said he would call back. I stared at the computer monitor, willing it to produce a response from Angela, and noticed that I had a new E-mail message. I downloaded it and read in surprise: *Tina Breckenridge drowned. Let her rest in peace.*

The screen name of the sender was pacific-1875@aol.com. I frowned at the message, wondering who was feeling threatened by my investigation. I clicked on Properties and printed out the entire message with all the cyberspace highway addresses it had traversed to arrive at my e-mail program. To my novice eye, it appeared that it had been sent from the library at 2:23 that afternoon via AOL on the Internet. I dialed the library number, got one of the volunteers, and identified myself. "I've received an anonymous e-mail message sent from the library. Do you know who might have been using the computers at two twenty-three?" She went off to check the computer log.

"There's no sign-in for that time," she reported.

"Would you or anyone remember who might have been in the library then?"

"Oh, no. We ask everybody to sign in, but we can't keep track. I'm sorry."

I thanked her and hung up. I wanted to know who had sent the message, but even more, I needed to find Tina's cell phone. I dialed the sheriff's office and asked for Angela. She had left for the day; could anyone else help me? I thought for a moment, remembered what Jared had said about the sheriff having a minor heart attack, and asked for the undersheriff with whom I'd established a good connection in the process of a recent child abuse case.

"Jeffrey Fountain."

"Jeff, Scotia MacKinnon. I'm sorry to bother you, but I've been hired to investigate the disappearance of Tina Breckenridge, the woman whose boat was found over near Sucia. I know the sheriff has closed the case, but I'm just trying to satisfy the family that it was an accident."

"Sure. How can I help?"

I hesitated. If I asked for the cell phone and he had it and turned me down, then it might be even harder to get hold of it. On the other hand, I wanted to check out the call log as soon as possible.

"Her husband wondered about her cell phone," I lied. "I know you went over the personal property that was on the boat, and he thought you might still have it."

"A cell phone? I thought all her stuff was returned to Paul. Let me look."

I waited, swinging my foot impatiently, re-reading the anonymous E-mail, realizing that it probably meant Tina had met with foul play. It was unlikely that she'd disappeared voluntarily and was sending the message herself.

"Yeah, it's here. Must have fallen out of the file box in the back of the drawer. The file notation says it was found next to her car at Roche. But I don't think it will be of much use to him."

"Why is that?"

"The LCD screen is crushed. Must have been run over."

One very bad day last year, my own cell phone had fallen out of my pocket and I'd run over it with the Volvo. To my surprise, even though it wouldn't transmit, it did still cough up the entire log of incoming call numbers that had been saved.

"Uh, I was going to see him tonight," I lied again. "Okay if I come by and pick it up?"

He hesitated. "Don't know why not. I'll leave it with the receptionist and you can sign for it."

Three minutes later I was standing outside the reception cubicle at the sheriff's office, staring at the ill-fated fluorescent lime-green Nokia cell phone. Splatters of mud marred the top of the device, and the detachable keypad cover was loose. The small viewing window had suffered major contusions and abrasions, but the screen was visible behind it. I pressed the On button. Nothing.

"Looks pretty dead to me," the receptionist offered, handing me a receipt to sign.

I scribbled my signature, put the phone in my pocket, and raced back to the Olde Gazette Building. Zelda had left. I sat down at her desk and pulled out the damaged unit. Tina's phone was identical to my own. I pulled the backup battery from my rucksack and replaced Tina's dead battery. Again I pressed the On button. There was a small hum and three seconds later "Welcome to AT&T" appeared on the LCD screen behind the crushed plastic. Both the battery

charge level and the reception bar were normal. I
keyed in my own number and burst out laughing when
my phone began chirping.

Hoping against hope, I pressed the Menu button,
and scrolled down to the Call Log. "Received calls"
popped up. There were two numbers. One was a local
prefix; the other was 410, which I knew was somewhere on the East Coast. Lily had said that Tina had
mentioned a problem with a client. Katy had said that
the disgruntled student lived on the East Coast. Both
calls had been received on April 19. I grabbed a pad
from Zelda's desk, copied the two numbers, pulled off
my own battery. I dialed the local number first, got
Tom's Taxi, and I pleaded a wrong number.

When I dialed the number, the one with the 410
prefix, a recording informed me that my number was
not on the list of calls being accepted by this number
and invited me to leave a message, which I did, without saying why I was calling. Whoever had called Tina
that Thursday night had a service called "Anonymous
Call Rejection."

I left my name and number, pocketed both cell
phones, and raced out of the building, half an hour
late for my date with Angela and the swimming pool.
I stepped outside, locked the door, and took a deep
breath. Finally, I had something concrete. I was exhila-
rated. This might be the first small indentation, the
trifling displacement that Jared had assured me
would emerge.

10

The women's locker room at the health club was empty. I peeled down to my birthday suit, fumbled in my gym bag for a towel and my black-faded-to-gray tank suit, and wriggled my way into it. I regarded myself in the full-length, anything-but-flattering mirror beside the lockers. I should get a new suit. The body inside the suit was not bad. Not a body that would ever win any beauty pageants or survive comparison with airbrushed photographers' models, but not bad. Five feet five inches, 135 pounds was what my private investigator's license said. After my seven-day bout in February with Montezuma's revenge while Nick and I were vacationing in his client's tangerine-colored villa on the west coast of Mexico, that was close enough. Good, round boobs. Strong arms and legs, although the winter seemed to have done something to the definition I'd had in the thighs last fall. At least, I preferred to think it was the influence of winter.

What I did need to do something about was my hair.

Not the color, which had always been some undefinable shade between blond and brown, but the length, which had grown out from a trim medium cut last summer to something shaggy hanging about my shoulders. I gathered it back into a ponytail and stared into the mirror.

Silly.

I pulled it on top of my head.

Better. Showed off my good cheekbones and added two inches to my height.

I'd make an appointment tomorrow for a cut. Something simple and easy to style. I glanced at my nails. Maybe go all out and have a manicure. And a pedicure too. If Nick could separate himself from the woes of Madame X, my bare toes might just be on view this weekend.

I glanced at the hand-printed sign on the wall above the mirror—PLEASE LOCK UP YOUR VALUABLES. THERE HAVE BEEN A NUMBER OF THEFTS RECENTLY—and stashed my clothes, bag, and shoes in the locker. After standing under the shower for two minutes, I draped the towel around my waist sarong-style and headed out to the pool.

Angela was still there, red Speedo cap covering her dark hair, tinted goggles over her eyes, swimming laps in the farthest lane. The only other swimmers were what looked like a scuba class in the far end. I eased into the lane next to Angela as she finished a lap. She smiled, waved, and continued her workout—a fast, graceful crawl that put to shame my far less energetic sidestroke. The water was a perfect eighty to eighty-two degrees. My exhilaration over the possibility of tracking one of Tina's students alleviated, at least temporarily, my sadness over her probable death, and I luxuriated in the clear aquamarine water.

Twenty laps later, I paused at one end. In the next lane, Angela effortlessly hoisted herself out of the water onto the edge of the pool and pulled off her cap and goggles.

"Thanks for joining me," she said.

"You look terrific." And she did. Sleek as a seal in a red Lycra one-piece. But then, Angela had looked terrific for all of the twenty or so years I'd known her—although Dr. Angela Morales, the San Diego Police Department's newly hired twenty-six-year-old medical examiner had been far less sure of herself then. Even less sure of herself than one Scotia Mac-Kinnon, also new to the SDPD, fresh out of San Francisco State University and the police academy and a recently divorced mother of a four-year-old. It was hard to say who took whom under her wing, but for ten years we shared a lot. My job frustrations and promotions from patrol to harbor patrol to detective on domestic violence cases. And then, for very personal reasons, back to harbor patrol. She saw me through my second marriage to Pete Santana, a fellow detective. And two years later helped me survive his death at the hands of a Mexican drug dealer.

After her broken engagement to a tall, craggy pilot in the Air Support Unit, she departed to teach forensic medicine at UCLA. I missed her immensely—even after I, too, departed San Diego and married a San Francisco stockbroker named Albert who liked to race fast yachts and collect classic cars.

And finally, we had a joyful reunion when she came to visit me in Friday Harbor and met Matt Petersen, a tall, blond, bearded giant of a commercial fisherman who fell head over heels in love and lust with her. Like his father before him, Matt fished the Fairweather grounds, an area that lies over a submerged mountain range some thirty-five or forty miles out from the southeastersn shore of the Gulf of Alaska. After their whirlwind courtship and Mexican honeymoon, Angela had accompanied Matt to Alaska for two seasons. Then, without explanation, she stopped going with him or visiting him while he was up there.

"You look great, too," she said. "You'd look even better if you'd get a new bathing suit. I hope you never let Nick see you in that."

With more effort and less grace than Angela, I hauled myself out of the pool and glanced down at the well-worn garment in question. It did seem to be a bit thin and, well, saggy, in certain spots. As for Nick seeing me *in* it, he never had. But since he'd seen me *out* of it, I didn't imagine it was a big deal. But then, Angela and I have always differed in our philosophies regarding the packaging of the female body. She belongs to the school of thought that says a man will do anything for you, or forgive you for anything, if you're wearing the appropriate sexy lingerie before he coaxes you out of it. I take the position that relationships are about values and respect and, within reason, it doesn't matter what you're wearing. Though I have noticed some revisionism creeping in lately. On my part.

"I've got a new Land's End catalog. It has some great suits. I'll bring it in tomorrow." Angela stood, reached for a big multicolored beach towel from the chair, and began to dry off. "How was your cruise to Montague with Nick?"

"The first part or the last part?"

"How about the *best* part?"

"The best part was the sail up there on Friday. Eight to ten knots of wind all the way. We got into the harbor and picked up a mooring buoy right in front of the marine park just before sundown."

"Followed by Sapphire martinis?"

"Followed by Sapphire martinis." I was silent for a minute, smiling, remembering the twilight interlude in the stateroom that had followed the martinis. I collected myself. "Followed by fresh halibut at the pub, followed by a moonlight dinghy ride back to the boat."

"Surely it didn't go downhill from there?" She wrapped her towel around her slender waist and sat in a chair at the edge of the pool.

I shook my head. "Not till Monday morning. We slept late, Nick made breakfast, and we were just about to leave when he got a call on his cell phone."

"A client in trouble?"

"Madame X got a DUI." I filled her in on the Cathy crisis and what had transpired since then.

She was silent for a long minute. I finished drying off.

Twice she started to speak and changed her mind. The silence was becoming awkward, because I knew what she was thinking and was too diplomatic to verbalize.

"It's okay, Angela," I said. "I'm going down there this weekend. We'll work it out."

"Good. You always do." She smiled, her teeth white in her tan face. "How's the Breckenridge case?"

"The only thing I know for sure is that a woman is missing. There's no body, no real suspects, many possibilities. And Jared says to keep a blank mind. Or maybe he said an open mind." I leaned back and drew my knees up to my chest. "But I may have a breakthrough." I told her about Tina's crushed lime-green phone and my resuscitation of the call log.

"Wonder Woman."

"We'll see where it goes. It may be a dead end. By the way, I don't suppose you have any idea what's in the sheriff's file on Tina?"

"Anything in particular you're looking for?"

"Rafie Dominguez told me the sheriff searched the *Alcyone* for drugs."

"Actually, it was Customs," she said.

"They find anything?"

She shook her head. "Clean as a whistle. There's a list of personal stuff they found on the boat. It's in the file. If you want to see it, I'll find a way to fax it over. You hear what happened to the sheriff this morning?"

"Jared told me. Was it really a heart attack?"

She shrugged. "Probably. He's hanging in there like a trouper. Refused to be taken to a hospital, or even to go home. Said it was just some indigestion from his own cooking while Jenna is off-island. I played bridge with Jenna Bishop last week. She says Nigel is overweight and his cholesterol is through the roof and he comes from the school that says that your blood pressure is okay if it's one hundred plus your age. Nigel is sixty-eight."

"Sounds like a recipe for disaster. You might end up with a new boss."

She smiled slyly. "Jeff Fountain would make a *fine* sheriff."

Jeffrey Fountain had been college educated in the Bay Area, and his politics were considerably to the left of his boss's. Of course, if Nigel Bishop were to become incapable of serving out his elected term, an acting sheriff would be appointed until such time as a new election took place. Angela's smile broadened. "And guess who's going to be first in line to take the tests for deputy if that occurs?"

"You?" I stared at her. "*You?* You're going to be a deputy? Angela!" I hugged her and we both shrieked with laughter. At the far end of the pool, three of the budding scuba divers pulled off their masks and stared at us resentfully. "Matt will *kill* you."

"Maybe yes, maybe no. Right now, he's happy as a clam with the big new Yanmar diesel he's just installed on the *Fairweather Princess*. And he's got a new crew this year—some humongous guy from Wisconsin who learns fast and does what he's told. I'm going to meet Matt in Sitka—and I plan to make the two weeks memorable." She stood and I followed her back toward the locker room.

We showered, dried off, and dressed.

"I have a proposition for you," Angela said, buttoning a burgundy velvet shirt over her snug-fitting blue jeans. "A&E did a bio on Richard Burton last night, with clips from *Night of the Iguana*. I'd forgotten what a good movie it is. How about we rent the video, order a pizza, and watch Ava Gardner seducing the beach boys?"

"Best offer I've had all day."

11

"Abigail's getting sued." Zelda flung the news over her shoulder as I came through the door of the Olde Gazette Building on Thursday morning. The musical notes emanating from the speakers on either side of her computer properly belonged in a funeral dirge, and I didn't know whether the operatic choice was related to Abigail's legal problems, some catastrophic event that had befallen the two missing canines, or impending disasters yet to be revealed.

"Who's suing her?"

"My new client."

"What client is that?" I glanced at the pink message slips. One from my mother, one from Petra Petrovsky von Schnitzenhoff, sister of the missing Harrison Petrovsky. Nothing from Nick. Nothing from the sailing student I'd left the message for last night.

"Edie, the woman who owns On the Edge that I'm doing the party for. M. J. Carlyle's wife. She claims Abigail's been slandering her around town and that she stole her dog, who's worth thousands of dollars."

"Sounds like your cohort had a busy day. Why did Abby steal the dog?"

Zelda scowled at the monitor. "This catering and events-arranging stuff is more complicated than I thought. The Beluga caviar has to be shipped up from Seattle. And they want French champagne."

"Why did Abby steal Edie's dog?" I asked again. "And what kind of a dog was it?"

"Part wolf, part husky, part Lab, part shepherd. Twice the size of Dakota, black as midnight, and answers to 'Lobo.' Abby claims she found the dog digging into the fox burrows, so she called the park ranger, who carted the dog off to the animal shelter."

"How to win friends and influence people." I began to leaf through the reports on the Breckenridges.

"Speaking of dogs, any word on Dakota and Sophia?"

"Nothing. They're dead. I know it." She clicked on the Save icon and swung around to face me. "It's all Rafie's fault, but he didn't mean to let them out."

"Don't give up yet. What about the background on the Quinces?"

Zelda turned back to her monitor. "We should have the report on Katy Quince back from DataTech in a bit, but I wouldn't hope for much on her husband, Danny. My friend Bernice, who works for the accountant, has had a sudden attack of ethics and wouldn't give me their SSN or a DOB. But that photo you took of Katy's bike was real clear. I took the tag number over to a friend of mine in the courthouse and got her DOB."

"Did you print the photos?"

"Oh, yeah, forgot to give them to you." She handed me the prints and turned back to her spreadsheet.

I filled a cup with coffee, went upstairs, and checked my calendar. There was just one appointment; it was at five o'clock with Paul Breckenridge to go over Tina's personal effects. I spread the photos on my desk. Like Zelda had said, the photos of Katy's yellow Ducati were astonishingly clear, as was the license tag. I scanned the shop and the house under construction and wondered again how her canvas business and her husband's yacht sales were paying for it all. The photos I'd taken at Roche Harbor were simply photos of the two boats and gave me nothing I didn't already know.

I filed the photos in the Breckenridge folder, made a list of Tina's personal and business belongings I wanted to see this afternoon, and stared for a while at the sociogram on the whiteboard. I added the name "Rafie Dominguez" and connected it to Tina and Katy, and then lingered over the name of "Stephan Breckenridge." I still hadn't heard from him. Paul and Lily had both mentioned that Stephan had gotten into trouble last year with his friend Sean MacGregor.

I typed an E-mail to Angela: *Thanks for the movie and company last night. Any info available on Stephan Breckenridge? Did the sheriff check Paul Breckenridge's alibi for the night Tina disappeared?*

I stared at my message for several minutes before sending it. Juvenile records were sealed. I wouldn't blame Angela if she refused. On the other hand, there might be something in them that would give me some clue as to what happened to Tina and why her "little problem" became a big problem.

There was an incoming message from Melissa.

Mother: I thought about our conversation Tuesday night and I don't think you were being very supportive. After all, I'm over 21 and I'm perfectly capable of making my own decisions. I wish you would stop treating me like a child. Grandma says that losing Gilberto is a major trauma and that I need several months to recover. Giovanni is going to help me get a waitress job at the Old Mendocino Lodge. It's really plush and I'll make lots of tips and then I can go back to school in the fall. Will you please call the dean of students and arrange for me to get Incompletes in my classes? Melissa.
P.S. Giovanni introduced me to a nice man here

*who is an artist. His name is Neptune and
he's going to paint a picture of my soul.*

I stared out the window and counted to ten and
then to ten again, and clicked on Reply to Sender.

*Dear Melissa, Since you are over 21 and an
adult, I would imagine that any request for
Incompletes must come from you. Good luck
with your new job. Love, Mother.*

Intermediate Parenting 301.

I walked downstairs to refill my coffee cup. Zelda
was flinging on her coat, a big smile on her face.

"They've been sighted! The dogs. Out at Roche
Harbor. I'm going out there right now."

I started to ask about the background on the
Quinces, but she was gone. I stared at the closed door
in frustration. The funeral dirge had run its course and
the office was silent. The door to Soraya's office was
closed; today was her day to be on Orcas dispensing
naturopathic remedies. Dakota's red doggie futon lay
in the corner of the office. I was glad its owner had
not passed on to canine heaven. The money Zelda
had spent recently for vet bills far exceeded what
more affluent dog owners would have expended. Dakota seemed to provide the one stable relationship in
Zelda's otherwise chaotic life. From what I could piece
together, her parents were both dead. Her stockbroker
sister in Los Angeles hadn't talked to her for more
than ten years because of what Zelda referred to as
"my Maui escapade." She had no children. And as far
as I knew, she had never been married. Dakota was
perhaps the only living creature that gave her unconditional love.

I emptied my coffee cup, washed it, and decided
not to pursue the issue of unconditional love in my
own life or why the one person who might provide it

for me hadn't called back last night. I checked my face in the mirror behind the door, remembered that I wanted to get my hair cut and maybe get a manicure and pedicure. I dialed Trudy's Salon. "I can do your hair at one-thirty, Scotia. And Suzanne can do your nails, but she wouldn't have time for a full pedicure. Maybe next week?"

"I'll check my calendar, Trudy. See you at one-thirty." If I wanted to impress Nick with snazzy toes, I'd have to do them myself. It was eleven forty-five and I decided to take myself out for an early lunch before the beautifying session at Trudy's. After last night's outrageous Deluxe Pizza with Everything from the Bistro Italiano, a bowl of vegetable soup at Madronna Landing was called for.

"Ask and it shall be delivered. And forget who delivered it." Angela laid a plain brown envelope on the table. "And here's the Land's End swimsuit catalog." She slid into the booth just at the moment the waitress brought my plate of meat loaf smothered in gravy. Angela stared at it, looked at the catalog, and said nothing. Always the mistress of the unspoken utterance.

"Don't say a word," I said, tucking into the meat loaf. "They were out of veggie soup."

"Wouldn't think of it."

"Are you lunching?"

"No. I just happened to see you come down the hill, so I made a summary of the info on Stephan Breckenridge and dashed over. What a morning! Anything new with the Hungarian hunk?"

I frowned and shook my head. "Nothing I want to talk about."

"I understand Lily MacGregor does hexes. Maybe you should have one put on Nick's ex. What's her name? Cathy?" She smirked and headed for the door.

I stared for a minute at the perfectly toned models

on the cover of the swimsuit catalog. All airbrushed,
I assured myself. I opened the brown envelope. Angela's meticulously handwritten notes contained a description of three offenses committed by Stephan
Breckenridge in the eighteen-month period prior to
his mother's disappearance. There was also a photocopy of the record of Tina's personal possessions
found on the abandoned *Alcyone.* I read the notes on
Stephan first.

> *Theft of a bag containing over one hundred
> CD's from a car parked at the Friday Harbor Airport. Stephan was with two other adolescents, the
> CD's were recovered, and no charges were made.*
> *Arrest for minor in possession of alcohol during
> a police raid on an unsupervised Halloween party at
> Cape San Juan. He was sentenced to 30 hours of
> community work and fined five hundred dollars.*
> *Arrest for possession of an illegal substance and
> for possession of drug paraphernalia at Brown
> Sugar Beach. He was fined a thousand dollars and
> was required to participate in outpatient drug
> therapy.*

The boat inventory held no surprises: a brown
leather purse with the usual female paraphernalia; the
contents of the navigation table and safety equipment
I'd seen yesterday; some foodstuffs that were probably
left over from the heavy-weather class; and a variety
of non-alcoholic beverages and containers of drinking
water. Nothing whatsoever that told me anything
about what had happened to Tina.

There was a note on the bottom of the boat
inventory:

> *Jeffrey Fountain said he verified with Paul's
> mother that Paul arrived at her apartment in Sedro
> Wooley at eleven o'clock on Thursday, April 19.*

He left on Saturday afternoon when he got a call from the sheriff's office. A.

I scraped the last wisp of garlic mashed potatoes off the plate, finished the ginger ale, and checked the time. It was one-fifteen. I headed over to Trudy's Salon, thinking about Stephan Breckenridge's records. The three "crimes" were sadly typical of many adolescent infractions in Friday Harbor, but I could see why Tina had wanted to get him off the island and into a boarding school. At the rate he was going, he'd never get out of drug rehab and she'd have to get a second job to keep up with his fines. I wondered if there was a bigger problem than bad choice of friends or the usual "nothing to do in Friday Harbor" complaint. Maybe this was the "little problem that had turned into a big problem" that M. J. Carlyle never had the opportunity to discuss with his sister.

I was back in the office at a little past three with my freshly painted fingernails and a new haircut resembling Paula Zahn's on a bad hair day. Zelda was not back and there were two messages on the machine, neither one from Nick. The first was from Jewel Moon chastising me for being so unsupportive of my daughter. The second was from Zelda, who reported in a sorrowful voice that they hadn't caught up with the dogs yet, but were closing in. Would I please turn down the heat and shut off the various pieces of equipment when I left.

My vertical file with current projects had two folders in it: the legal document relating to the missing Harrison Petrovsky and notes for a report that was overdue for my insurance broker client. The latter involved alleged whiplash injuries on a claim filed by a woman on Lopez. I'd done two days of surveillance over there. The woman appeared to be in great pain most of the time, and I saw nothing that would make her claim fraudulent.

Reports are anathema to me. I'd sooner track a scumbag drug dealer in a monsoon or engage in hand-to-hand combat with a Siberian tiger than type up a report for a client. Particularly an insurance report. I pulled the folder onto my desk and began to review the pages of scribbled notes I'd taken over the past two months. The hateful project was finished by four-fifteen and I turned my attention to Anastasia Petrovsky's missing heir.

Anastasia's estate was being handled by Friday Harbor attorney Carolyn Smith. She had retained me to find the missing son and heir, who had sailed away from Friday Harbor last year on the 40-foot gaff rigged cutter *Ocean Dancer*, bound for New Zealand. I, in turn, had retained a private investigator in New Zealand. A long-lost Tongan soul mate of Harrison's had complicated the search, and my Kiwi PI almost caught up to them in Australia, then lost them when they sailed on for the Indian Ocean. Anastasia's will stipulated that no assets could be distributed until all beneficiaries were either located or determined to be dead. Harrison's sister, Petra Von Schnitzenhoff, had tried a number of shenanigans, including petitioning to have her sibling declared dead. According to the most recent communication, last week Harrison's son in Seattle had received an e-mail from his father describing *Ocean Dancer*'s passage across the pirate-infested South China Sea and its arrival in Singapore. Carolyn was now requesting that I put special effort into locating Harrison in Singapore and securing his signature on a document that would allow the assets to be distributed and Harrison's share held in escrow until such time as he returned.

I sat for a minute, staring at Carolyn's letter, then pulled out my San Francisco phone directory and flipped to the "H's", where I found a number for H & W Secu-

rity, my old employer in San Francisco. H & W special-
ized in security and investigations involving maritime
cases—thefts, fraud, disappearances, arson—and had
provided a place to hang my investigative hat after
Albert's fatal heart attack. It had also allowed me to
accumulate the one thousand hours of supervised investigation I needed to get my PI license.

Bob Hiller was out, but Joe Wallace took my call
immediately.

"Scotia! Are you coming back?"

"Not this week, Joe," I said. "How's the family?"

The twins were in college, he reported, his wife had
finished her law degree, and he was planning to retire
in five years. "Come back to San Francisco and I'll
make you an heir apparent. Or an heiress apparent.
Or something."

"I'll keep it in mind. Meanwhile, I need the name
of a contact or a PI in Singapore."

"Singapore? Yeah, as a matter of fact, last January
we had a seaman that jumped ship in Singapore and
took along a case of jewels belonging to the captain's
sweetie. We actually got them back for her. Hold on.
I have the file right here. We hired a nice Chinese
gentleman. His name Wang. H.W. Wang." He gave
me a phone number and an E-mail address, we exchanged more pleasantries, and I turned my attention
to composing a message to Mr. Wang, requesting his
services to track down my elusive target, with a copy
to Carolyn Smith.

The sky had darkened and tree branches rustled
against the window. I would have loved a cup of tea,
but it was four-forty. I tidied up my desk, locked up
and shut down everything per Zelda's instructions, and
headed out to the Breckenridge residence on Hyacinth Lane.

12

I finished my visit to the Breckenridge household, a large old brown-shingle that needed somebody to take care of a lot of delayed maintenance, a little before six o'clock on Thursday afternoon. I drove slowly back to town under overcast skies. Paul had been quietly cooperative, almost passive, and we'd gone through all of Tina's clothes and jewelry, personal items and file cabinets. I'd selected some recent photos of Tina and a number of files to bring back to town. I had asked about a life insurance policy and a will and had received a negative on both. Ditto a safe-deposit box. Nor had I found a diary or journal nor any old letters. I'd examined her car, the Ford Windstar minivan the police had found in the parking lot behind the hotel at Roche Harbor. It was washed and polished, and the inside carpet looked clean enough to eat off. Paul said he had been planning to sell it, but had decided to keep it for Stephan, who would be sixteen next year. I'd given him the damaged cell phone; he accepted it absently and stared at the crushed face.

Stephan hadn't been home, but Paul had promised, once again, to ask him to call me. I had also stopped to talk to the neighbors on either side of Paul's place. The sixtyish couple at 180 Hyacinth Lane thought they remembered seeing Tina's car in the driveway around

seven o'clock that Thursday night. They did not see
the car leave and hadn't noticed that it was missing
the next day. The young family on the other side had
taken the five o'clock ferry to the mainland and saw
nothing.

On the way down to the port I stopped at the hard-
ware store to buy some non-skid tape for *Dragon-
Spray*'s companionway steps. After another stop at the
Corner Grocery for the *Seattle Times*, six cans of
Fancy Feast for Calico, cream of asparagus soup and
a loaf of Moroccan peasant bread for me, I parked
the Volvo in the lot. The file storage box Paul had
provided to transport Tina's records was on the passenger seat. I was too tired to go over them tonight,
but I didn't want to leave them in the car, so I ended
up hauling the groceries and the box out to G dock
in one of the dock carts.

DragonSpray was rolling lightly against her lines in
the wind. There were lights on *Pumpkin Seed*; through
the uncurtained windows I saw Henry and Lindsey
chatting over cocktails. They waved, and I returned
the greeting and unlocked the hatch covers on the
companionway.

The cabin was cold so I turned on the heater. Groceries stowed, cardboard box tucked away behind the
table on the settee, dry vermouth and soda chilling in
the galley, I changed into sweats and browsed the
TV's satellite channels. I settled on CNN and the latest bad tidings from around the world, which included
an earthquake measuring 7.4 on the Richter scale that
had caused devastation in Japan. Another quake of
5.4 was recorded near Mexico City. The infamous Pacific ring of fire.

On that happy seismological note, I switched off
CNN and surfed through the early-evening offerings,
which included *I Love Lucy* reruns, images of earth
from a NASA satellite, and both Geraldo and Larry
King engaged in shouting matches with their evening's

guests. Wondering whatever had happened to civilized discourse, I hit the Power Off button and stared at the telephone. It was seven-thirty.

Okay, so Nick hadn't called.

He was a busy maritime attorney with demanding clients. He was a caring man who would always be there for his family . . . even if that family included a neurotic daughter and an ex-wife who had left him for her financial consultant. We had known each other long enough that I didn't have to wait for his call.

I could call him.

A woman with a chirpy voice answered on the second ring. I was struck dumb. It wasn't Nicole's voice, so it had to be Cathy. But why was she answering Nick's phone?

"Uh, hel . . . hello." I cleared my dry throat and stopped stammering. "May I speak to Nick?"

"Who is this?"

What the hell business was it of hers?

"Scotia MacKinnon. May I please speak to Nick?" May I please speak to my lover, the man I spent last weekend with, the man you abandoned.

"Well, we're late for our dinner reservation. Could you call back?"

I nearly bit my tongue and remembered Angela's remark about hexes. "I'd like to speak to Nick. Now."

There was a silence, then voices in the background. "Scotia?"

"Hi, there. How's it going?" Ms. Cool here.

A long sigh. "Scotia, glad you called. I've been running like a maniac and trying to get a minute all day to get back to you. This isn't a real good time. How late are you going to be up?"

"Probably eleven."

"Talk to you before then." The line went dead. I stared at the phone, then slammed it back into the cradle, grinding my teeth. *Merde*! *Merde encore*! He hadn't had time to call me for three days, but he had

time to take his ex-wife out to dinner. I wanted to
scream. I wanted to throw something. I wanted to
kill him.

After a bowl of soup, salad, a glass of white wine,
and three slices of the peasant bread, I still did not
feel like a rational adult. I tidied up the galley and
tried to read the *Times*. It was useless. I threw the
paper on the floor and cast about for something to
take my mind off the image of Nick and Cathy dining
in a romantic Seattle bistro. I stared at the cardboard
box of Tina's files for five minutes, then brewed a cup
of Red Zinger, emptied the contents of the box onto
the table, and sorted it into piles.

Paid invoices for both the household and Pleiades.

Quicken financial records for the past three years.

Statements from a mutual fund and a savings
account.

Along with the Pleiades client list, class reservations, and class evaluations, I found a Pleiades promo-
tional brochure printed on pale blue paper. Tina's
image was on the front: a smiling, perky Sally Field
face with long, curly dark hair. The nose was pert and
just a shade too short, but the chin was strong and
determined. The brochure detailed her sailing and
boating background and credentials and listed the
class schedule for the rest of the year. Classes that
would never take place.

I stared at a brochure and the stacks of paper. They
represented five years of work and dedication to in-
structing women how to properly trim a sail and read
a chart and spring a boat off the dock in the wind.
Now the woman behind it all was gone. I brewed another cup of tea and began my perusal of the paper
remains of Tina Breckenridge.

The household bills and invoices yielded nothing
out of the ordinary. Ditto the paid bills for Pleiades,
which included normal boat-type work: a bilge pump
installation by a local marine mechanic; haul-out,

power wash, and bottom paint for *Alcyone* performed by an Anacortes shipyard; replacement of sail slides and installation of lazy jacks on *Electra*. The discovery of the two files on the mutual fund and the savings account had been an obvious surprise to Paul, and he had stared at them for a long minute but had not said anything. The mutual fund was in Tina's and Stephan's names in the amount of $38,572; the savings account, again in both their names, had a balance of $18,000.

I leafed through the Pleiades mailing list, found names, addresses, and phone numbers for women from across the United States, Mexico, and even Europe. There was a file of class evaluations, the majority of which were positive. Only a few of the comments indicated that the Pleiades classes had possibly offered more than some of the women had been prepared to learn or perform: "The anchor was too heavy for me and I'm going to leave this to my husband." "I hadn't realized we were going to be sailing in a storm." I leafed through the file to find the evaluations on the class Katy Quince had completed the day Tina disappeared.

There were none.

Either Katy had never given them to Tina, or they had disappeared with her. I called Katy and got her machine. I left a message asking to see the missing evaluations and turned to Tina's financial records.

The Quicken printouts were orderly and complete: check registers, transaction records, cash flow records, profit-and-loss statements. I have a basic knowledge of accounting, but after spending the better part of two hours reviewing the various documents, for the life of me I couldn't figure out how Tina had been able to accumulate the fifty thousand dollars represented by the savings account and mutual fund, in addition to nearly twenty-five thousand in the Pleiades checking account.

At the very bottom of the box I found the color

photos of Tina that Paul had said I could bring back
with me. One was the close-up shot she had used on
the brochure, but it was in color and I realized her
eyes were the rare shade of spring violets. The other
photo had been taken from a distance; Tina was standing against the mast on a sailboat, wearing a white T-
shirt, dark blue shorts, and boat shoes. Her driver's
license described her as five feet six, weighing 124
pounds. She looked slender in the photo and had long,
well-shaped legs.

My neck muscles were tight and my lower back
ached. *DragonSpray*'s settee in the main salon, however beautiful, was not designed for heavy-duty office
work. I gingerly extricated myself from behind the
table, stretched, and put everything except the list of
the last class members back in the box. It was nine-
thirty. Nick had said he would call by eleven. Rain
was dripping on the deck. I should have been sleepy,
but I wasn't. The silence in the cabin was oppressive.
I stared at the phone, then pulled on a sweater and
my foul-weather jacket, laced my feet into hiking
shoes, tucked my hair under a black knit cap, and
headed out for a walk.

Pumpkin Seed's lights were still on, but the curtains
had been drawn. I wondered where Calico was. I
walked carefully up G dock, and over to the main
dock. A tall figure in dark clothes was leaning against
the phone booth beside the port building, receiver
tucked into the crook of his neck. I cut across the
small park above the port. This was the postage-size
plot of grass and rocks where high school students
hung out when they played hooky. I considered the
similarities between Friday Harbor and the fishing
community on Cape Breton Island where'd I'd
grown up.

Both were small towns near the ocean, though Friday Harbor was far more protected than the east coast
of Cape Breton, where the winters could be brutal.

Both communities were once dependent on fishing as a way of life. The teenagers I grew up with sailed dinghies and went to the movies. Just about everybody experimented with cigarettes and sex at one time or another, and my cousin had gotten in big trouble for making off with a bottle of his uncle's home-brewed beer. Nobody had been hospitalized for alcohol poisoning or arrested for possession of drug paraphernalia. But nearly thirty years had passed since I'd left Cape Breton. Perhaps drugs and alcohol had become the recreation of choice there, too.

I walked up Spring Street to Second, then uphill past the courthouse and the lighted community theater, where a high school performance of *The Emperor's New Clothes* was in rehearsal. The Olde Gazette Building was as dark as I had left it. I continued along the deserted road, wondering if Zelda had found Sophia and Dakota. Past the public works building and the library, I turned left on Park Street. About the time I got to Blair, the light rain turned to a downpour. I hastened downhill on Spring Street, then cut over to the stairs behind the American Legion Post and stopped off to use the rest rooms in the port building. I hurried back to *DragonSpray*, the hood of my jacket covering half my face, and found Calico crouched under the canvas dodger, impatiently awaiting my return. I unlocked and followed her below.

No blinking red light on the answering machine announced a message from Nick. I hung my wet jacket and pants to drip dry in the head, and slid gratefully into flannel pj's. After opening a can of Fancy Feast for my still damp feline, I slipped an early Emmy Lou Harris CD in the player and checked for E-mail on my laptop. There was one message.

Your not listening. Drop the Breckenridge case or you'll wish you had.

Like the first message, it was sent from the library

through the Internet and had the same screen name: pacific1875@aol.com. It had been composed at 4:10 that afternoon. It certainly wasn't the first time I'd received a menacing message, but it was unsettling. Who thought I was getting too close to something? Paul? Katy? Stephan? Was the message connected to why Stephan still hadn't called me? I tried to ignore the goose bumps on my arms. Without serious police assistance, which I was unlikely to get, the E-mail would be hard to trace. I printed out the message and put it in my rucksack. I would ask Zelda to see if she could track down the sender.

It was ten forty-five. Calico was curled into a furry ball on my white comforter, one paw covering her eyes. I checked the locks on all the hatches, stared at the phone for a while, then crawled into bed with Travis McGee. I stared sightlessly at the pages, unable to stop thinking about Tina. If it weren't for the menacing e-mails, I would have been willing to write the whole thing off as either too much wine and a fall overboard or a wife and mother who'd had enough and taken French leave. But the e-mails were putting a different spin on it. I had to face the fact that Tina Breckenridge was dead, and the only thing left for me was to find out who had killed her and why. I moved Calico to one side, put the portable phone next to my pillow so I'd be sure to hear it when Nick called, turned out the light and closed my eyes.

I did not sleep well, and dream time was spent fleeing from stalking white tigers that morphed into faceless, hooded enemies who lured me into dead-end streets. I awoke to the heart-sinking realization that Nick had never called back.

I listened to the steady patter of rain on the cabin roof, stared into the bleak darkness of the night, and let the tears fall.

13

Friday morning was pink and clear after the rain, but I overslept and awoke at seven forty-five to a dullness of brain and spirit. Calico was gone, apparently having departed through the porthole that I leave open for her at night. I snuggled under the down comforter and watched the rays of morning light filtering through the portholes. I refused to think about why Nick had not called back. The only engagement I had, if you could call it that, was the Bikram yoga class at eight-thirty. I made an executive decision to deprive my body of the life-enhancing experience of the twenty-six asanas today, switched on the Canadian marine weather radio station, and gazed around the cabin.

Like the main salon, the captain's cabin was crafted of mahogany with leaded-glass cupboard doors. The portholes were round and brass and had become verdigris with the years, a lovely greenish patina that forms on bronze or brass surfaces after long exposure to sea air. Alongside the wide double bunk was the intricately carved wooden dragon Nick had given me for my last birthday. A birthday weekend we'd spent over in Oak Bay at the old Beach Hotel, taking high tea at the Blethering Place Tea Room, then running back through the spring shower to our room to make love all afternoon.

The weather forecast was for partial sun in the

morning and showers in the afternoon, then clearing and sunny on Saturday. My gaze fell on my laptop computer, and I remembered the second threatening E-mail. I threw off the comforter and scrambled out of bed. Half an hour later, clad in my rainy-day attire of blue jeans and a brown wool sweater, I gulped an OJ, stuffed a copy of the e-mail message in the pocket of my foul-weather jacket, and locked up *DragonSpray*.

At the Olde Gazette Building all appeared to be back to normal. Coffee was brewing and a cheery fire crackled in the little woodstove—a welcome addition that Zelda had acquired last winter in exchange for the brochure she designed for the island chimney sweep. The uplifting sounds of something light and semi-classical filled the office, and Zelda was back in place, resplendent in a white poet's shirt, long jade-green cotton skirt, and black boots. A far more feminine outfit than her customary attire. Her long hennaed hair was neatly coiffed in an elegant French twist. Ornate silver-and-turquoise earrings dangled from her earlobes.

She twirled around on her steno chair as I came in, a smile on her face. "We found them," she announced with glee, nodding toward the sleeping black dog.

"So I see. Both alive and well?" There were three pink message slips in my mail cubby. The first was from Nick. "Sorry about last night. Didn't get in until late. Will call later." I gritted my teeth, muttered my favorite French expletive, and read the other two messages, both from M. J. Carlyle, both from last night: the first at seven o'clock, the second at nine-thirty, both asking me to call ASAP. I frowned, wondering why he hadn't called my cell phone. While there were areas on the island where cell phones didn't function, they usually worked down at the port and I always kept mine with me, and turned on. I had checked it last night and again this morning.

"Did you talk to M.J.?" I asked.

"No, I took both messages off the voice mail. He sounded upset. Nick called a few minutes ago. What's going on with your sweetie, anyway? He sounded awful."

I shrugged noncommittally, afraid to think about why Nick hadn't gotten home until late and sounded awful. Zelda took one look at my face and switched to the subject of the recovered canines. "When Rafie and I got to Roche Harbor yesterday, they were gone again, but one of the gardeners saw them heading out toward the tennis courts. We spent the whole afternoon looking and had almost given up when Rafie got a call on his cell phone from a woman out at the very end of Westcott Bay Road."

"None the worse for wear?"

"Dakota looks okay, but Rafie took Sophia to the vet this morning. She's suffering from exhaustion. Maybe he's learned not to let her out. But never a loss without some small gain."

"Such as?" I glanced again at M.J.'s urgent messages. Probably wanted a report on my investigation.

She batted her eyelashes. "I stopped at the store at Roche Harbor to get a snack and I met this luscious Frenchman. His name is Jean Pierre Zola. He's from Martinique and he's the skipper on a big yacht that's anchored out near Henry Island. After I got Dakota safely back home, Jean Pierre took me to dinner."

So that was the source of the glow.

"He's going to pick me up after lunch and we're going for a hike up Mount Finlayson."

"Sounds delightful." I glanced dubiously at her long skirt.

"Not to worry. I brought a pair of blue jeans."

"What's with the background check on Katy Quince and company?"

"I'll query DataTech right now. Oh, I almost forgot!

Abigail's in jail. She got arrested this morning at American Camp."

"So the sheriff finally had enough. Are you going to bail her out?"

"I offered to. She vows she's going to fast until On the Edge leaves. Won't accept anything except water."

"If she continues to refuse bail, she'll be fasting down on Whidbey Island."

"How come?"

"The jail here is for temporary holding only. Once she has a hearing, she'll either be released or moved to Coupeville. What are the charges, anyway?"

"Destruction of personal property. Assault. Creating a public nuisance and resisting arrest. The sheriff himself came out to try to talk sense to her, and she ordered him and the deputy to leave with some very colorful language. At least, colorful language for Abby."

"Sounds like she had a busy morning."

"The sheriff had to handcuff her and haul her away kicking and screaming and swearing to tell his old mother what he and his cousin did on the senior trip in 1952."

Law enforcement on a small island. Unique.

Coffee cup in hand, I hurried upstairs and hung my foul-weather jacket on the ancient coatrack, where it began to drip on the scarred planks of the old floor. I dialed the number M.J. had left. A recording advised me that M. J. Carlyle was unavailable and invited me to leave a message, which I did. If he'd wanted to speak with me so urgently, he could at least have left his cell phone turned on.

The phone rang downstairs and I heard Zelda bewailing the price of caviar.

I read Nick's message again. Patience is not one of my virtues. I don't believe that all things come to she who waits. I wanted to know what Cathy was doing at Nick's last night. I wanted to know why he had found it necessary to take her to dinner and why he'd arrived back too late to call me. I wanted to be reassured that he still loved me, unconditionally or otherwise.

Fearful of hearing a female voice again, I called the condo in Seattle, but got only his voice on the answering machine. I dialed the number for his office on Queen Anne Hill and reached his assistant, who said he would be in court all day. She expected him back about five. I left a message and hung up. The phone rang. It was Jared Saperstein.

"I've got a craving for Mexican food. How about some *chile verde* at Pablo's? I hear he hired a new cook." Mexican food would be better than sitting around waiting for Nick to call. "Eleven-thirty?"

"See you there."

I spent the next hour reconciling my checking account. Several years ago I'd signed up for on-line checking, which allowed me access to my account balances any hour of the day or night and was supposed to make child's play of reconciling my bank statement. Which it would have done if my handwriting wasn't so illegible that several payees downloaded into my check register as gibberish. I had also managed to confuse the check numbers in the computerized check register. Thus, the check for moorage to the port was downloaded with the same number as the check to the shoe store. And the check to the laundry came back with the same number as a check I'd sent to Melissa. And on and on, ad nauseam.

I finished a little after eleven, tried unsuccessfully to reach M. J. Carlyle once more, and checked for incoming e-mail. There was a message from Mr. Wang in Singapore. He would be pleased to associate with me in locating Harrison Petrovsky. Would I please transmit the documents in question by E-mail. I forwarded the message to attorney Carolyn Smith, asking that she electronically forward the document file to Mr. Wang.

The DataTech report on Katy and Danny Quince was in my cubby when I went downstairs. I scanned it quickly. It covered only Katy; there was nothing on her husband. I left printouts of the two anonymous e-mails with Zelda to see if she could discover who had sent them. It was past eleven-thirty before I made it to Pablo's.

The tiny restaurant smelled of onions and garlic and corn tortillas. All eight of the wrought-iron tables were occupied. Jared was reaching for a tortilla chip from the wooden bowl as I hung my wet jacket on a hook and slid into the red vinyl booth across from him.

"Sorry," I said breathlessly. "I'm a terrible time manager."

"It's okay. I just got here ten minutes ago." He dipped a corn chip in the green salsa. "I decided to write up a brief article on Abigail's arrest."

"I suppose her arrest will be in the sheriff's log."

"Oh, yes. She'll probably love it. She's been writing a letter a day to each of the three papers, vilifying the visitors from Seattle and predicting everything from famine to tsunamis if they're not expelled. She's using three different names. The woman is indefatigable."

"Should keep your readership up."

"You must be talking about Mrs. Abigail. I saw the *Gazette* this morning."

"Hello, Pablo." Jared smiled up at the brown-skinned man in a white apron standing by our table. "One and the same. How's the *chile verde* today?"

"*Excelente.* Shall I bring two?"

Jared glanced at me. I nodded.

"Two orders of *chile verde* with flour tortillas and two lemonades," Jared said.

Pablo took the menus and disappeared into the kitchen.

"You look dejected, my dear," Jared said, sprinkling salt on a tortilla chip. "How's the Breckenridge case going?"

"I've interviewed everyone connected to her except her son and a friend of hers who works at Roche Harbor. And I've gone through all her personal effects and business records." As I was speaking, I remembered that in my distraught state over Nick, I'd forgotten to bring Tina's files and records to the office. *Merde*! "Paul couldn't tell me whether any of her clothing was missing, but nothing looks disturbed. Her purse was found at home, and her cell phone was discovered in the parking lot at Roche next to her car. No recent withdrawals from a bank account. No credit card activity since the day she disappeared. She's either dead or she took absolutely nothing with her."

"Want to know my theory?"

"Sure."

"I think Tina got tired of being a fishing widow and took off. She wouldn't be the first island woman to do so."

I told him about the two anonymous E-mails.

He raised his eyebrows. "That could change the color of things. However, it's possible she might not want you to look for her. Women are quite good at that." He smiled. "My esteemed London friend dealt with several disappearing women. In *The Disappearance of Lady Frances Carfax*, Lady Frances was a middle-aged beauty who disappeared from Lausanne. In her case there was a suitor, a large, swarthy ruffian of a man with a horrendous scowl, who had been pursuing her."

"No wonder she decamped."

"And then there was the lovely Hattie Doran, a vivacious American tomboy who married Lord Robert St. Simon and then vanished. The police thought it was foul play, and their first suspect was the cast-off lover of Lord Robert, a hotheaded female by the name of Flora Miller."

"Tina may have been a tomboy, but as far as I know, she wasn't being pursued by anyone, villainous or otherwise. Nor have I uncovered any cast-off—"

My cell phone rang, forestalling further Holmesian musings. It was Angela. Her voice was crisp and un-emotional. I thanked her and absently pressed the End button. I stared blankly at the phone and then at Jared.

"Scotia, what's wrong?"

I shook my head, bewildered, trying to make sense of what Angela had said. Wondering what it could have to do with Tina's disappearance. Berating myself for not having moved faster to discover why Tina had disappeared. Berating myself for oversleeping this morning. Berating myself for everything.

"It was Angela," I said slowly. "M. J. Carlyle's body has just been found on the rocks out at Brown Sugar Beach."

PART 2

In much wisdom is much grief: and he that increaseth knowledge increaseth sorrow.

—Ecclesiastes 1:18

14

Brown Sugar Beach is a pristine, driftwood-laden, pocket-size strip of sand and gravel tucked below the bluffs at American Camp. It lies within a national historic park where, in 1859, the United States and Great Britain narrowly avoided an all-out war over the shooting of an itinerant pig. I could well imagine that the beach and the prairies above the beach would provide an eye-catching background for On the Edge to digitalize its latest line of high-tech sportswear.

As I scrambled into my jacket and raced out of Pablo's after Jared, my mind was working overtime, trying to comprehend that my client was dead. What had M.J. wanted to tell me when he called last night? Was his death accidental or intentional? And what did it have to do with Tina's disappearance?

I climbed into Jared's van. We barreled out of the parking lot and sped up Spring Street. Jared made a screeching left onto Mullis Street and gave me a look.

"Before you get too wound up, Scotia, don't dismiss the possibility of an honest-to-goodness accident. Those bluffs are highly unstable all the way out to the lighthouse. If Carlyle had been trying to set up a fancy shot too close to the edge, he could have easily tumbled down and hit a rock."

"I know," I said dully. "But I just don't believe it was an accident."

And now I would never know what M.J. had wanted to tell me. Just as he had never found out what Tina had wanted to tell him before she died. The sunny morning was giving way to overcast skies. I stared out the side window at the well-kept frame houses and fenced green pastures as we drove the eight miles or so to American Camp in silence. The entrance to the parking lot was blocked off with a wooden gate, and the lot was jammed with cars: Two white Chevy Blazers with the Sheriff's Department decal, the EMT van, several sedans and minivans, three rental cars from Island Auto Rentals. An unfamiliar man in a dark blue parka with an On the Edge logo on the collar was sitting on a stool beside the gate.

Jared flashed his *Gazette* ID card. The sentry read it, returned it, and reluctantly opened the gate and closed it behind us.

We parked beside a dark red Chevrolet sedan. Jared grabbed his camera from the backseat and locked the van. "You know where Brown Sugar Beach is?" he asked.

I pointed toward the southwest and led the way, jogging down the gravel drive and onto a shortcut through a thick stand of Nootka rosebushes, then back onto the main trail, which used to be barely wide enough for two hikers to walk abreast. The trail had been widened to at least five feet. The width, I imagined, necessary to transport photographic supplies and models' wardrobes to On the Edge's shooting site.

No wonder Abby had blown her cool.

A dozen people were clustered along the bluff overlooking the beach. Several of them turned to stare as we approached. A red-haired man was holding the leash of a huge black dog that I assumed was the infamous Lobo. An oval of yellow crime scene evidence tape marked off one section of the bluff top, but none had been put in place across the trail that led down to the beach. I hesitated and stared down as Jared bolted past me. The tide was out, and the brown uniforms of three of San Juan County's finest were gathered around an inert figure at the south end of the beach. I darted past two shivering and shapely models clad in purple-and-red Lycra hiking pants and matching sports bras and followed Jared down the sandy, twisting path to the beach.

I glimpsed two women halfway down the beach near the largest pile of driftwood—a tall, perfectly made-up blonde in a purple jacket and black pants standing with arms akimbo and a brown-skinned woman in a faded blue sweatshirt and blue jeans who was crying. Both were gazing toward the distressing scene at the end of the beach. At our approach, the blonde jerked her head around and stepped in front of Jared.

"I'm sorry, you can't go any farther. There's been an accident."

Jared flashed his press card once again. "*Friday Gazette*, ma'am. What time did the accident occur?"

"I found him a while ago. He was dead. I don't know what time it happened. I don't care who you're with, I said you can't go any further." Her blue eyes flashed with anger. I stared past her to where the sheriff's group was still huddled around my late client. One of the brown uniforms detached itself and headed our way. It was Undersheriff Jeffrey Fountain.

"Mrs. Carlyle, may I have a word with you?" The blonde glared at Jared, then followed the deputy. I stared after them.

Mrs. Carlyle? I had forgotten that Lily said M.J. was married. And if he was married, what had he been doing with the woman at George's on Tuesday night? The same beautiful brown-skinned woman who was now talking, between sobs, with Jared? I edged closer.

". . . about an hour ago," she said in a ragged voice. "It was an awful morning. First it was raining, and then we couldn't find M.J., but Edie insisted on doing the shoot without him." She took a deep breath.

"Then I discovered there was a whole trunk of clothes missing. And the stupid dog was chained up and wouldn't stop barking. So Edie called a break and took him for a walk and that's when she found M.J." Overwhelmed by sobs, she shook her head and covered her face.

"Edie is his wife?" Jared asked quietly.

The woman shook her head violently and scrubbed the tears away with the back of her hand. "No! I mean, yes, but they're getting a divorce."

"What is your position with On the Edge, Ms.—?"

She swallowed hard. "I'm Olivia Camille. I'm in charge of wardrobe. And I'm—I was M.J.'s fiancée."

"When did you last see M.J., Ms. Camille?"

"Last night," she said dully. "We had dinner at the Topsail, then he left the hotel about nine. He went to meet with her, with Edie. They've been trying to work out a property settlement and he said he had a new proposal. He never came back last night."

"Do you know where he—" Jared began, but he was interrupted by the return of the undersheriff and the widow Carlyle.

"Ms. Camille, I'd appreciate it if you would wait with the rest of the crew up there." Fountain nodded toward the top of the bluff and the group of curious onlookers above us.

"Please, I just want to see him. Just for a minute." The tears began to flow again.

"I'm sorry, that's not possible just now. Please wait with the others. I'll need to talk to all of you." His tone allowed no dissent. Olivia Camille turned and stumbled across the piles of driftwood, tripping and nearly falling when a log shifted beneath her feet. She stood there, hands over her face, unable to move.

My heart wrenched with the memory of the night Pete was shot and I, also, had watched the love of my life being carried away in a body bag. I ran after her, grasped her elbow, and guided her over the slippery driftwood and up the path. "I'm Scotia MacKinnon, Ms. Camille. M.J. hired me to find out what happened to his sister, Tina."

"I know," she said brokenly as we climbed the sandy path. "He told me. He knew it wasn't an accident. Like I know *this* wasn't an accident. M.J. was a very experienced hiker. He wouldn't have slipped. Somebody pushed him."

She turned and stared down at the beach. Jared had followed us up the trail. The EMS unit had transferred the body of my handsome client from the fatal black rocks to a black body bag and were now climbing the trail with it. I reached into my jacket pocket for a business card and handed it to Olivia. "Call me if you want to talk," I said.

She nodded and stuffed the card into the pocket of her blue jeans without looking at it. I followed Jared back across the green prairie, up the hill past the flag-pole and the laundress's quarters of the old fort and back to the parking lot.

Jared started the engine, and we stared at each other for several minutes without speaking.

"Looks like a simple disappearance was not so simple," he finally said.

Jared dropped me at the Olde Gazette Building with a promise to keep me advised of any new information on M. J. Carlyle. New Millennium was silent and empty, Zelda no doubt out scaling mountains with her new French beau.

One client down. Now what? For all intents and purposes, with my client deceased, the Carlyle/Brecken-ridge case was closed. Interrupted almost before I'd begun the investigation. I grabbed the DataTech back-ground reports on Katy and Daniel Quince from my cubby, where I'd left them before dashing off to have lunch with Jared. Upstairs, I unlocked the door to my office, hung up my jacket and inserted a Paul Lanz

CD in the player, hoping the music would mend my fragmented mind. I tossed the DataTech report on top of the other files and papers on my desk that I'd been expecting to return to after lunch and studied the white board with its interconnecting lines and circles, searching for a pattern. With the black marker I added the names "Edie Carlyle" and "Olivia Camille" and connected both of them to M.J.'s circle. The phone rang. It was Paul Breckenridge.

"You hear about M.J.?" he asked.

"Yeah. I just came from the beach."

"You think it was connected to Tina's—to Tina?"

I stared at the white board again, the hint of a pattern forming in the farthest recesses of my brain where I process illogical ideas, intuitive bits of information, and other data that don't lend themselves to reasonable consideration.

"If it wasn't an accident, Paul—and we should know as soon as the autopsy is done—then I would hazard a guess that Tina's disappearance wasn't voluntary. In which case, the question would be, Who wanted them both out of the way and why? Any new ideas?"

"I've been thinking about that for the last three hours." I heard a televison newscast in the background. "You know," he continued, "before this, I kind of let myself believe that she'd just done something stupid and maybe did have an accident with the boat. It happens, even when you've been on the water for as long as she had. And then when you asked if she might have decided to go away, that really threw me. But now, I dunno." There was another silence. "Anyway, what I called for was to say I'd like you to go on with the investigation. I don't know what your fees are, but I'll find the money somewhere. Because the other thing I've been thinking is . . . suppose something happens to Stephan?"

If Tina and M.J.'s deaths were related, and if there

was some kind of family connection, then his fear was appropriate. "Or yourself."

"Yeah."

I quoted him my fee schedule and told him M.J. had already given me a retainer.

"I can handle anything from here on out."

"Then I'll stay on it. And I *must* talk to Stephan."

"He's off-island for some kind of field trip today and tomorrow, but I'll ask him to stop by on Monday morning. I think he's got gym or something light first period. I'll call the school and tell them he's going to be late. How about eight-thirty?"

I glanced at my calendar for Monday. It was wide open. "Eight-thirty is perfect. And, Paul, keep a close eye on Stephan. As close as you can."

There was a long silence, and I thought he had hung up.

"I'll do that," he said finally.

I wrote the Monday appointment on my calendar and was about to attempt the pursuit of that random thought about Tina that was still lurking in the back of my mind when Nick called. My stomach turned over at the sound of his voice.

"Scottie! Glad you're there. I called earlier, but I only got the machine and I decided we'd done enough phone tag for the week. Sorry about all the chaos here."

"Is the chaos contained?" My chirpy voice gave no hint of the awful night I'd spent waiting for his call or the tears at four A.M.

"Probably two steps forward and one back. Sorry I didn't call back last night. I didn't get home until almost eleven."

"I hope it was a pleasant evening." Like hell I did.

"It was *not* a pleasant evening. Nicole got tickets to see a play, and she wanted the three of us to have dinner together, which was the first mistake. After a couple of glasses of wine, Cathy started reminiscing about old times and stuff we did when the kids were little, and I'm thinking, Oh, shit, I know where this is leading. Then Nicole got all teary-eyed and said, couldn't we please just get back together and be a family again?"

It wasn't the first time Nicole had tried to play marriage counselor. "Textbook stuff, Nick."

"What do you mean?"

"Every kid in the world who's been through a divorce wants Mummy and Daddy to get back together. It makes the fairy tale come out right. How did the evening end?"

He sighed. "I excused myself to make a phone call, and by the time I got back to the table, we had to rush off to the theater. I don't want all this mess with Cathy to get in the way of our relationship. But I couldn't just abandon her with the DUI." There was a pause and a long sigh. "Scottie, if you can live without the Mozart concert, I'd just like to get out of Seattle for the weekend. Tony's flying up to the island Saturday morning and I can hitch a ride. Would you be available for some R and R?"

Would I! "I can arrange it." I wanted to shout for joy.

"How about you come out on Saturday afternoon, we'll go for a hike, then sit in the hot tub and gaze at the Milky Way? I'll even turn off the phone and cook you a five-course Hungarian dinner. We can do whatever you want on Sunday, and Tony's not coming back till Monday morning. Is it a date?"

"It's a date!"

I hung up the phone and stared out the window, contemplating the weekend at Nick's house on Mount Dallas. My erotic reverie was interrupted by a call from my mother.

"Scotia, I've been trying to get hold of you for days."

"I left a message with Giovanni and I left a message on your answering machine."

"Well, I didn't get either of them. I called to talk about Melissa."

"Where is she?"

"She's just started working at the lodge. She's very excited about it and I wish you would be more supportive. That beastly South American terrorist really broke her heart. I don't think she's in any shape to go back to classes yet."

"She'll recover, Mother. Gilberto is a soccer player, not a terrorist, and there's no need for her to lose a semester of school."

"He's a monster. And school isn't everything, young lady. Her inner child is grieving, and her reading with Melantha showed that she's got a lot of unresolved issues around Gilberto. They've been together in many former lives."

"Does that mean she has to spend present and future lives with him as well?"

"Sarcasm doesn't become you, Scotia." She sniffed. "I've set up a weekly appointment with Melantha to cleanse Melissa's aura. And she's going to join our Thursday night class. Melissa has a wonderful sense of rhythm. She'll make a wonderful belly dancer."

I counted to five. "I'm sure she would, Mother, and after she finishes college that might be one of her options." Over my dead body. "Right now, I'd appreciate it if you would encourage her to go back to school instead of wasting fifteen credits."

"I believe that it's up to Melissa to make her own decisions. Besides, it will be nice to spend time with her. I missed so much of her childhood when you two were in San Diego. And how are you doing, my dear? Still digging up dead bodies?"

I refrained from reminding my mother that the reason she hadn't shared much of Melissa's childhood was that she and Giovanni had spent seven years in

Assisi in an old Italian farmhouse Giovanni had inherited from his grandmother. One "not really safe for children, dear," she'd informed me when I had suggested that Melissa spend a summer vacation with her. Giovanni would probably still be painting his unsalable watercolors of old Italian stables and my mother dancing on the hillsides by the light of the moon if the big earthquake hadn't leveled the farmhouse while she and Giovanni had been visiting cousins on Capri.

"I don't often stumble over dead bodies, Mother." Present case excepted. "Most of my stuff is insurance work, as you know."

"Did you ever find that boy who sailed off to the South Pacific? What was his name? Like that actor in *Raiders of the Lost Ark*? Ford something?"

"I'm still working on Harrison's whereabouts. I'll keep you posted."

"Thank you, dear. And I'll meditate for Melissa this evening and try to locate her spirit guide. Perhaps you could come down sometime soon. By the way, are you still seeing Nicholas, that handsome lawyer from San Francisco?"

"He lives in Seattle now. I'll be seeing him this weekend."

"That's nice, dear. Bring him down to Mendocino. We should try to be more of a family. I do wish you and Giovanni could let bygones be bygones."

My Call Waiting signal sounded.

"Yes, Mother. Take care of yourself." I pressed the Flash button. Whoever had called hadn't wanted to wait, and whatever sparks of intuition had been surfacing earlier had been frightened off by my mother's remonstrations. My mind was a blank, a state of mind that may have been prized by Sherlock Holmes but wouldn't go very far toward solving what was looking like a double homicide. I glanced at the white board and remembered that Joy Johnson had never called back. I found her name in the phone book, and she answered on the first ring. Yes, she would be happy to talk to me about Tina. She was working on Saturday, but could see me on her lunch break at noon at the café. *Merde*. Nick's name was penciled in for Saturday. Oh, well. It wouldn't take long, and his partner, Tony, was not an early riser.

I entered the appointment on my calendar and picked up the DataTech background on the Quinces. The report was disappointing and added little to what I already knew about Tina Breckenridge's sailing instructor. Katy had been born in Camden, Maine, thirty-eight years ago, the daughter of Emerson Quince and Louella Reynolds Quince. She'd graduated from Camden-Rockport High School and completed two years at the University of Maine in Orono. She'd had had four addresses in Santa Cruz, California. She had been employed by a Santa Cruz sailmaker, had married Harold Huguenot of Santa Cruz and had subsequently used the name of Kathryn Huguenot until she moved to Seattle. She had an ATM card, a Visa card with a balance of $3,569.25, and a checking account with a balance of $340.21 at Bank of the San Juans. There was no mention of a divorce from Harold Huguenot. She had worked for North Sails in Seattle for an eight-month period before coming to Friday Harbor seven years ago. Neither Kathryn Quince nor Kathryn Huguenot had any record of citations or arrests. The five-acre parcel of property on Meadow Road was recorded in the name of Kathryn Mary Quince. Katy looked squeaky clean. But what about her husband? Zelda had stapled a note to the last page of the report: Nothing on a Daniel Quince. Like the dude doesn't exist. I took the liberty of asking DataTech to run a check on Harold Huguenot. Hopefully by tomorrow. Z.

I filed the report in the Breckenridge-Carlyle file and cleared my desktop. My stomach rumbled, a rude

reminder that Jared and I hadn't eaten even one forkful of the *chile verde* before I'd gotten the call from
Angela. I thought about my erudite friend, who was
most likely whiling away the evening, if not the night,
with Allison Fisher. My clock chimed six times and I
realized that I was faced with an empty Friday
evening.

I called my friend Meredith Martin, who works for
U.S. Customs.

"I'd love to join you for dinner, Scotia, but there's
a DEA agent here and I'm probably going to be tied
up until eight or so."

"How about we meet at George's at eight and we
can take it from there?"

"You've got it."

Meredith and I had met last fall when I was investigating a child custody case with international implications, and we had become friends. She had been
divorced for ten years, had an eighteen-year-old son,
and had recently married a San Juan Island contractor
with two young children.

I stared at the phone and thought about the body
bag on the beach at American Camp. I dialed Angela's number at the sheriff's office and asked about
the report on the Carlyle autopsy. "I just heard the
undersheriff say it's not in yet," she informed me.
"But you might be interested to know that Eden
Bell Carlyle came in and filed a formal theft report
on a missing wardrobe trunk that disappeared from
the van they had left parked at American Camp
this morning."

"Not surprising, with all the petty theft on the
island."

"I'm out of here in half an hour," she said. "I just
have time for a quick drink before my meeting for the
church bazaar tomorrow. Want to meet at George's?"

It sounded like my evening was going to run in
shifts. We agreed on six forty-five. I locked up and

trotted down to *Spray* for a change of clothes, something a little more classy than the brown sweater and mud-stained blue jeans I'd worn to Brown Sugar Beach.

15

George's was a haze of blue smoke, all the tables filled, the decibel level rising by the second. Billiard balls snapped into side pockets on the green baize table at the back of the room. Trying not to inhale, I pushed my way through the wall of bodies around the bar, searching for Angela's head of curly dark hair.

"What'll it be, Scotia?" Lindsey, Henry's fiancée, was bartending.

"Dry vermouth and soda." I spied Angela at the end of the bar. She was chatting with Peg O'Reilly, the forthright owner of the Netshed who had advised me to let sleeping dogs lie. Peg met my eyes, then turned aside and said something to Angela, who glanced my way and began inching toward me through the crowd, glass mug of amber brew held shoulder high.

"You got your hair cut! I love it!"

"Thanks. How's Peg O'Reilly?"

"She says hi."

"That's certainly more cordial than our last encounter."

"Yeah, she told me. But since Carlyle's death, she thinks something funny's going on. And she thinks the sheriff will probably conclude M.J.'s death was an accident, just like Tina's. She was Tina's godmother, you know. Are you going to continue with the investigation?" Angela unbuttoned her periwinkle-blue polar-fleece anorak, revealing the black T-shirt she wore with well-fitting blue jeans. Her lips were a lovely shade of dark watermelon. Angela has deep brown eyes and thick dark lashes, and I, blessed with the blue eyes and pale, straight lashes of my Celtic fore-bears, am very envious of her. Even in my crisp white shirt, clean blue jeans, and freshly painted fingernails, she outclassed me by a mile. I'd hate her if she weren't my best friend.

"Yes I am," I said. "But I'm working for Paul now. I hope I can close it before he goes back to Alaska."

"Speaking of Alaska, I'm leaving for Juneau a month from today to spend some time with Matt."

Lindsey pushed my vermouth and soda across the bar. I turned back to Angela and spied Zelda at a table along the windows. She was with a dark-haired man in a white fisherman's sweater. They were holding hands, heads very close together. I also noticed that the newly widowed Edie Bell Carlyle and the red-haired man I'd seen on the bluffs at American Camp were seated at a table next to Zelda and her friend. The new widow did not appear to be overly saddened by her estranged husband's recent death. I wondered if she had an alibi for whenever M.J. had met his maker.

"You haven't been to Alaska for two years, have you?" I said.

Angela took another sip of the ale. "Right. And Matt was afraid I wouldn't go up this year, either." She took another sip of the ale and sneezed. "Sorry. I'm allergic to this smoke."

"Makes two of us."

She pulled a tissue from a pocket and blew her nose. "I never told you why I didn't want to go back, did I?"

I shook my head, sipping the vermouth and soda.

"I love Matt a whole bunch, and I know fishing in Alaska is really important to him, even though he's got enough money. It's important that he keeps on doing just what his father did. Probably more important, since his son's an engineer."

Matt had been married previously and had two children: a girl and a boy, both in their early twenties, both living over on the mainland.

"I got the impression Alaska fishing's not your cup of tea."

"Your impression was mostly right," she said. "It's not just floating around on a boat full of dead fish that I hate. God knows, I've seen enough dead things in my life. It's that I'm married to a madman who goes out in any kind of weather. Rain, wind, snow, sleet—you name it, and Matt's out there. Broken poles, broken windows, hatch covers washed overboard. He couldn't care less." She shivered. "The last time I was up, we got caught in a horrible storm. We were headed back into Sitka. There were gale warnings out and it was blowing fifty knots. The seas got bigger and bigger, and pretty soon it was just a monstrous black wall of waves and spray and clouds. In some of the gusts the wind meter hit sixty and seventy." She took another sip of her ale and I saw how pale her face had become. " I can't tell you how many times we were blown over. I didn't stop praying for five hours and I vowed if we made it into port in one piece, I'd never go back again. I'm not made of the same stuff as Tina Breckenridge."

"It can be fierce out there," I agreed, watching a new set of arrivals burst through the front door of the tavern. "What changed your mind about going back?"

"Matt's promised to be a lot more cautious about the weather. Besides, I miss him desperately when he's gone, and I don't want some outback Alaska woman to get her mitts on him."

"Sounds like you're protecting your investment. How's the sheriff feel about your taking time off?"

"His cousin's wife is our night dispatcher, and while

I'm gone she'll get to work days. Otherwise, he probably wouldn't have approved it."

The new arrivals to the tavern were Mac MacGregor and two men in plaid wool shirts. I'd seen one of them at the Netshed on Wednesday. The other one I didn't know. The threesome paused for a minute inside the door, then elbowed their way through the crowd and managed to create space for themselves at the bar.

"Hey, Lindsey, darlin', how about some service down here?" Mac's big voice carried clearly over the jukebox. He had both hands on the bar, palms down.

Lindsey glanced warily at the men, dried her hands, and approached with a smile. "What'll it be, boys?"

"Three pitchers of your best booze, three baskets of those giant cheeseburgers with fries, and a table."

"Three pitchers of brew, three giant cheeseburgers coming up." Lindsey smiled at Mac and started to move away.

"Not quite so fast there, sweetheart," Mac roared, reaching across the bar and grabbing Lindsey's wrist. "I said we wanted a table. No reason for us to stand, is there, while the fucking tourists are sitting down?"

Lindsey looked down at Matt's hand and frowned. From somewhere at the other end of the bar a man in a dark green sweatshirt stood up and began to make his way toward Mac. It was Henry, Lindsey's betrothed, and I prayed he'd have the smarts not to take on the town's biggest bully.

"If you know what's good for you, Mac MacGregor, you'll put your hand on the other side of that bar and take your ugly snout out of here." The gravelly voice of Peg O'Reilly came from over my left shoulder. There was a widening circle of silence around the three men, and all eyes turned to Peg. "If you want to cause a ruckus, take your sorry ass out to the Hunting Club. We've had enough trouble from you for one week."

Mac released Lindsey, turned slowly and stared at Peg.

"And take your friends with you," she snarled. "I've had a hard day and I came here to socialize, not to watch a goddamn prizefight."

"Now, now, Peg, no need to be nasty." He glanced at his friends, scanned the suddenly quieted room, and shrugged. "Come on, boys. Don't look like we're wanted here."

Peg watched them elbow their way toward the door, took another sip of her drink, narrowed her eyes, and headed for the billiard table. Kenny Rogers's velvety voice reminded us that it's important to know when to hold 'em and when to fold 'em. Lindsey smiled at Henry across the bar and winked.

"Score one for Peg," Angela said with a giggle, emptying her mug of beer. "I have to leave. Tell Meredith I said hello. And if you two are having dinner, I recommend the Drydock. They do a great cioppino on Friday nights."

She gave me a quick hug, donned her parka, and made her way through the boisterous crowd.

It was eight-fifteen. I pulled my cell phone from my pocket and called Meredith at the Customs office.

"I know, I know," she said. "I'm late. Just finishing up. I'm not really in the mood for George's. Can we meet somewhere else?"

"See you at the Drydock."

The restaurant was cozy, tranquil and welcoming. Red-checked tablecloths covered the round tables. Flickering white candles lit the small, low-ceilinged room. Meredith was waiting for me in the entrance, her long mane of naturally blond hair tucked under a becoming dark green beret. The waitress ushered us to a table overlooking the harbor. We ordered a carafe of Washington State Chardonnay and the cioppino.

"God, what a week!" said Meredith. "A guy from

Vancouver was caught peddling B. C. Bud out of the Topsail Inn, and our cutter intercepted a sailboat from Victoria with a cargo of cocaine. And to top it all off, it's my birthday. Mark was going to cook a cozy dinner at home tonight." She stared moodily out the window at the lights of the approaching ferry.

"What happened? You guys have a tiff?"

"No, and it's not his fault. His ex was supposed to have the kids this weekend, but she canceled on him last night. Said she was having a party and it wouldn't be appropriate for the girls to be there. God knows what kind of a party she was having. What could he do? To make up for their not going to their mom's, he agreed to a sleepover with six ten-year-olds."

"Aside from the weekend cancellation, how's everything going?"

"Actually, quite well. Jeremy's graduating and going to spend the summer with his dad in Tacoma. Neither of Mark's girls seems to resent me, and both of them made the honor roll this semester. Life could be worse." Before the wedding, Meredith had confided that it took a lot of soul-searching on her part to accept Mark's proposal of marriage and take on two prepubescent females.

"Maybe you're just wiser about childrearing this time."

"That could be. My current parenting philosophy is that life's too short to get upset about little things. When Jeremy used to refuse to clean up his room or help with chores, I always made a federal case out of it. Now, I just close the girls' door, put on a Dolly Parton CD, and do the dishes myself. Takes a lot less energy in the long run."

The waitress brought the carafe of white wine and a wicker basket of sourdough. She filled our glasses and I reached for a piece of bread. Meredith smiled and took a sip of the Chardonnay. "Anyway, in another seven or eight years they'll leave home and I'll have the gorgeous man to myself." She buttered a piece of sourdough. "I see you got your hair cut. And your nails done. You look terrific. You have a hot date with that handsome attorney this weekend?"

"He's coming up on Saturday."

"Lucky you," she said. "Your daughter in college, Nick's ex in San Francisco, and his kids all grown up and out of the house. Must be heaven."

I stared at Meredith, thinking about Nick and the return of the ex-wife, his neurotic matchmaking daughter, my rebellious daughter waitressing down in Mendocino, aided and abetted by my bohemian mother. I burst out laughing. Meredith stared back at me, wineglass in hand, then joined in.

"Pure soap," I gasped, wiping a tear from my eye. "Romance in the twenty-first century. Single parenting, irresponsible ex-spouses, rebellious adolescents. Meredith, we should sell our lives to a sitcom: gorgeous blond customs officer with handsome new husband whose ex-wife cancels out at the last minute. Or this one: female private eye trying to solve a missing persons case and possible homicide, crying in her wine over her significant other, who is consoling his cute blond ex-wife in a Seattle bistro. Take your pick."

"How do you know Nick's wife is cute and blond? You ever meet her?"

"Nick has a picture of her and the two kids at the house on Mount Dallas. And right now she's in Seattle."

"What's he consoling her about?"

I explained about the DUI while the waitress served our salads. Meredith frowned at her salad, then looked at me.

"Did I hear you mention a homicide?"

"Tina Breckenridge's brother, M. J. Carlyle, hired me to investigate his sister's drowning. This morning his body was found at Brown Sugar Beach."

"M.J. Carlyle was your client?"

"Sure was."

"Good grief! I didn't make the connection. You think Carlyle's accident is connected to his sister's disappearance?"

"Maybe, maybe not. I should know more in a couple of days when the time and cause of Carlyle's death are determined." I sampled the arugula from the top of the salad. "Sounds like you're on a big case, too."

"Actually, two cases. One's a very suspicious fishing trawler that spends too much time in Juan de Fuca Strait. Owned by a Canadian with a history of drug smuggling. The coasties are keeping an eye on it. The other case is more of a puzzle. Somebody is supplying B. C. pot to the U.S. mainland on a regular basis, but we can't figure out the pipeline. The DEA sent an agent over. She's pretty sure they're using either some of the small San Juan Islands or the Gulf Islands as a drop-off point, like the rumrunners did during Prohibition." She sighed. "We don't have the resources to monitor every island in the county. And, frankly, I wonder if it's not a waste of time to try. The U.S. drug market is worth somewhere around $150 billion a year. And the so-called War on Drugs is costing U.S. taxpayers almost $20 billion annually. Even when we bust somebody, it's just the tip of the iceberg."

"You think drugs should be decriminalized?" I asked idly, remembering the high price my second husband Pete, had paid for trying to enforce the unenforceable on the U.S.-Mexican border.

"I'm sure it will shock you to hear a customs officer say this, but, yes, I do. The people who want drugs will always find ways of getting them. Even if they have to kill and steal and prostitute themselves to support their habit. For God's sake, pure cocaine is retailing for about thirty-eight hundred dollars an ounce and the dealers are making a profit of over eight hundred percent!"

Meredith's voice had risen. The conservatively

dressed older couple at the next table looked up from their platters of fish and frowned at her. The waitress brought our bowls of steaming cioppino and we began to eat in silence.

"How's Melissa doing?" Meredith tore off a large chunk of the sourdough and dunked it in the sea-food stew.

I drew a deep breath and summarized the domestic drama unfolding down in Mendocino with Jewel Moon and Giovanni.

"Give her a week," Meredith said with a chuckle. "She'll be more than ready to return to classes. Toting trays and waiting on the hoi polloi isn't all she thinks it is. I know. That's how I used to pay my tuition." She emptied her wineglass and refilled it from the ca-rafe. "I hear Abigail Leedle got arrested at American Camp. You think her Corona cohorts or some other Hate the Tourists group had anything to do with your client's accident? Maybe some kind of harassment that got out of hand?"

It was a mean question that had been lingering in the back of my own mind. I had wanted to keep it there. "I'd hate to think so. Zelda was busy with a new boyfriend. Lily MacGregor is a Corona," I said slowly, remembering Lily's admission that she had had a crush on M.J. when they were kids.

"If it wasn't something the Coronas set up, that leaves Mac MacGregor, doesn't it?"

I stared at her. "Mac? You mean because of the bar fight at George's on Tuesday night?"

"I was there. Mac was very drunk and very mad. He's not going to forget what his wife's childhood sweetheart did to him in front of his cronies."

16

Sunlight streaming through the starboard porthole woke me at nine o'clock on Saturday morning. Calico's purring beside my pillow sounded like a buzz saw in my pounding head. I cautiously opened my eyes and tried to reconstruct the night before. After we left the Drydock, Meredith and I had stopped at the Spinnaker for an Irish coffee, and I'd learned more than I had ever wanted to know about the British Columbia marijuana industry. That the B.C. lower mainland had an estimated twenty thousand growers of marijuana, nearly half of which were located inside Vancouver city limits. And that the retail price for B.C. Bud in Los Angeles was $6,000 a pound. The figure seemed a bit exorbitant, but somewhere after the second Irish coffee, I'd learned that the amount of THC—the chemical that causes the buzz in marijuana—was rumored to be 20 percent or more in B.C.-grown marijuana, compared to 5 percent found in most Mexican marijuana. That also sounded a bit exaggerated, but apparently the B.C. growers had their southern competitors beat hands down.

As we were about to order the third coffee with double whipped cream, David Kean and Rafie Dominguez came in from the theater, all smiles. They insisted on our sharing their good mood and a number of highlights from the Anthony Hopkins movie they'd just seen, and we closed the bar up. It was two-thirty before I made it back to G-73 in the pouring rain.

I moved Calico to the other pillow and contemplated my day: an appointment at noon with Joy Johnson, Tina's best friend, and then a drive out to Nick's place on Crow's Nest Drive. I'd better get moving.

I provided a Fancy Feast breakfast for Calico, grabbed a quick shower on *DragonSpray* instead of trekking up to the showers at the port building, and painted my toenails candy apple red. After drying my newly styled hair, I applied some makeup and opened the hanging locker for something that would captivate the love of my life. Or the man I hoped was still the love of my life. I pulled on a long dark red skirt and white sweater and wished I didn't feel threatened by Nick's ex or get queasy from thinking about the two of them together under the encouraging eye of daughter Nicole. I packed a few necessities for a weekend at Nick's and checked my appearance in the full-length mirror. Angela and Meredith were right: my new haircut was dynamite.

Maybe Paula Zahn on a *good* hair day.

I arrived at the Marina Café promptly at noon. Only one customer—a large forty-something woman with peroxided blond hair going gray—was the right age to be Joy Johnson. She motioned me to join her without smiling.

"I'm Joy." She had blue eyes and a large square face covered with a web of fine wrinkles. Her blue overalls fit loosely over a white T-shirt, and she wore white Adidas with red stains on them.

"I'm Scotia MacKinnon. Thanks for meeting me."

Joy had just begun making her way through a gigantic cheeseburger and fries. I handed her my card and pulled out a chair. "I've been hired to investigate Tina Breckenridge's disappearance. I thought you—"

"Disappearance, my foot! Somebody wanted that

girl out of the way. And when M.J. hired you, that same somebody offed him."

No reticence about this lady. "You have anybody in mind?"

"No, but don't think I haven't lost sleep over it." She took a huge bite of the cheeseburger. Her hands looked like they had spent a lot of time in hot water. Ketchup dribbled out of the bun and onto her plate. She chewed and swallowed. "Tina was my best friend in the whole world. She wouldn't have hurt a fly. And she didn't fall overboard. You want some coffee?"

"No, thanks. Just had breakfast. Okay if I record this?"

"Go ahead."

"How long have you known Tina?"

"Since seventh grade at Ballard Middle School."

"You and Tina went to Alaska together?"

"Yep. Two high-flyers on a wild adventure. Tina worked for a boatbuilder in Ballard for a while after high school, then she took some business classes in community college to please her mom. But it wasn't her thing. So we took off, north to Alaska."

"Where in Alaska?"

"Kodiak. And it almost turned into a disaster."

"How so?"

"Horny fishermen, too much booze and drugs, no jobs."

"But you stayed?"

"Shit, we had nothing else to do. No jobs, no money to live on or get back home with. If it hadn't been for Paul Breckenridge, it might have turned into a Thelma and Louise rerun. Tina was tiny and built like a brick shit house. I felt like her bodyguard after the sun went down. Which is pretty early in Alaska in the winter." She paused, chewed on a french fry, her gaze far away. "Tina knew Paul when she was a little kid in Friday Harbor. He got us jobs on the crab boat he was work-ing on, the *Ice Queen*."

"How long did you work on the *Ice Queen*?"

"Three years total, then I fell in lust with another crab boat skipper—and married him. Five years later, he went out in a storm when any normal man would have been laid up in Lazy Bay or getting snockered at Henley's. The boat went down off Cape Chiniak. All souls lost, and he hadn't paid the last premium on the insurance policy. Which is why I'm still slaving over a hot grill at the hotel. Oh, well—win some, lose some. At least Tina had the sense not to go north again after she got married. Even if it was the worst mistake of her life."

"Marrying Paul?"

"Yeah."

"Why was it the worst mistake of her life?"

She devoured three more french fries and looked at me speculatively. I waited while she took a long swig of coffee.

"Because she didn't love him."

"Why did she marry him?"

"Stephan was born seven and a half months later. You figure it out."

"I see." So Tina and Paul's had been a shotgun marriage. I waited for further explication, but none was forthcoming.

"After you moved here, did you and Tina see each other often?"

"Usually got together once a week. Sometimes at her place, sometimes at mine."

"Would you say the sailing school was successful?"

"If you want to call catering to a lot of rich women a success. I told Tina there was no way she could charge so much for a week or a weekend on a sailboat. I was wrong. After three years she had a long waiting list. That's why she hired Katy."

"How did Tina and Katy get along?"

"Tina said Katy didn't know as much about sailing as she thought she did and had a bad attitude to boot.

But she couldn't find another woman instructor to replace her. And she needed Katy for the three- and four-day classes, where she made the most money."

"What can you tell me about Tina's state of mind in the weeks before she disappeared?"

Joy sighed, stared out the long windows overlooking the fuel dock. "Tina started getting depressed around last Christmas. Said it was the weather. Said she needed more sunlight. Then she started drinking too much wine. I drove her home from George's one night when she couldn't walk. She promised me she wouldn't drink alone." She paused. "Stephan was getting pretty surly. He threatened her with a knife once." Her big wrinkled face tensed and she swiped at her eyes. "Tina's not being around has put a big hole in my life." She wiped away more tears and checked her watch. "Look, I have to go. I'm training a new salad chef. I'm sorry I can't help you. I hope to God you find out what happened to her." She picked up my card, put it in her big black pouch of a purse, and left.

I watched the large, full-bodied woman make her way between the tables and out the door above the dinghy dock. Then I stood up, nearly colliding with a magenta-haired young woman heading for the table I was vacating. She was dressed in a black leather vest over bare skin and black leather jeans studded with metal. Three other young people followed her, all similarly attired, all sporting body piercings in eyebrows, nipples, and belly buttons. The foursome flung their backpacks on the table, and silence fell over the café as they lined up at the order counter, their costumes loudly incongruous at a dining spot where the rest of the patrons wore blue jeans and sweatshirts.

I stashed the tape recorder in my rucksack, wondering if black leather and pierced belly buttons were the future of Roche Harbor, and headed out to the house on Crow's Nest Drive to spend the rest of Saturday afternoon with Nick.

17

Tall red geraniums swayed gently in the late-afternoon breeze outside the bedroom window. Nick lay sleeping, snuggled against my back. Sliding carefully out of his arms, I sat up and pulled the mint-green sheet up to my neck. Propped against the padded leather headboard, I gazed across the wide indigo expanse of Haro Strait to the Trial Island light and beyond to the snow-topped mountain range on the Olympic Peninsula. Just north of the entrance to Baynes Channel a sailboat changed course. For a minute or so, the white headsail fluttered as the boat came through the eye of the wind, then settled in on the new tack, and the vessel heeled to leeward, sails taut. Further west, the orange disk of the sun was about to sink behind the tall, purple gray mountains on Vancouver Island.

The waters of Haro Strait are deep. Two hundred, three hundred, even four hundred feet in places. Many of the rocky, volcanic cliffs and ledges and glacial outcroppings of the islands that rim the strait rise vertically from the dark, watery depths. Northwest of San Juan Island, the swift ocean currents veer north and flood up Boundary Pass, past Waldron and Orcas Islands. Mingling with the waters of Georgia Strait, they continue rushing northwest past the city of Vancouver and up Malaspina Strait on the edge of the British

Columbia mainland. No matter the month, the waters that ebb and flood and hurl white frothy water against black rocks are neither tropical nor welcoming.

The third Thursday in April could have been a turning point for Tina Breckenridge. Dispirited over her constant conflicts with Stephan, weary of being both mother and father, unhappy with her sailing instructor, she could have returned to *Alcyone*, cranked up the engine, cast off the dock lines, and headed out of Roche Harbor into the darkening night. The nighttime cruise would have been an escape. An opportunity to get away and drink a bottle of wine out of sight of well-meaning best friends.

It would have been cold. There would have been a wind, probably out of the northwest. She would have motored over to Reid Harbor on Stuart Island, four miles or so from her berth at Roche, dropped anchor, and opened a bottle of wine. And after the third or fourth glass of wine, before crawling into her bunk, she might have gone topside to check the anchor, slipped on the wet deck, hit her head, and gone overboard.

There would have been no one to see her slender, stunned body slip into the black, forty-five-degree waters.

The outgoing currents would have carried her unconscious body out of the mouth of the tiny harbor, into the vicious tide rips of Speiden Channel into Haro Strait and on to the Strait of Juan de Fuca. And finally it would have been carried out past Race Rocks and into the icy, whitecapped waters of the north Pacific.

Such a scenario would explain the missing body. But if she were anchored, how did the boat get to Sucia on its own? Or did she fall overboard while she was pulling up the anchor and—

"Penny for your thoughts, lovely lady."

Nick stretched his long body beside me, yawned, and ran a finger down my bare arm. I shivered.

"It's this case I'm working on."

"Your client from *On the Edge?* What's his name? Carlyle?"

"*Was* his name. He had a fatal accident yesterday. Exit one client. Now I'm working for the disappeared's husband, Paul Breckenridge."

Nick sat up and stared at me. "Fatal accident as in dead? Fatal as in murdered?"

I shrugged. "Could have been accidental. I don't know what the sheriff's found out. He doesn't share confidences with me. The estranged wife was not exactly tearful. That role was being filled by Carlyle's lovely mistress."

"So you have a disappearance, a death, and a love triangle on your hands? I thought you didn't want to take on that mean stuff anymore."

"I don't. But if I know our sheriff, this will go into the same file of 'accident, case closed' as Carlyle's sister's disappearance. And that rankles. A woman is gone. If it was an accident, so be it. If M.J. hadn't died, and a thorough investigation turned up nothing, we could have assumed she drowned."

"But now you can't. Any suspects for a double homicide?"

"Not really." I briefly described my interviews with Paul and Katy and Joy Johnson, and Joy's proclamation that Tina was not in love with Paul.

"Maybe she had something going with someone else and took off. Maybe her husband found out and did her in."

I nodded, lost in thought. Homicides motivated by infidelity account for a significant percent of deaths— crimes that are often committed by an estranged spouse or spurned love. I glanced at Nick and thought about his ex and her mental instability. Suddenly I wondered if she knew where he was spending the weekend. He seemed to read my thoughts.

"No, Cathy doesn't know where I am. And since

we're on the topic, I know you're uncomfortable with what's been going on the past week."

"Yes, I am."

"I want you to know that I'm doing what I'm doing out of respect for all the years I spent with her. Because she's the mother of my children. Not because there's anything left between us. At least on my part."

"And on hers?"

He looked uncomfortable and folded his arms across his chest. "She wants to try again."

A frigid wind swept over my naked body. I shivered and pulled the sheet closer around my shoulders.

Nick put an arm around me, his brown eyes serious. "Scottie, don't look like that. I told her it would never work. What we had is ancient history. She's moving out of the condo on Monday. She's going back to Nicole's until she figures out what she wants to do."

I stared at him. "You mean she's been staying with *you*?"

"She was staying with Nicole, but Nicole's boyfriend is coming for the weekend, so I gave Cathy the guest room. That's why I came up here."

"Whatever happened to hotels?" I said spitefully. "Isn't that where divorced spouses normally stay?"

"Cathy doesn't have any money. And she doesn't want to take any from me."

How convenient. I wondered what had happened to the generous property settlement she'd gotten.

He shook his head. "*Listen* to me, Scottie. You're the one I want to be with. Not her."

I truly wanted to believe it.

And I tried, all the rest of the afternoon and evening. I made every attempt to erase the image of Cathy bedded down in Nick's cozy guest room overlooking Elliot Bay, bathing in his shower, sipping coffee in his breakfast nook. I showered and dried my hair and donned the pale blue silk kimono Nick kept in his closet for me. I sipped the chilled Fumé Blanc he brought to the bedroom and tried to concentrate on the Breckenridge-Carlyle puzzle. I thought about what Nick had said about Tina being involved with someone else.

It is virtually impossible to keep an illicit relationship secret on San Juan Island. If Tina were involved with someone while Paul was in Alaska, did she leave her car somewhere overnight where it would cause comment? Or was it purely love in the afternoon? Did Stephan know about the liaison? Or one of his friends? Would Stephan have told his father? If Paul had found out, what would he have done?

I consumed the second glass of Fumé Blanc while Nick added the finishing touches to a pot of fragant vegetable soup. "Family lore has it," he said with a grin, grinding black pepper over the pot, "that *grandmère* got the recipe from her outlaw lover from the mountainous Bakony region of Hungary. Long before she met my grandfather, of course."

"Of course."

"This, however, is *not* an old family recipe," he said, transferring sauce-covered pieces of chicken paprika from a large white carton to a blue-flowered casserole. "In the interest of spending more time with you, I picked it up from Tino's Deli. Tino also talked me into his world-renowned rum-raisin crepes with whipped cream and chocolate sauce. At least, they're world-renowned according to Tino. I didn't tell him my mother considered hers to be of the same caliber and wouldn't share her recipe with anyone."

I smiled, remembering how jealously my grandmother had guarded the ingredients for the chocolate cream puffs that she would whip up in her big, old-fashioned kitchen. I wondered where her recipe book was.

Nick lit two tall candles on the long refectory table in the window alcove overlooking the water. The old ivory linen tablecloth was a family heirloom, as were the china and sterling. And somewhere between my first taste of the soup of the Bakony outlaws and the last morsel of the rum-raisin crepe, I managed to tuck the nagging discomfort of Nick's Madame X and the increasingly tangled web of the Carlyle-Breckenridge matter into the furthermost recesses of my investigative mind.

We moved into the living room after dinner. The night had grown cool, so Nick built a fire in the fieldstone fireplace and brought a carafe of coffee and two cups to the table in front of the leather sofa. Darkness had fallen, and the only lights to be seen were two flashing markers far out on the water.

"I was going through an old trunk this week," Nick said, pouring coffee. "I found some sheet music I haven't played in years. Including some Mozart. I realize it's not Gerard Schwarz, but I'd be happy to play for you."

"I'd love that, Nick." I watched his tall figure move over behind the piano. Playing the piano was one of Nick's passions. His mother had been a music teacher and he'd been playing since he was a small child. In January we'd gone to an estate auction here on the island and he'd found a lovely old baby grand that fit into the corner of the living room. I added milk to my coffee, then settled deeply into the down cushions on the sofa and closed my eyes.

I'm not terribly educated about classical music, but Mozart I do know because Albert loved symphonic music and we had season tickets to the San Francisco Symphony. Nick began to play and I quickly recognized Concerto No. 21. He followed it with what is, for me, Mozart's signature piece, *Eine kleine Nacht Musik*, then switched to Chopin. One of the sonatas, I thought, watching Nick's curly salt-and-pepper head bent over the keyboard. I sipped my coffee and luxuriated in the pure happiness of being exactly where I wanted to be with the one person I most wanted to be with.

It didn't get any better than this.

18

At seven-thirty on Monday morning I dropped Nick at the Roche Harbor airstrip, where his partner already had the Piper Arrow ready for takeoff.

"I'll try to get everything tied up with Cathy's DUI today and move her back over to Nicole's," Nick told me. "Maybe you could come down next weekend. We could do something special. Maybe go out to the coast. I'll call you." He gave me a quick kiss, grabbed his bag from the backseat, and was gone, running across the rough airfield to the plane. The sky was cloudless, with only a zephyr of wind. I watched them taxi to the end of the field, turn, motor down the length of the runway, and lift off into the pale sky. In thirty to forty minutes, they would land at Boeing Field, and by nine o'clock they'd be back in the office and the world of maritime torts and undersea salvage.

I drove back to the road and through the Roche Harbor arches and headed into town, fondly replaying our weekend. On Sunday we'd begun the day with mimosas in the hot tub, watching a tiny red tug laboring up the strait with two huge barges. Later, while I showered, Nick took my car into town to get the *New York Times* and we spent what was left of the morning and the early afternoon perusing the news of the world over eggs Benedict and a fresh fruit concoction on the deck, accompanied by the marmalade cat that hung out at Nick's when he was on the island. In the late afternoon, we'd ambled down the hill for a walk through the state park and been rewarded by the appearance of two pods of orcas.

It was clearly my turn to prepare Sunday supper, and I'd shocked both Nick and myself with a repast of tortilla wraps from Saturday night's leftover chicken, sliced avocados, and a fabulous Jamaican sauce. We'd devoured it with glasses of chilled Mirror Pond ale while watching *Clear and Present Danger* from Nick's collection of Harrison Ford videos. And then it was bedtime. Dawn arrived long before my psyche was inclined to return to the real world of clients and suspects and unsolved cases.

Just before I got to Boyce Road, an old black truck lumbered onto the road in front of me and I screeched to a halt. The driver gave me a salute, the exhaust belched a huge cloud of smoke, and I was trapped behind it for the remaining five winding miles into town.

It was a few minutes before eight when I got to the Olde Gazette Building. The big first-floor space was pungent with the rich aroma of fresh coffee. But the usual opera music had been replaced by something symphonic: Vivaldi, I thought. I sniffed appreciatively, rested my rucksack on the floor near the mail cubbies, and filled a cracked yellow cup with steaming black liquid. Zelda was hunched over her computer keyboard, intent on an early morning Internet search.

"New brand of coffee?" I inquired, adding a few drops of nondairy creamer.

"Kona Coast Gold." She twirled around on her steno chair. "Left over from the On the Edge party Saturday night. There was a lot more booze and cocaine consumed than coffee."

I stared at her. "You mean they still had the party after M.J.'s accident?"

"Can you believe it? It was totally bizarre. Edie

Carlyle rented this humongous house at Eagle Cove. I don't know what she's doing rattling around out there by herself. Or maybe she's not by herself, judging by the way she was all over Jerome."

"Who's Jerome?"

"One of the male models. Anyway, about half the crew showed up and didn't seem to care a whit that one of their number had bitten the dust the day before. They reminded me of a bunch of androids."

"Including Edie?"

"Especially Edie. Jerome was passing around a sack of B.C. Bud. Edie got stoned out of her mind, and she's not nice when she's stoned. Never stopped bitching about being questioned by what she fondly refers to as our 'redneck sheriff.' "

"Did M.J.'s girlfriend put in an appearance?"

"Olivia Camille? No. And apparently several of the female models were also absent. They don't like their boss. They call her Edie the Ogre. Easy to see why M.J. was divorcing her. She's as likable as a great white shark on a rampage." Zelda's computer beeped; she turned to frown at the screen, clicked on the Print icon, and continued. "About midnight, when I was cleaning up, she got into it with the photographer. Something about keeping his hands off the local women. He was as drunk as she was stoned, so it wasn't pretty. I also heard some scuttlebutt about M.J. Maybe he wasn't as nice as he was pretty."

"Such as?"

"M.J.'s first wife was filthy rich, and when they got divorced he got a big chunk. Including alimony. Apparently Edie also had a bunch of money of her own and he wanted half. But she made him sign a prenuptial."

"Sounds like a smart thing to do."

"Yeah, but he was saying it was coerced, since she didn't present it until the day they got married and then he didn't have legal representation."

"I see," I said thoughtfully. "How did the food and entertainment go?"

"Super. Except that she didn't like my eggplant caviar."

"I thought they ordered Beluga."

"It was sixty dollars an ounce. It was a fixed-price contract, so I improvised."

"I see." I sipped the Kona Coast Gold and surveyed Zelda's Monday morning attire: a vividly embroidered white shirt over an ankle-length black flounced skirt and black leather shoes with wedge heels. A lot of silver and turquoise bracelets. Her hair was held back with a narrow black velvet ribbon, very Alice in Wonderland. If Alice had had hair the color of raw carrots. Also very feminine, very un-Zelda, whose getups ran the gamut from heavy metal to Chinese concubine. "You're looking very ladylike this morning."

"Jean Pierre likes women in skirts."

"And how is it going with the Frenchman?"

"*Magnifique.*" She batted her lashes at me and smiled. "Jean Pierre's teaching me French."

Given Zelda's cadre of international suitors—Hans in Germany, Boris the ex-KGB agent from Vancouver, now Monsieur Zola—she had a better deal than a year at Berlitz.

"In addition to being a spectacular lover, he's found me a new client. I'm going to arrange a surprise birthday party next week on the yacht he skippers for some dude from Seattle. It's a Gatsby party. Everybody is supposed to dress in twenties costumes. Lawn tennis attire. The women in gauzy white dresses, men in white pants. The invitations are already out. All I have to do is provide the champagne, music, food, and flowers."

"No cocaine?"

"No cocaine. Jean Pierre says his boss hates drugs."

"How unique." I emptied my coffee cup, rinsed it in the sink, and pulled my mail from the cubby: a phone message from Jared Saperstein saying he'd call back, four solicitations from charitable organizations; and the latest edition of *P. I. Magazine*. I wished Zelda well with the Gatsby party and suggested that she stick with Beluga this time.

"They don't want caviar. But I've got to find a bartender and some serving wenches."

Upstairs, I stashed the rucksack under my desk, turned on the heat and the old Art Deco lamp on my desk. Having spent the weekend among Nick's far more lavish furnishings, I thought the office looked drab this morning. The cushions on the wicker chairs from Pier 1 imports had faded and I'd forgotten to water the ficus. The leaves were already yellowing. I stared at the scarred wooden floor, considering a new rug. The phone rang. It was Jared.

"You got my message?"

"I did."

"Want to make a second try at Pablo's? A little before noon? I've got a big story to share with you."

"See you there."

I spread the message slips on the desk, noted that the cover story of *P. I. Mazagine* was on the consumer popularity of a software surveillance program that monitors everything your employee, child, or spouse does online. I was about to water the ficus when I heard a tentative voice behind me.

"Ms. MacKinnon?"

I glanced at my appointment book for Monday morning, saw my notation, "Stephan Breckenridge, 8:30," and turned to face the tall young man in an oversized black T-shirt, baggy blue jeans, and black felt hat.

I extended my hand and looked into a pair of deep-set dark brown eyes. The long sideburns and thin Van-dyke beard made for a Tim McGraw look-alike, and the straight, longish hair was the same dark brown as that of his recently deceased uncle. His blue jeans were wrinkled and stained over the knees, and a bulky backpack weighed down his left shoulder.

"Thanks for coming by, Stephan. Have a seat." I motioned him to one of the wicker chairs. He glanced around the office, put the bulging backpack on the floor, and slouched into the chair. He was very handsome. Handsome and sullen.

"Dad said you're trying to find out what happened to Mom." He pushed the black felt hat back on his forehead.

I nodded and reached for a yellow lined pad and the tape recorder.

"You have to record this?" he asked.

"I'd like to. Is that okay?"

There was a long silence that I interpreted as reluctance. "Well, yeah, I guess." He frowned.

I gently pressed the red Record button.

"Stephan, tell me what you remember about the day your mother disappeared. It was a Thursday."

He took a deep breath. "It was the last time I saw her."

"Anything special you remember about that morning? Anything you talked about?"

He blinked and blinked again and rubbed one eye. "We had a big fight."

"What was the fight about?"

"I wanted to go to a party that night. But I wouldn't tell her where it was."

I waited for him to continue.

"She always wanted to know who I was with and where I was going," he said with a defensive edge to his voice. "Sometimes she'd call up and check on me. She was always looking over my shoulder. It was embarrassing."

Tina sounded like my kind of mother. During Melissa's adolescence I had always checked up on her, confirmed with the other parent that she was where she said she would be. It had infuriated her, but at least I'd never gotten a call in the wee small hours advising that she was incarcerated or worse.

Stephan stared at me. "Okay, okay. Parker's cousin was coming up from Seattle. He was going to bring some beer, and a bunch of us were going to get together at his dad's cabin on Cady Mountain."

"Does Parker have a last name?"

"Benjamin."

"Is he a friend of yours?"

"Yeah, kind of."

"And you didn't want your mom to know about the party?"

"Why would I? She'd just go ballistic." He stared at me defiantly. "Look, I know the last couple of years were hard on her. But they sure weren't easy for me either."

"In what way?"

"After being home-schooled since I was a kid, it was a major change to have to go to regular classes. And it's not like I'm learning anything. Except for my English classes, I'm just putting in time."

"Your mother wanted you to go to school off-island. How did you feel about that?"

"I didn't think it was such a hot idea, but I could have lived with it. But my dad refused. He went to high school here, so it was good enough for me. He's clueless."

"So you and your mother were arguing a lot?"

"Every day she wanted to know what I'd done in school, where I'd gone after school, was I smoking pot, was I drinking beer. It drove me crazy! I told her to get out of my face."

"What happened after your fight that Thursday?"

"She wanted to drive me to school, but I told her not to bother. I hitched a ride with one of our neighbors."

"When were you going to see her again?"

He shrugged. "Sometime that night, I suppose. Or maybe the next day."

"How were you going to get home, if you'd been drinking?"

"I could have hitched a ride. Or stayed with somebody."

"Did you sleep at home on Thursday night, Stephan?"

He slouched lower in the chair and folded his hands together. "No. I stayed with Parker," he said in a low voice.

"Where does Parker live?"

"About a mile out of town."

"So you didn't know that your mother wasn't home Thursday night?"

"No, I didn't. Why are you asking me all this stuff? Katy Quince saw her after I did, didn't she?"

"Do you think Katy had something to do with your mom's disappearance?"

He shrugged. "Not really."

"Did your mother ever talk about Katy?"

"Yeah, she was always complaining about her. She said Katy was a sloppy sailor and a pain in the ass." He slouched lower in the chair, and a small smile played around his mouth. "But she sure has a cool bike."

"The Ducati?"

"Yeah, a Monster 900. Electric fuel injection, inverted forks, dual disc brakes. Man, it's so cool!"

"You like bikes?"

"Yeah, Parker's been showing me how to fix them. He works on Katy's bike." He sighed. "My dad was going to get me one, but my grades were pretty bad last semester, so Mom wouldn't let him. Katy let me ride the Monster once, but I never told my mom. She'd have had a fit."

"Is Parker a classmate?"

"He's out of school. He's sort of a mechanic. Fixes bikes and boat motors and stuff like that. He lets me hang out with him." He sat up in the chair, glanced down at the tape recorder, then at his watch. "I've got a class at nine-thirty. Could you turn the recorder off now?"

I touched the Stop button. He pulled the backpack onto his lap, unzipped the top pouch, and took out a long, narrow wooden box. Without looking at me, he put the box on the edge of my desk and slowly re-zipped the backpack.

"A long time ago, my mom gave me a key to her safe-deposit box at the bank. She said if anything ever happened to her, I should open the box and read what was inside. So after the memorial service last week, I did. I found this."

He touched the wooden box tentatively. "I'd like it if you'd keep it. I don't want my . . . my dad to see it." The defiance had gone out of his eyes, and he looked like a small boy about to cry.

He pushed the box across the desk, stood, and flung the backpack over his shoulder. "I'm sorry I couldn't help."

I touched the box. "I'll keep the box until you want it back, Stephan." I reached into the desk drawer for a business card. "Call me if you think of anything else."

He snatched the card and hesitated at the door. "You're wasting your time, Ms. MacKinnon. My mom's not coming back." He bolted out the door and clattered down the stairs.

I reached for the wooden box, opened the small metal clasp, emptied the contents onto the top of the desk. There were three items: a colored snapshot of two people and two white envelopes.

The slender, smiling young woman in the shapshot had long, dark, wavy hair. She was standing beside a tall, broad-shouldered man who had one arm around her shoulders. I mentally compared the woman in the snapshot with the photos of Tina I'd found at Paul's house last week. The young woman was Stephan's mother, without a doubt. I stared at the tall man by her side. Even though probably twenty years had passed, it could not have been Stephan's father, Paul. What was most disturbing—or perhaps most illuminating—was that the resemblance between the tall man in the photograph and the young man who had just left my office was stunning. I turned the snapshot over. There was nothing on the reverse side to identify the man.

The larger envelope was addressed in broad, sprawling black letters to Tina Carlyle, in care of Lily Mac-Gregor, Friday Harbor. It had a Seattle postmark of fifteen years ago, and no return address. I opened the envelope and read the letter that had broken Tina's heart.

Dear Tina,
I am writing this to you because I was too much
of a coward to tell you in person. You see,
before I returned to Dutch Harbor last fall, I
became engaged to a woman in Seattle. It is
not something I can break off. I am not going
to ask you to forgive me for not telling you.
I don't imagine that you can. I did not mean to
fall in love with you. I will not try to see you
again, but I will always remember every
precious minute we spent together.
                    Best wishes always,
                              J

I took a deep breath, physically experiencing the pain that J's letter must have brought to its recipient.

The smaller envelope read "Stephan" in precise, neat handwriting with blue ink. It had probably produced its own heartbreak to the recipient and I understood why Stephan had not wanted it to fall into the hands of Paul Breckenridge.

> *Dear Son,*
> *If you are reading this, it is because I have gone*
> *away from you. The man in the photo is your*
> *father. He does not know of your existence, so*
> *please do not blame him. I have tried to give*
> *you a good life. I am sorry it didn't always work*
> *out. Both Paul and I love you very much.*
>   *Your mother*

I reread the two letters and considered their implications. Piecing together what I'd learned from Paul, Lily, and Joy, I was able to construct a scenario that made sense of the mementos Tina had left for her son. Tina had met someone while she and Joy were in Alaska. John? Jim? Jeremy? She must have been pregnant when she and Joy returned to San Juan Island at the end of the crabbing season. Lily said that Tina began dating Paul Breckenridge a week after she came back. After receiving J's letter, marriage to Paul Breckenridge must have seemed a viable option to raising the child on her own. The marriage had to take place quickly if Paul was to believe the baby was his.

I read Tina's letter to Stephan again. What did "gone away from you" mean? A statement about the inevitability of death? Or a note of farewell preceding a voluntary departure? I mentally replayed my conversations with Joy and Lily. Had the secret of Stephan's father remained Tina's alone, or had she shared it with one or both of her friends?

I expanded the sociogram on the whiteboard to include Parker Benjamin connected to Stephan and Katy, and finally, recalling my conversation with Meredith on Friday, I added Mac MacGregor connected to M. J. Carlyle.

I replaced the two letters and the photograph in the

box, locked it in my bottom desk drawer, and took my empty coffee cup downstairs. New Millennium was flooded with late spring sunlight and the sound of violins.

"No opera music today?"

"Jean Pierre hates opera music. He bought me some new CD's."

"Nice. What's the piece?"

"Bach. One of the Brandenburg Concertos. I don't remember who's playing it."

"How're you doing on that report on Harold Huguenot?"

She stared at me blankly. "Harold who?"

"Huguenot. The guy Katy Quince used to be married to. Your note said you'd ordered a background check on him."

"Oh, him. I'll have it just as soon as I find two servers for Saturday night. I'll put it in your cubby. I'm having lunch with Jean Pierre, and then I'll probably take the afternoon off."

I refilled my coffee cup, climbed back up the creaking stairs, and checked my E-mail.

I found two new messages, one of them a cruising update from my friend Rebecca Underhill aboard *Gypsy Wanderer*. They were in Barra de Navidad doing laundry, topping off the water and fuel tanks, and awaiting the arrival of one of Lars's friends. The weather had been hot and humid, they had had to motor virtually all the way from P.V., and she missed the horses. If I saw Gregg, please ask him to E-mail her and tell her what was going on at the ranch.

I typed back that I had seen Gregg a few days ago, waiting near the ferry dock with the ranch's new red wagon pulled by two shiny black draft horses resplendent in silver-and-black-leather harnesses.

The second message was from Melissa:

I just quit the job at the hotel. I'm going back to school. Waitressing really sucks. Everybody treats you like you're a servant. Would you please call the dean and make up something, so I don't flunk out. And I'm sorry I got mad at you. Can I come to Friday Harbor for Memorial Day? I miss you. Love, M.

I smiled, stuck a Post-it reminder on my appointment book to call the dean of students at St. Mary's College, and went off to meet Jared for lunch. Maybe he would have an update on the Carlyle accident.

19

"Two and a half million dollars in cocaine. Transported on a tuna fishing boat in bags marked 'Azúcar de Colombia.'" Jared chuckled. "Right out of the old rum-running chronicles." He chuckled again and attacked the plate of *chile verde* Pablo had just served with the hope that we would get to finish our lunch today.

The big feature article Jared was working on was not the M. J. Carlyle accident, as I had hoped, but a huge drug seizure by the U.S. Coast Guard. A Canadian fishing trawler carrying more than two tons of cocaine that had been intercepted in the Strait of Juan de Fuca.

"They were using the same pickup and drop-off spots that were used during Prohibition. But this skipper wasn't as smart as the rum runners in their go-fast boats used to be."

"Two and a half million represents a lot of cocaine," I said, spooning the chile verde onto a warm tortilla. "Sounds like organized crime to me."

"My thoughts exactly," Jared said. "No one person, particularly a Canadian fisherman, could finance a two-ton cargo of cocaine."

"Anybody know where it was coming from or headed to?" I asked, wondering if the case Meredith Martin had been working on was related to the seizure.

"Nobody's talking yet," Jared said. "But my guess is the cargo came up the West Coast on a mother ship and the trawler skipper went outside to meet it. And at a much bigger risk than transporting B. C. Bud."

"I hear the Canadians aren't terribly concerned about marijuana and our so-called War on Drugs."

Jared peered at me over his glasses and reached into the black leather portfolio at his feet. "My friend Ian, the guy I told you about that lives up on Santiago Island, just sent me some interesting statistics on these 'illegal drugs' the U.S. is ostensibly at war against. Listen to this: "Deaths from illegal drugs, between 10,000 and 15,000. Deaths attributable to 'legal drugs' in the same year: tobacco, between 200,000 and 400,000, depending on who's doing the reporting; and alcohol, at least 100,000." Would you like to guess the leading cause of death among fifteen- to twenty-year-olds? Not marijuana, not cocaine, not crystal meth, but— alcohol. And yet your average, middle-of-the-road, hardworking U.S. citizen thinks we are being menaced by illegal drugs grown in some dirty Third World country by people with skins darker than ours."

"How does B. C. Bud fit into that profile?" I asked. "It's not being grown in a dirty, smelly Third World country. It's being grown a few miles across the border from where we're sitting."

"Some of the growers are independents, but Ian says in many instances the pot farms have been organized by bikers and Asian gangs. The authorities know that however much gets confiscated, it's just the tip of the iceberg. There's no way the U.S. is going to win this latest version of the war." He sopped up the remainder of the *chile verde* with a tortilla. "But I'll bet you didn't agree to have lunch to hear me pontificating on drugs, now, did you?"

I smiled. "Tell me what you know about M. J. Carlyle's accident."

"In lay terms, as it will appear in the next *Gazette*,

the ME's report lists a brain concussion, which would be consistent with the fall to the rocks. But he also said Carlyle received a blow to the side of the head by a small blunt object, which could have caused unconsciousness or death."

"So somebody knocked him out and then pushed him over."

"Possibly. Approximate time of death is 2300 hours last Friday."

"Eleven P.M. An hour and a half after his second call to me and his departure from the inn to meet his estranged wife."

"Yes, but get this," Jared continued. "The ME thinks one of the blows to the head occurred several hours later than the first one, and there was no internal bleeding from the last one."

"So he died from the first blow, then some time later, got transported to American Camp and thrown down on the rocks. Does Edie Carlyle have an alibi?"

"Claims M.J. came out to the house she's renting at Eagle Cove about nine-thirty, left a little after ten, and after that she spent the rest of the night with Jerome, her number one model. Jerome confirms her story."

"All neat and tidy. M.J. is dead, and there's no need for a property settlement."

"Could be." Jared forked up the last of his saffron rice, patted his mouth with the red cotton napkin, and beckoned to Pablo for the bill. "I need to head out. Allison and I are going over to Orcas today."

I reached for my purse and pulled out my wallet. Jared stayed my hand. "This one is to make up for last Friday. Next one's on you."

I followed Jared out to the street. He pulled a pipe from his jacket pocket. "You're feeling frustrated, aren't you? A missing woman, perhaps dead, plus one dead client. And you're wondering who's next?"

"It's just that I can't get a lead, a real thread of

anything to follow. Everybody tells me the same things. What a wonderful mother she was, what a wonderful sailor she was, her husband worshiped the ground she walked on, and she had no enemies. The worst thing I've heard about her is she was a stickler for boat safety. I can't find even a *hint* of a motive."

He pulled a small brown-paper package from his pocket and handed it to me. "The Lady Carfax case. Thought it might be of interest to you." He gave me a peck on the cheek and headed off toward the ferry terminal.

It was one-thirty when I got back to the Olde Gazette Building. Zelda and Dakota had left and the office was silent. The background on Harold Huguenot was in my mail cubby. It was less than inspiring. The subject had been born and raised in the Santa Cruz, California, area, was currently employed as a rigger by a Santa Cruz marina, had married Kathryn Mary Quince twelve years ago, the marriage was dissolved seven years ago, and he had remarried last year. Harry had two moving violations in the past three years, but no criminal record. He did not owe any state or federal taxes. According to his latest driver's license, which he had renewed two weeks ago, his current address was 245 Sand Dollar Road in Santa Cruz. Harry Huguenot was not Danny Quince. So who the hell was Danny Quince? I checked the notes from my first interview with Paul and found a listing in the phone book for Inside Passage Yacht Sales on Plimsoll Lane in Friday Harbor. A call to the number got an answering machine inviting me to leave a message, which I did not do. I added Harold Huguenot's name to the sociogram on the white board and connected it to Katy Quince. Now what?

I noticed the Post-it reminder on my calendar and called the dean of students at St. Mary's. As I expected, the dean was cordial but noncommittal. It was against school rules and considered an inexcusable absence to be away from classes except in cases of illness or death in the immediate family. I explained the situation, and she asked that Melissa come by her office as soon as she returned. I transmitted the gist of the conversation in an E-mail to Melissa, reflecting that my little girl was going to have to face some grown-up music. On her own.

I was about to close up the office and take a walk out to Plimsoll Lane when the phone rang. It was Zelda.

"I've got to talk to you. Right away." She was talking in a stage whisper.

"What's up?"

"Jean Pierre and I had lunch on the yacht."

"What yacht?"

"*Maia.*"

"Jean Pierre's yacht?"

"No, no. Jean Pierre's just the skipper. *Maia* belongs to this guy from Seattle."

Alcyone, Electra, Maia. Three of the Pleiades, the "seven sisters" of Greek mythology, sometimes called the Sailors' Stars. I wondered what the connection was.

"And?"

"Jean Pierre had a couple of beers and started talking about a woman his boss used to bring on board. You know, like for an afternoon or a night."

"Hanky-panky on a yacht is not unheard of, my dear."

"Yeah, but when he started describing the woman, she sounded really familiar. About thirty-five, dark hair, has a teenage son, likes to sail. Sound familiar?"

"Tina! My God! What's Jean Pierre's boss's name?"

"Tyrell. Jonathan Tyrell. He's married and he lives in Seattle. I snooped around and found a picture. It's Tina. The one that was in the paper with the obituary."

Jonathan. The "J" of the Dear Mary letter? Stephan's father? Could it be?

"Where are you? Can you find an address and phone number for Tyrell? And bring the picture in?"

There was no response. I heard a masculine voice in the background. "Be right up, Jean Pierre," Zelda shouted. The connection went dead. I pressed the End button and considered what Zelda had told me. A man by the name of Jonathan Tyrell from Seattle had entertained a woman matching Tina Breckenridge's description on a yacht named *Maia*.

I wondered if Tina had intended to expand the fleet to include all the stars. If Zelda was right in her identification—and if Jonathan Tyrell was the "J" of the long-ago letter—he had broken his word not to see her again. Had Tina been carrying on a clandestine relationship with *Maia*'s owner all these years? If so, how did she keep it secret? Particularly from her best friends. Or did they know more than they had told me?

I added Jonathan Tyrell to the sociogram, locked up the office, and headed out for a walk to Plimsoll Lane to check out Danny Quince. I had no idea what might come of any investigation into the Tina/Jonathan/Paul triangle, but I was beginning to get a funny feeling about the Quinces.

The office for Inside Passage Yacht Sales was closed and locked. When I got back to *DragonSpray*, Calico had eaten her tuna-chicken concoction and departed. I was just about to add the soda to my vermouth over ice when I heard a tapping on *DragonSpray*'s hull. "Permission to come aboard?"

It was Zelda. I opened the hatch covers. "Permission granted. My, but we're getting nautical."

She let out a giggle. "Jean Pierre's teaching me. He says protocol is important." She climbed on deck and down the companionway and flung herself on the settee. She had on a navy blue windbreaker and was still wearing the embroidered shirt, but the ankle-length skirt and wedge heels had been replaced with faded blue jeans and boat shoes.

"I've got it." She pulled a five-by-seven inch photograph from the depths of her large black-leather handbag. "There. Isn't that Tina Breckenridge?"

I picked up the photograph. It was a color version of the one that had appeared in the *Gazette*. There was no mistaking the laughing violet eyes, the wavy dark hair and high cheekbones. The inscription across the lower right-hand corner said, "Love, T."

"That's Tina Breckenridge. Would you like something to drink?"

"What are you drinking?"

I told her.

"I'll have the same without the vermouth."

"How did you happen to find this picture?" I moved over to the galley, pulled the tray of ice cubes from the minuscule freezer, extricated two. I covered them with soda, added a twist of lime.

"When Jean Pierre started telling me about his boss's paramour, it seemed almost too much of a coincidence, but when he mentioned that Tyrell used to have a crab boat in Alaska, all of a sudden this lightbulb went on in my brain. Just then Jean Pierre got a phone call from his boss, so I went to use the bathroom—I mean the head—and I decided to do some snooping. Tyrell's got a whole office set up on the yacht. I found the picture in a frame on the credenza behind his desk. The dude should thank me. If his wife had found it, I should think he'd be in deep *caca*."

"How long has Jean Pierre been working on *Maia*?"

"About a year, I think."

"Where was Tyrell today?"

"He went down to Seattle. He's coming back tonight."

"Do you think Jean Pierre knows who Tina was? That she was married and then that she drowned?"

"I don't think so. He just called her *la femme*. But I got the impression that the romance had been going on for as long as he'd been on the boat. And the odd part was he didn't seem to know anything had happened to her. But I think *Maia* was down in Seattle for a month and they just brought her back up."

"So he might have missed the newspaper articles," I said. "What do you know about this Tyrell?"

"Jean Pierre says the guy made a stack of money crab fishing in Alaska. Spends about six months a year on *Maia*. But he does a lot of entertaining. Sometimes he charters a float plane and flies the guests in to where he's anchored. His wife gets seasick, so she flies in and meets him after they get to their destination. The surprise birthday party I'm arranging is for her."

"Was today the first time you've been on *Maia*?"

She nodded. "It's really plush, Scotia. Ninety-something feet long. Oriental carpets and teak doors and brass fittings everywhere. It's even got a formal dining room. It was designed way back in the twenties by somebody named Garry or Geary."

"L. E. 'Ted' Geary," I said. Geary was a fabled marine architect from Seattle, famous for the magnificent wooden motor yachts he designed in the twenties and thirties for some of the most prominent individuals of the era.

"Yeah, that's it. It's got this huge deck where they're going to have a jazz band and dancing on Saturday. This dude must have more money than God."

"Ninety feet is a lot of boat. Does Jean Pierre handle the boat all by himself?"

"When they go further north and are out for several weeks, Jean Pierre's brother, Emile, comes along."

"Such a literary family. Does he have a sister or cousin named Emma?"

"Huh?"

"Never mind. How long is *Maia* going to be at Roche?"

"They're leaving in about ten days to take her up to Alaska for the summer. Jean Pierre's been working on the engines every day. Twin 334 somethings."

"Did your sleuthing aboard *Maia* happen to include a phone number for Tyrell?"

She produced a slightly wrinkled business card with a flourish. "Name, address, and e-mail address. No phone number."

I read the card. The address was in Seattle.

"What time is Tyrell expected back?"

She pulled up the sleeve of the shirt and checked her watch. "Jean Pierre should be picking him up at the airport just about now."

Mentally I reviewed the crisscrossed lines on the sociogram in my office. Was Tina headed out for a tryst with Jonathan Tyrell the night she disappeared? Did she get waylaid by someone or something? Or did she, in fact, have a tryst with Jonathan and never make it back? Worse yet, did Tina tell Jonathan about Stephan, and Jonathan in turn make a confession to his wife? Then I considered the balances in the mutual fund and savings accounts and posed the meanest question of all: had Tina been blackmailing Jonathan Tyrell?

"You happen to know Tyrell's wife's name?"

"It's Helen. I ordered a hundred white balloons with her name on them for the surprise party."

I retrieved the portable phone from my bunk in the captain's cabin, dialed Seattle information, and was rewarded with the phone number of Jonathan and Helen Tyrell.

A woman answered.

"Mrs. Tyrell?"

"Speaking."

"This is North Saanich Engine Repair," I said in my best Canadian imitation. "We're ordering some parts for *Maia*. I need to check some prices with your husband, and I'm afraid we've misplaced his cell phone number. Could you possibly help?"

"Certainly. Hold on." There was a silence, then the soft voice produced the number.

I thanked her, hung up, and dialed the number.

"Jonathan Tyrell." The voice was a confident, deep baritone.

I identified myself and told him I was investigating the disappearance of Tina Breckenridge. "I understand you knew her. I wonder if it would be possible to talk to you."

There was a long silence. "Mr. Tyrell?" I said.

"Tina worked for me a long time ago. In Alaska."

"Would it be possible for us to meet?"

Another long silence. "Of course," he said in a neutral voice. "I'll be glad to help any way I can. I'll only be here for a few days. We're anchored on the yacht *Maia* at Roche Harbor. Come out to the customs dock at nine o'clock tomorrow morning. We'll pick you up."

I pressed the End button on the phone and glanced at Zelda. She gave me two thumbs up. "You're good, boss. Really good."

"All in a day's work. Would you please run a background on the Tyrells as soon as you get in tomorrow?"

"Will do."

"I picked up some wild mushroom soup and fresh sourdough at the Corner Grocery. And two pieces of carrot cake. Want to share?"

She smiled. "Love to. Jean Pierre made a gorgeous seafood salad for lunch, but that feels like eons ago. I can't stay late, though. Rafie and I are taking the dogs for a run early tomorrow."

I warmed the soup while Zelda set the small table and recounted the brief history of her romance with Jean Pierre Zola and her hopes for the future.

"So this is the love of your life?"

"I hope so," she said wistfully. "I'm really tired of a different man every other month. And Jean Pierre is so . . . so European. Even though he was born on Martinique."

"You said Tyrell wants to take *Maia* to Alaska. What will that do to your romance?"

Her face became the picture of gloom. "I don't want to think about it. Jean Pierre said maybe he could arrange it so I could go with them. As a cook or something." She giggled. "I didn't tell him I'm the world's worst. Do you think you could get along without me for a couple of months? They'll be coming back in August."

The thought was both disturbing and sad. On the professional level, Zelda's computer skills were extraordinary and I couldn't easily replace her. On the personal level, life around the Olde Gazette Building would be far less interesting without her unpredictable behavior and outrageous comments.

"I could get along, but I'd miss you a lot, my dear."

"I really don't want to leave the island," she said wistfully. "And at the same time, I don't want to lose Jean Pierre. I did our horoscopes. I'm a Gemini and he's an Aquarius and we have a five-nine sun sign pattern. That's about as good as it gets."

"I see." The soup was steaming. I refreshed my vermouth and soda and ladled the soup into bowls. I refrained from reminding her that as far as astrology was concerned, she'd also been dazzlingly compatible with Boris.

"I saw David and Rafie on Friday night," I said, topping off her glass of club soda. "Are they getting on better now that Sophia's back home?"

She stirred one of the wild mushrooms in the soup and sampled it. "Yes and no. Rafie seems to get more paranoid by the day. He's looking over his shoulder all the time. He mentioned once about his papers being illegal and said he wanted to talk to you."

"I'll be happy to speak to him, but I'm not an attorney. Is he thinking of going back to Mexico?"

"Maybe. Rafie thinks David doesn't trust him."

"I guess they'll have to work it out."

"Yeah. You know what, boss?" She blotted up the last drops of the soup with a piece of sourdough. "I think Lily was right."

"About what?" I asked, prepared for one of her lightning conversational switches.

"About Tina. About her essence being here. I think Tina's dead."

"She probably is," I said slowly between swallows. "And all I can do now is try to establish how and why. If I—"

Zelda's cell phone interrupted me. "Maybe it's Jean Pierre," she said breathlessly, scrambling to extricate the device from the depths of her handbag. I gathered up the soup bowls and put them in the sink, ground coffee beans, and found plates and forks to serve the carrot cake. Judging by her face, if the caller was Jean Pierre, he was not delivering good news.

"Are you really sure?" Zelda was frowning and chewing her lip. "Maybe you should wait until he cools down and then talk about it. Okay, okay. I'll be home in an hour. Come on over." She pressed the End button and dropped the phone back in her bag.

"Jean Pierre?"

"No, Rafie," she said. "He's packing up and moving out of David's house and wants to stay with me until he finds another place to live."

"Another tiff?" I said, pouring the steaming water over the coffee.

"David found a whole wad of cash in Rafie's underwear drawer. Like several thousand dollars. He accused him of turning tricks."

I stared at her. "What an awful accusation!"

She shrugged, took a bite of cake. "Didn't you know? That's how they met in Mexico. The all-inclusive, escorted tour to Yelapa."

I hadn't known. We finished the cake and coffee in silence, and I declined Zelda's offer to help with dishes before she left. My galley is efficient, but squeezing in two people is pushing it. I closed the companionway hatch covers, poured another cup of coffee, and put on an Anne Murray CD. While I washed up the dishes, I thought about the two people I had already interviewed who could have known about Tina and Jonathan Tyrell: Lily MacGregor and Joy Johnson. The relationship had been going on for at least a year, and it's a rare woman who can get involved with a new man and not tell *anyone* about it. I wondered if either of them knew Jonathan was Stephan's father.

There was only one way to find out.

At the MacGregor household I got the answering machine, but Joy Johnson answered on the second ring. She sounded surprised to hear from me. It was a long shot, but I decided on a direct approach. "How long had Tina been seeing Jonathan Tyrell before she disappeared?" I asked.

I heard a sharp intake of breath and a long sigh. "For about three years."

"Can you tell me about it?"

After a long pause, she described how Tina had run into Jonathan by accident at Roche Harbor. "She was with some of her students. One thing led to another. Jonathan was living in Seattle and he started bringing his boat up every few weeks. His wife doesn't like boats. She's a musician with the Seattle Symphony. He'd call Tina every time he got in, and Tina couldn't say no."

"How did she keep Paul from finding out?"

"He was in Alaska from May to October, sometimes later. Tyrell usually didn't come up in the winter."

"What about Stephan?"

"She didn't think he knew."

I threw her another curve. "Did Jonathan know Stephan is his son?"

Another intake of breath and a longer silence this time. "I don't know. I told her she should tell him, but she said she never would. She didn't want him to feel obligated to her."

"Is there anything else about Tina you didn't tell me?"

"I didn't think it was important for you to know about Stephan," she said sullenly. "Jonathan's a jerk. He's always been a jerk. But he would never hurt her." There was a silence, then she threw *me* a curve. "If you want to know what happened to M.J., ask Lily MacGregor where Mac was last Thursday night." She broke the connection.

I slowly replaced the phone in the cradle. Joy was the second person to suggest that Mac MacGregor had something to do with M.J.'s death, an idea I found outlandish. A bar brawl was one thing; homicide was something else altogether.

As I reached to turn off the reading light behind the table in the main salon, I noticed the small, brown-paper-wrapped package done up in string that Jared had given me. It was a leather-bound first edition of *His Last Bow* by Sir Arthur Conan Doyle. I smiled, put the small volume on the bed, and pulled on flannel pj's.

Calico had returned and she snuggled along my leg. I turned on the light over my bunk and opened *His Last Bow*. It was a collection of stories and included the two cases Jared had mentioned: "The Adventure of the Cardboard Box" and "The Disappearance of Lady Frances Carfax." The first one concerned the receipt of a "gruesome packet" by a respectable maiden lady of fifty, and I moved on to the second story, immediately drawn into the search for the handsome missing woman of limited means with remarkable old Spanish jewelry. One step behind the tall, dark, bearded ruffian who was also in hot pursuit of the missing woman, Holmes and Watson moved from London to Lausanne and Baden and back to London, where, thanks to Holmes's last-minute brainstorm in the gray of the morning, Lady Frances was rescued from a terrible fate at the hands of her kidnappers. I closed the book, turned out the light, and thought about Jared's suggestion, which now seemed prophetic: that perhaps there was a suitor somewhere in Tina Breckenridge's life. Tomorrow I would see that suitor, but I was sure that sadly, unlike the fortunate Lady Carfax, it was too late to rescue Tina Breckenridge.

20

"I doubt that random motion brought you here," Tyrell said. "Who told you I knew Tina Breckenridge?"

It was Tuesday morning. Jean Pierre had been waiting at the customs dock in the impeccably maintained little tender with the white lapstrake hull. We had made small talk while he transported me across the harbor to the elegant classic white yacht lying at anchor just off the Seattle Yacht Club's outstation, where Tyrell had been pacing on the main deck. Jean Pierre had disappeared to what I assumed were the crew's quarters, and I'd followed Tyrell into his office.

Now he stood behind the huge polished wooden desk in the office on the upper deck of the old vessel, leaning back against the credenza, arms crossed over his broad chest. His face was that of a man who'd spent a lot of time out doors. Craggy, tanned, and lined. He was tall and had a large, sturdy body, the kind of body a woman likes to lean against or be embraced by. Well-trimmed dark brown hair going gray at the temples. Eyes the same soft brown as Stephan's. His soft burgundy corduroy shirt in a herringbone weave was tucked into well-worn khaki-colored canvas trousers. While he hadn't appeared exactly happy about my arrival, I hadn't detected any hostility, and he'd grudgingly agreed to my recording our interview. I was sitting in one of the two stationary swivel chairs in front of the desk.

"Before his death, Tina's brother, M. J. Carlyle, hired me to look into her disappearance," I said, ignoring his question.

"Tina's brother? Dead?" His confident voice went suddenly hoarse. "I didn't know. How did it happen?"

"His body was found on the rocks at American Camp. The cause of death was a blow to the head. I'm working for Tina's husband now. Could you describe the nature of your relationship with Tina?"

"Tina worked as a deckhand on my crab boat for four months in Alaska more than fifteen years ago." He eased himself into the executive chair behind the desk.

It was a nice try. "I understand you had a more recent relationship with her. A romantic relationship."

He stared at me for several minutes, a variety of emotions playing over his face. I hoped he never had to take a polygraph test. "Apparently you've been talking with Joy Johnson," he said in a harsh voice. "That . . . that *woman* is an incorrigible busybody."

"In what way?"

"Tina and I had a reasonable and harmless relationship. Nobody was getting hurt. Then that Johnson bitch started mucking things up." He made a visible effort to control his anger.

"Mucking things up how?"

"Everything was fine until last fall. Then Tina said she couldn't go on living with Paul any longer." He turned abruptly and stared out the porthole, shoulders hunched. Over his shoulders I could see a barge move across the harbor and into Mosquito Pass. "She wanted us to be together. She asked me to divorce my wife. I know the Johnson woman was behind it."

"Were you going to divorce your wife, Mr. Tyrell?"

"Of course not," he said, turning back to face me. "It was ridiculous. I couldn't possibly have . . . there was no reason to mess up four people's lives. Five, if you count her son." He leaned back in the chair and steepled his fingers. "Stephan got into some sort of trouble around Halloween last year and for a couple of months she stopped talking about leaving Paul. Then right after Christmas it started again. She said it was immoral to keep on living with someone she didn't love."

But not apparently immoral to have married him. I let the silence settle around us, considered the advisability of telling him that Stephan was his son. The wake from the passing barge rocked *Maia* gently.

"How often do you come up here?" I asked.

"I spend a week here every couple of months. I'm a trustee for the yacht club." He motioned toward the window and the well-kept docks and buildings on Henry Island. "Sometimes my wife joins me with some of our friends," he added almost defensively.

"Does your wife know about your relationship with Tina?"

"Of course not." He frowned.

"I understand your wife is a musician."

He raised his eyebrows, but did not ask how I knew. "Yes. A pianist with the Seattle Symphony. Very talented and totally dedicated."

"Do you have children, Mr. Tyrell?" I hadn't planned to ask the question; it came from out of nowhere.

A look of pain came over his face. "No, I . . . we don't, we couldn't. What does that have to do with Tina?" he said harshly.

"Nothing, actually. I apologize for asking. I'm not here to criticize you or judge you, Mr. Tyrell. I was hoping you might tell me something that could help my investigation. There are a lot of unanswered questions surrounding Tina's disappearance." I hesitated, thinking about the unaccounted-for funds in Tina's savings account and mutual funds. "One of the questions has to do with money. Did you ever loan Tina any money?"

"Yes, I did," he said. "I provided the start-up money for Pleiades and . . . from time to time I gave her a little something to help the cash flow. But that was strictly between Tina and myself." He glanced at the recorder. "This is never to go any farther."

"When did you last see Tina?"

"The first weekend in April. Two weeks before she . . . before her boat was found."

"Could you describe the occasion to me?"

He cleared his throat and chewed on his lower lip. I wondered if he was going to throw me out. The boat continued to rock. He stood up again and leaned against the credenza behind the desk, hands in the pockets of his trousers.

"It was the first time I'd been up since New Year's. The first Friday in April." The harshness had disappeared from his voice. "Paul had gone to see his mother. Stephan was spending the night with a friend. Jean Pierre picked her up at the customs dock and we motored over to Prevost Harbor." He paused and stared vacantly past my head. Stuart Island lies northwest of San Juan Island and has two small bays: Reid Harbor on the south and Prevost Harbor on the north. A trail connects the bays, both of which are popular anchorages in the summer and are virtually deserted the rest of the year. Either would be a good choice for a clandestine winter rendezvous.

"The rain had stopped by the time we got into the harbor. We anchored and had the place to ourselves. The moon came out and the stars were gorgeous. Tina was in a strange mood." He paused, lost in reverie. "Almost devil-may-care. More open, more . . . more erotic than I'd ever known her. Jean Pierre fixed fresh crab and spent the evening in his quarters. Tina and I went to bed about ten. A storm came up during the night. I checked the Canadian weather report about five A.M. It was blowing fifty knots in Haro Strait, out of the southeast. We waited until eleven, but it was still blowing a gale. And flooding. I wanted to wait a few hours more, but Tina insisted we start back."

"Trying to get around Turn Point in weather like that would be a challenge," I said. "The currents are vicious there."

He nodded. "Tina was nervous. Not about the weather, or the boat, but because she was supposed to pick Stephan up by noon and take him to tennis practice or something, and she was going to be very late. We got into a disagreement. She said this was it. She was tired of sneaking around, and she couldn't live a double life anymore. We got back to Roche Harbor and anchored around one o'clock. She was crying. I hugged her, and then she pulled away and Jean Pierre took her back to the dock. I told her I'd call her the next day and we would talk." He stared at me with vacant eyes.

"And did you see her again?"

He started to speak but appeared to be having difficulty forming the words.

"No, I didn't . . . that was the last time. I stayed around for another week. She didn't answer her cell phone and never returned the messages I left. I didn't want to call the house. Finally, we took the boat back to Seattle." He paused. "Tina did try to call me the night before her boat was found. Helen and I were out to dinner with friends. She didn't leave a message, but I found her number on the incoming call log. I called back the next morning, but there was no answer. It was too late." His eyes were bleak.

"When did you find out about her disappearance?"

"My sister has a cabin on Orcas. She saw it in the local newspaper and called me. I couldn't believe it. Still don't believe it. Tina's just too good with boats to have had an accident."

"Your sister knew about your relationship with Tina?"

"Yes. We're very close."

"Might she have divulged the relationship to your wife?"

"Absolutely not. The two don't get on very well."

"Did Tina ever say or do anything to indicate she was suicidal?"

He hesitated. "She was depressed after Christmas. She said she couldn't go on like this anymore. But nothing specific, no."

"Does Jean Pierre know about Tina's disappearance?"

"I told him last night after you called. He was shocked." He took a deep breath and swallowed with difficulty. "You must believe I would never have harmed Tina. I . . . I did love her."

I believed him, although love and violence are not mutually exclusive.

I had no more questions. I thanked him for his time, gathered up my rucksack, and Jean Pierre ferried me back to the dock with a minimum amount of small talk. I didn't know if he knew that Zelda was my research assistant or that my visit was thanks to his indiscreet comments. It probably didn't matter.

I stood for a minute on the dock, watching the wake of the tender as it made its way back to *Maia*. Jonathan Tyrell was standing on the bow of the lovely old yacht, staring toward shore. I knew it would be a long time before he forgot the last night he'd spent with his mistress. And as I made my way up the main dock and across the parking lot, I was haunted by the thought that we never know when a hug is a last good-bye.

When I got to the Olde Gazette Building, the air at New Millennium fairly crackled with electricity. I was feeling depressed from my meeting with Jonathan

Tyrell and should have known better than to inquire of the back of Zelda's head how things were going.

"I had a horrible night," she snapped. "Rafie moaned and complained about David until two A.M. and Sophia barked until four o'clock."

I made sympathetic murmurings and retrieved the printed report and several telephone messages from my mail cubby. One was from Nick.

"In addition to not getting any sleep last night," Zelda rambled on, "I can't find a bartender or any servers for the Gatsby party. You'd think with all the bitching that goes on around this island about lack of jobs, somebody would be happy to put on a gauzy white dress and pass the stinking hors d'oeuvres. And to make things worse, Shel's coming up to the island this weekend. I haven't had a chance yet to tell him about Jean Pierre."

Sheldon Wainwright, a Port Angeles ship's pilot, was Zelda's backup boyfriend for those dry spells between more exotic romantic episodes.

"I'm sure you'll think of something," I said, reading Nick's phone message. "I made a reservation on the float plane for Thursday evening at seven. Can you come down? We could go out to the coast for the weekend." My spirits were immediately elevated. I poured a cup of coffee and leaned against the counter, sipping and speed-reading the one-page report from DataTech on Jonathan and Helen Tyrell. Both appeared to be outstanding and upright residents of a fine address in the Lake Washington area of Seattle, with nary a traffic violation or other transgression against society to mar their existence. The house had no outstanding liens, there was a joint savings account of just under a hundred thousand dollars, and an obscenely long list of stocks and mutual funds owned by the couple. There were also four properties in San Francisco and three in Los Angeles in the name of Helen Caulfield Tyrell. As I read over the list of holdings, I suspected that Helen Caulfield had been able to maintain Jonathan Tyrell in a manner to which he had become accustomed, and I understood why he would have been loathe to disturb the status quo, even for his beloved Tina.

"Did you hear about the photographer from On the Edge?" Zelda whirled around on her chair, smirking, her outlook on the day suddenly improved. I shook my head, inching toward the stairway.

"On the Edge's photographer was arrested last night for soliciting sexual favors from a minor. The jerk had the bad luck to pick on the daughter of the commissioner from Orcas. When Abigail found out, she laughed so hard she peed in her pants."

"Is Abby still in jail?" I asked.

"No, she was released on her own recognizance with a stern warning not to return to American Camp until On the Edge has left the island."

My phone started ringing, and I raced up the stairs and unlocked the door. It was Angela; Katy Quince had had a motorcycle accident early that morning and had been medevaced to Island Hospital in Anacortes with a broken arm, multiple contusions and abrasions, possibly a concussion. The sheriff was checking the motorcycle for malfunctions.

"How did it happen?"

"Apparently she lost control of the bike when she turned off from Rouleau onto Roche Harbor Road. Hit a tree head-on."

In and of itself, the accident could be just that. In the context of my investigation, it was one more "accident" involving someone close to Tina. I shivered. Who would be next?

I called Nick, who was with a client, and left a message on his voice mail that I would be on the 7:00 Puget Sound flight on Thursday, arriving at the Lake Union terminal at 7:48.

The other two messages were from Olivia Camille, M. J. Carlyle's fiancée, and a number I didn't recognize. Olivia answered on the first ring. Her voice was steadier than on the day I'd talked with her on Brown Sugar Beach.

"Ms. MacKinnon, I thought of something that might be important. When M.J. and I were having dinner the night before he died, he said he had to call you. He seemed really upset."

"Any idea what he wanted to tell me?"

"I've been trying to piece it together, but it didn't make any sense until last night."

"What happened last night?"

"After we finished shooting, we were all having a beer at George's. Jerome—he's one of the models—was bragging about the B. C. Bud he got last week. From somebody named Katy. I really wasn't paying attention, then I woke up early this morning and suddenly remembered M.J. saying he had to let you know about Katy."

"Could her name have been Katy Quince?" I asked, staring at the lines and circled names on the white board.

"I don't remember. I think he just said Katy." I heard an annoyed female voice in the background. "I hope this helps, Ms. MacKinnon. I've got to go now."

I thanked her and hung up the phone, ready to jump up and down. If the Katy M.J. had wanted to call me about was Katy Quince, Tina's sailing instructor was peddling dope in Friday Harbor! Had Tina found out and raised hell? And stepped on the wrong toes? Or had she been involved in it? Was that the little problem that had turned into a big problem?

I glanced down at the phone number on the other message slip and did a double take. It was the number I'd gotten off Tina's crushed cell phone!

Dr. Veronica Walker answered on the second ring

and confirmed that she was one of the students on *Alcyone* the Thursday Tina disappeared. Yes, she had left a message for Tina. I asked why.

"I took the sailing fundamentals course from Tina last summer and I was *so* disappointed when I found out that she wasn't going to be teaching the heavy-weather class. But I came all the way from Baltimore, so I didn't know what to do. That woman, Katy, was a perfect witch the whole week."

"What exactly happened, Dr. Walker?"

"It started on Wednesday afternoon. She did a lecture on sail balance and control. Then we went out and practiced trimming the sails, and I just didn't get it. She acted like I was stupid."

"Did anything else happen?"

"On Wednesday night I was so upset about her rudeness I couldn't sleep. About midnight, I went up on deck. I was sitting in the cockpit when all of a sudden I saw another boat pulling up beside us. It was a powerboat with a cabin and bridge on it. Something like a Bayliner. There were two people on it. Two men. Or maybe a man and a woman. Then, all of a sudden, Katy was yelling at me to get below. I went back to bed, but I was so angry I couldn't sleep. I never heard the boat leave, but it wasn't there in the morning."

"Did you see the name of the boat anywhere?"

"There were two words in the name. I think one of them was 'Angel.' I couldn't see the rest of it. It was too dark. When I asked about the night visitor the next day, Katy explained that the other boat had dragged its anchor. She apologized for yelling, but I was still mad."

"Did anything else happen?"

"When we were sailing back to Roche Harbor," Veronica went on, "one of the other women was at the wheel. She sailed too far off the wind and we did an accidental jibe. I got hit in the shoulder really hard."

A jibe occurs when the helmsperson steers so that the stern of the boat goes through the eye of the wind. An accidental jibe done without proper preparation by the crew can be dangerous.

I recalled Lily's comment about Tina getting a call from a disgruntled client. "Did you talk to Tina before you left?"

"She wasn't there when we got back, so I called her from the airport in Friday Harbor and left a detailed message and asked her to send my money back. But she hasn't. Do you work for her?"

I explained Tina's disappearance and my investigation. She was silent for a minute, then I heard, "Oh, my God, I didn't know. Oh, that's terrible."

I thanked her for answering my questions and she hung up.

The pieces of the puzzle were beginning to fall into place like a row of cherries on a Vegas slot machine. I suspected that what Veronica had seen, which had so upset Katy, was a drug delivery boat. That tied in perfectly with the possibility that Katy Quince had been running drugs into the San Juans under cover of the sailing classes.

What I didn't know was how Tina fit into it.

I called Island Hospital in Anacortes, was connected to the nurses' station and presented myself as Katy's sister. Mrs. Quince's condition was stable, I was advised, and she would most likely be discharged the next day. Would I like to be connected to her room? That wasn't necessary, I said, since I was going to visit her that evening. I inquired about visiting hours and hung up. I then dialed Inside Passage Yacht Sales and got the same recorded message I'd gotten the day before. So, Katy was in the hospital in Anacortes and Danny was nowhere to be found. It was time to pay another visit to Canvas by Quince.

Before its proprietor returned.

*　　*　　*

One way to obtain information you're not supposed to have is to pretend that you're entitled to it. And pretending that you have a perfect right to be someplace you don't is also often equally effective. As any agent in place knows, part of the right to be someplace involves dressing for the occasion and or presenting the appropriate props. When I arrived at Canvas by Quince at two-fifteen, one of the trucks I'd seen on my last visit was parked in front of the house-under-construction and I heard hammering from inside the house. I retrieved my lock picks from the rucksack, buttoned up my gray striped coverall that said DUSTBE-GONE on the back in red embroidery, and covered my new haircut with a red bandanna.

From the back of the Volvo where I kept them for such occasions, I extracted the vacuum cleaner, mop and bucket, and lamb's-wool duster. I left the cleaning equipment propped against the Volvo and marched up to the house. Neither the short bald-headed man with crooked teeth nor the thin red-haired one with a pocked face who were laying the hardwood floor seemed to care one way or the other when I announced I was there to clean for Ms. Quince. I grabbed the cleaning equipment and made tracks toward the shop door, which was fortunately out of sight of the house.

Although I hadn't utilized my breaking and entering skills for a number of months, I hadn't lost the knack, and five minutes later I was inside. It appeared that the shop's owner had departed either in haste or in anger or both. Several cabinet drawers were open, two bolts of green canvas lay on the floor in front of the cutting table, and a broken beer bottle had come to rest under one window. The contents of one drawer, mostly large spools of blue and green thread, lay scattered on the floor toward the back of the shop.

Dutiful cleaning lady that I was, I retrieved the beer bottle and dropped it in the nearest waste container and connected the vacuum cleaner. Mop and bucket leaning against the door, lamb's-wool dusting wand in hand, I pirouetted around the shop, opening drawers and cabinet doors, searching for any concrete evidence that would support my suspicions and implicate Katy Quince in a drug-running operation or any foul play toward Tina Breckenridge. Something I could go to the sheriff with and get him to listen to me. Or to U.S. Customs or the DEA.

I was to be disappointed. Aside from a high level of disorganization, I found nothing of interest except the missing set of applications and class evaluations from *Alcyone*'s last heavy-weather sailing class. Veronica Walker of Baltimore, Maryland, had been either more observant or more of a whiner than the other three students, all of whom gave high ratings to the four-day nautical experience. I glanced over the labels on two file cabinets, most of which said STORAGE, all of which were unlocked. I hastily riffled through the folders and found only files of old tax returns and paid bills, none of which were in the name of Danny Quince.

The vacuum still blaring away, I moved toward the computer and heard the mop fall to the floor. I turned with a dry throat and watched the door open. It was the shorter, bald-headed floor layer.

"Excuse me, ma'am, do you happen to know when Mrs. Quince might be coming back? We finished the floor and she promised to pay us today."

I waved my dusting wand over Katy's printer and smiled. "I understand she'll be back on the island tomorrow. You might check back then."

He frowned, thanked me, and left. A couple of minutes later I heard an engine start up. I stared at the closed door, then moved over and slid the barrel bolt into place. I would rather have to explain why I had locked myself in than be surprised by the return of the mysterious Danny Quince.

Katy's computer was an older model. I turned it on, praying it would not require a password that would exceed my high-tech skills. My prayer was answered, and I checked the programs on her Windows desktop, searching for a word-processing program that might produce some files. Or a financial program or some E-mail. I was rewarded with the last two, although it appeared that accounting was not Katy's forte. There was little of interest besides records of client billings and payments. It wasn't until I downloaded her E-mail that things got interesting.

There were five messages in the In box, ten in the Out box, and more than fifty in the Trash bin. The message that attracted my attention was in the Trash and had been sent through Blue Water Communications, one of the new local Internet service providers, with no subject reference. It included forty-seven first names and phone numbers, all with Friday Harbor and Orcas prefixes. The screen name was benj@bluewater.net. The message was brief, with no signature: *You'll have to take care of these till I'm clear again.*

I printed the message, gathered up my props, and was out of there. Next stop, a woman at Blue Water Communications who owed me a big favor. I called her from my cell phone on the way back to town.

"I'm not supposed to do that, you know."

"I know, Ruth, but the information might save a life."

I heard a small click as she put the receiver on the counter, a long silence, then she was back.

"That E-mail account is in the name of Parker Benjamin," she said in a low voice, and provided a post office box number in Friday Harbor. "I've got another customer now." The line went dead, and I drove back to town vainly trying to remember where I'd heard the name Parker Benjamin.

21

"Parker Benjamin? Yeah." Zelda looked up from the thick book of historical costumes she was leafing through. "He was busted about a week ago for selling dope. I hear he's out on bail."

Three more cherries in the slot machine.

It all fit. When Parker Benjamin got arrested, Katy took over his customers, one of which was the male model named Jerome from On the Edge. Zelda's phone rang and I raced up the stairs and pounded out a message to Angela. *Can you find out who posted bail for Parker Benjamin?*

I stared at the screen, the name nagging me from another context. And then it came to me: Stephan had mentioned hanging out with Parker Benjamin, the bike mechanic! I dialed Lily's number at the Secret Garden. Yes, she knew Parker Benjamin. He was three or four years older than her son, Sean. Parker had graduated two years ago after a long history of truancy. Parents divorced, mother remarried, father an oil tanker pilot and away from the island for long periods of time. Parker hated his stepfather and he lived in his dad's house by himself. Used to hang out at the port a lot and at Sunken Park. "He likes to tinker with cars and motorcycles. I've heard he's actually a good mechanic," she said. "He used to work for one of the garages, but I think he's got his own business now. He just got arrested, didn't he?" She hesitated. "Sean told me Stephan's been hanging out with Parker. I don't know if Tina knew or not. And for what it's worth, Parker's been dating the sheriff's niece."

I thanked her and dialed the sheriff's office. He was in and took my call. I told him what I'd learned about Katy Quince and Parker Benjamin and the East Coast student and my apprehensions regarding Tina. "We've got everything under control, Miz MacKinnon, and I do thank you for calling."

Under control? "What do you mean, 'under control'?"

"Mr. Hudson's case will be heard in due time."

"What about Katy Quince?"

"I have no evidence that Ms. Quince has done anything illegal."

"What about the list of names and phone numbers I found?"

"Just fax that over and we'll take a look at it."

"Was there any evidence of foul play on Katy Quince's bike?"

"Little brake problem," he said. "Could of happened to anyone."

"What about M. J. Carlyle's death at Brown Sugar Beach? Is that all under control, too?"

"Mr. Carlyle had a nasty accident. Very unfortunate, but nothing to get in a twist over. Is there anything else I can help you with?"

I gritted my teeth and assured him there wasn't and called Meredith Martin at the Customs office. She was far more receptive to my theories of drug trafficking and distribution in Friday Harbor, but she was in the middle of a special assignment this week that could mean a promotion. "Whatever they're up to, it's probably small potatoes. The drug market in Friday Harbor isn't exactly large."

It might be small potatoes in terms of a national War on Drugs, but if Tina was involved or found out about it, it could have provided a motive to kill her. I was on to something and no one would pay any attention! *Merde! Merde a la treize!*

I put my feet up on the desk and reviewed what I knew: Veronica, the disgruntled Pleiades student, had seen a powerboat approaching *Alcyone* when they were anchored at Sucia; M. J. Carlyle had tried to call me the night he died with information about Katy; Jerome, the On the Edge model, had named Katy as his source for B. C. Bud; and the list of names I'd printed from Katy's computer could be a list of drug customers that Parker Benjamin had forwarded to Katy when he got busted. What I didn't know was who was driving the delivery boat Veronica had seen at Sucia? Danny Quince? Where was he now?

I checked my E-mail before closing up and found three messages. The first was from Mr. Wang in Singapore: he had located *Ocean Dancer* at the Golden Lotus Marina and had conducted continuous surveillance on the vessel for thirty-six hours, but had not seen Harrison. How long did I want him to continue the surveillance? I forwarded the message to Carolyn Smith and asked how much she wanted to spend.

The second E-mail was from pacific1875@aol.com. It had been sent from the cybercafé over on Caines Street. *Tina. M.J. Katy. Who'll be next? How many do you want on your conscience?*

I read it, infuriated that there was some watcher out there. Someone who seemed to know every move I was making. And worse yet, knew what had happened to Tina. I whipped around, pawed through the phone book to find the cybercafé number, and asked the female with the little-girl voice who answered the phone to please trace who had sent a message at 2:32 that afternoon. The little-girl voice assured me that was against company policy. I asked to speak to the owner. She was the owner. I thanked her for nothing and hung up. I printed out the message and turned to the last E-mail, which served to raise my spirits somewhat. It was from Angela in response to my inquiry as to who had posted bail for Parker Benjamin. It consisted of two words: *Danny Quince.*

Another jackpot! Danny Quince had bailed out Parker Benjamin!

I buzzed Zelda on the intercom.

"You ever find out anything about those two anonymous E-mails I left on your desk?"

"Not much. They were sent locally, but the sender used public computers for all three, went on the Internet and then through AOL, so I couldn't go any further. I imagine you'd need a subpoena to trace them. Sorry. I'll be leaving in a few minutes to get the banquet permit for the Gatsby party. You need anything before I leave?"

"That's okay. See you tomorrow."

I was just about to call it a day and lock up when the phone rang. It was Paul Breckenridge.

"I don't know where Stephan is," he said, his voice full of fear.

I glanced at the anonymous E-mail that had just come in and got goose bumps on my arms. "When did you last see him?"

"Yesterday afternoon. We had an argument."

"What was it about?"

"I want Stephan to come to Alaska with me for the summer. He refused. He slammed out of the house, and I haven't seen him since."

"Did you check with his friends?"

"Hell, I don't even know who he's hanging out with now. I called Lily MacGregor. He wasn't with Sean, and she hasn't seen him. She suggested I try Parker Benjamin, so I went out to his dad's place, but there was nobody there."

"What about the school?"

"The principal checked with all his teachers. He wasn't in any of his classes today."

"Does he have a girlfriend?"

"If he does, I don't know who it would be."

I hesitated, wondering if Stephan's disappearance was connected with his discovery that Paul was not his father. Stephan had said he didn't want Paul to know about it, and I wanted to honor that request. At least for now. "Did you call the sheriff's office?"

"Yeah. I talked to Jeff Fountain. He says not to sweat it. Teenagers get mad and run away every day and are usually back in twenty-four hours. He's going to keep his eyes open."

I fervently hoped Jeff Fountain was right. "Call me if you don't hear from him tonight."

"I will. You better send me a bill for your time and expenses so far. We'll probably never know what happened to her."

"I've got some new information that might be related to Tina. One of the crew at On the Edge reportedly bought some B. C. Bud from Katy after Parker Benjamin was arrested. I've also come across what looks like a customer list Parker sent to Katy by E-mail. And I've been in touch with one of Tina's students who saw a boat meeting *Alcyone*, the boat Katy was teaching on, the night before Tina disappeared."

"Drug running," he said dully. "Tina probably discovered what was going on and they killed her. And M.J. must have found out and they killed him. Shit!"

"I've given what information I have to the sheriff. And I'll mail a complete report tomorrow, Paul."

There was a silence. "I don't know what I'll do if anything happens to Stephan." He hung up, and I stared at the buzzing phone, perplexed, angry, frustrated, and not a little frightened.

I'd parked the Volvo out front, so on the way down the port I drove by Inside Passage Yacht Sales. The door was still locked and a Closed sign hung at half mast. Was it a slow week for megayachts or had Danny Quince flown the coop?

22

I was up early on Wednesday morning after another restless night. Calico hadn't shown up for either kitty supper or a sleep-over; I hoped she'd spent the night with Henry. I brushed my teeth and stared at my sleepy face in the mirror and tried not to feel guilty for going off for the weekend with Nick when I had an unsolved case on my hands. But the truth was, I didn't know where else to go with it. Katy Quince was hospitalized; Danny Quince was nowhere to be found; Parker Benjamin had already been arrested; and the sheriff was stonewalling. I had to agree with Joy Johnson that Tyrell was probably a jerk but wouldn't have harmed Tina. I hesitated to call his wife unless I had reason to believe that she'd known about the liaison with Tina. And I didn't. As for the three anonymous E-mails, those were scary, but they were also a dead end. I hadn't heard from Paul, and I hoped that meant Stephan had returned home last night.

I replaced the cap on the toothpaste, pulled a pair of sweats over my pj's and walked up to the showers at the port facilities. As far as I could remember, I had no appointments scheduled, and I was in no mood for twenty-six asanas, so my plan was to do some invoicing, talk to Carolyn Smith about how far we were going to take the Singapore surveillance, organize some files, and take off about three-thirty. Tonight, I wanted to pack carefully for my weekend with Nick, have time for a shower and shampoo, give myself a fresh pedicure, and get a good night's sleep so I'd look fresh and dewy-eyed when Nick picked me up.

Henry, still in pajamas and unshaven, was drinking a cup of coffee on the back deck of *Pumpkin Seed* when I returned to the dock. Lindsey, in the galley, waved to me through a cabin window.

"Morning, Henry. Did Calico spend the night with you?"

"She did. And she's already had her breakfast and departed."

"I'm leaving tomorrow afternoon for the weekend. Back on Sunday. Will you keep an eye on her?"

"I'll be happy to. Lindsey's taking a few days off and going to the mainland to buy a dress for the big occasion next month. I'm not going anywhere."

"Ah, the wedding. That's pretty exciting."

Lindsey came out on deck and offered me a cup of coffee, which I accepted. I wished her well with her shopping, then took the coffee below, put on some music, and continued my preparations to meet the world. I was drying my hair and singing along with Kenny Rogers when I realized I hadn't actually talked to Nick since he'd left the invitation on the answering machine. He'd probably been busy. I stashed the hair dryer in the cupboard above the sink and got dressed, wondering exactly how I was going to pack if I didn't know where we were going.

For no particular reason, I made a real breakfast of orange juice and soft-boiled eggs, rye toast and coffee. I carried it up to the cockpit. Neither Henry nor Lindsey was in sight. The sun was warm and springlike on my face, and I nibbled on the toast and considered the consequences of calling Katy Quince and confronting her head-on with my suspicions about her drug trafficking before I flew down to meet Nick. If I was right, at best I'd get an outright denial, and at worst, if she was back on the island, a bullet in the head. Not a good plan.

At the Olde Gazette Building a lilting duet that I identified as something by Stravinsky poured from the quadraphonic speakers. I wondered if opera was gone for good.

"There's a glitch with the caterer," Zelda reported, deep in the throes of events arranging. "She ran out of fennel seeds."

"Did you find your serving wenches?"

"Lindsey's going to help. Jean Pierre's going to bartend. And I'll probably have to pass the hors d'oeuvres." She shuffled several pieces of paper with names and addresses and squinted at the one on top. "What I can't figure out is why Allison Fisher's name's on the guest list."

"Perhaps Captain Tyrell wants to mingle with the natives," I said. "Is Jared's there as well?"

She checked the list. "No," she said, watching me regard my empty mail cubby. "And I found out last night the people I've been house-sitting for are coming back in two weeks. Jean Pierre is leaving right after the party to take *Maia* up to Alaska with his brother. Jonathan and Helen will fly up to Sitka and meet the boat. So if he can clear it with his boss, I think I'm going with him."

"What about Dakota? Is he going too?"

"No, he can go out to Rebecca's ranch and hang out with Big Boy."

Big Boy was a large Bernese mountain dog currently in the care of Rebecca Underhill's son, Gregg. I gave her shoulders a quick hug. "I'll miss you, but I'd probably do the same thing if I had a chance."

The phone began ringing, and I climbed the stairs and unlocked the door. The intercom buzzed. "It's Paul Breckenridge," Zelda said.

"Good morning, Paul."

"Stephan didn't come back. I filed an official missing persons report," he said dully.

I thought for a moment. "Didn't you say Tina had an aunt in Seattle?"

"Her Aunt Patsy. I tried calling, but I didn't get an answer. I'm leaving for Alaska next week, and I've got to do some work on the boat today."

"What about your family, Paul? Is your father alive? Do you have any brothers and sisters?"

"Dad passed on five years ago. And there's just me; no brothers or sisters."

"Why don't you give me Aunt Patsy's number? I'll keep trying to call her. Call me when you get back from working on the boat."

He gave me the number, and I dialed, praying for at least an answer. Somewhere down in Ballard, the phone rang fourteen times. I listened to each ring and tried to convince myself that Stephan had just gotten angry with his dad and gone off to sulk for a few days.

I spent the rest of the morning organizing files and prepared three invoices for investigative services and expenses, including one to Paul Breckenridge. I decided to forgo lunch and work straight through. My desk was clear by two-thirty. About to close up shop, I realized there'd been no word from Melissa since she fled the Old Mendocino Lodge and the rigors of waitressing to return to the campus at St. Mary's for the last week of school. I had just begun an E-mail to her when my phone rang.

It was Nick. "Hi, sweetie," I said.

"Scottie, I don't know how to tell you this." His voice was very serious and I felt a sudden chill. A feeling of here we go again. "Cathy tried to OD on Zoloft last night. I'm at the hospital. I'm afraid I'll have to cancel our weekend plans."

I stared at the phone, speechless. Zelda came clattering up the stairs, opened her mouth, took one look at my face, and scribbled a note on my yellow lined pad.

"Scottie, are you there? Did you hear what I said?" His voice was sharp and impatient, as if I were a child. "Cathy is very ill."

I listened to Zelda clatter back down the stairs and the front door closed. "I heard, Nick. I'm very sorry. Is she going to be all right? How can I help?"

"There's nothing you can do," he said brusquely. "I just have to keep an eye on her. I'll call you later when I get out of here. Oh, don't forget to call Puget and cancel your flight." That was it.

I pressed the End button on the phone, a swarm of questions buzzing in my head. I was shocked and frustrated and angry. Shocked that Cathy would do what she did; frustrated and angry because I was always playing second fiddle. Was divorce anything more than a legal document? When did the responsibilities end? How long would Cathy's attempted suicide keep Nick at her bedside? Or was that the point of it all?

Dazed, I called Puget Sound Air and told them I would not be on the 7:00 P.M. flight to Seattle on Thursday nor would I be returning to Friday Harbor on Sunday afternoon. And no, I didn't want to reschedule the flights. I gathered up my rucksack and was about to turn off the lamp on my desk when I saw Zelda's note. "Rafie's hysterical. I'm off to play amateur psychologist."

Listlessly, I locked up my office and went downstairs. New Millennium was silent. I went by the post office to mail the invoices and picked up my personal mail. I had a stomachache and I trudged down to the port. Calico was waiting on *DragonSpray* and followed me below. I stared at my suitcase, on the settee in the main salon waiting to be packed, and wanted to throw it against the wall. I tidied up the boat and considered doing some laundry, then decided that one of the reasons my stomach was unhappy was that I hadn't had any lunch. Calico convinced me she had also skipped lunch, so I opened a can of mixed grill for her and prepared some microwave macaroni and cheese for myself. I had just begun my tasteless repast when the phone rang. I grabbed it, hoping it was Nick, hoping Cathy had made a miraculous recovery and he was free to see me. Hoping for anything.

It was Zelda. She sounded scared. "Scotia, Rafie is almost incoherent. He says he can't stay here and he can't go back to Mexico and he doesn't have any reason to live. He says he *has* to talk to you. It's about Katy Quince and Tina Breckenridge. I think he knows something."

I sat up, forkful of macaroni and cheese poised in midair. "Where is he?"

"Still at my house. Please come out, Scotia. I don't know what to do for him and he's afraid to go to the sheriff."

I was in no mood to play Ann Landers, but I sensed that whatever was bothering Rafie was more profound than a lovers' quarrel.

"I'll be right there."

Rafie wasn't *almost* incoherent, he was *completely* incoherent. He sat huddled under a white afghan on the long, wine-colored velveteen sofa in the living room of the large, Tudor style house Zelda was care-taking at Davison Head. In his right hand he clutched a wadded-up piece of dirty paper. His white shirt was stained and wrinkled. His long black hair hung un-bound, and he kept pulling it over his face like a veil. His teeth were chattering. Sophia paced in circles around the living room, occasionally emitting a frantic bark, her large white body reflecting nearly as much distress as her owner. Dakota had retreated to a far corner of the living room and lay quietly, his silky black head between his paws.

Zelda tiptoed about in her jade-green satin pajamas, brewing chamomile tea and serving it in bone china cups. I pulled aside the linen drapes and gazed out the window overlooking Speiden Channel. A flagstone walk meandered down the hillside to the dock, where a small gray powerboat bobbed in the waves. For ten minutes or so, I let my imagination roam and tried to imagine what it would be like to have *DragonSpray* tied up at the dock, to live in such a house with Nick. Zelda joined me at the window, and we stared across the water until Rafie's teeth chattering dissipated and he began to talk.

"*Lo vi todo*," he wailed. "*La noche de jueves.*"

I pulled an upholstered side chair nearer to the sofa. "What did you see on Thursday night, Rafie?"

"My car, I leave it behind the hotel. After dinner with David, I go there and I see them. They have a big bag. *En el suelo.*" He shuddered and pulled the hair closer around his face. Sophia moved over and curled up on the floor at Rafie's feet.

Realization dawned. "Are you talking about the Thursday night Tina Breckenridge disappeared?"

He nodded, staring at the floor.

"You went out to the parking lot and saw a big bag on the ground. Who was there?"

"*La pelirroja*," he wailed, bordering on hysteria. "*Y un hombre muy flaco.*" The redhead and a very thin man. In his anguish his English was deteriorating. I hoped he didn't exceed my fundamental grasp of Spanish.

"Who did you see, Rafie? Katy Quince? Or her husband?"

"Her husband. I no see Katy."

"What happened then?" I asked in a quiet voice, afraid of losing him completely. Zelda sipped her tea and stared at Rafie with unblinking wide eyes.

"The man he laugh, and say *perdón*. He say they are taking the sail to be clean." He sighed deeply. "I get my car and start to drive to home. When I get out to *los arcos*, I remember I leave my *cartera* on David's boat. So I go back." He gathered his mane of hair into his left hand and twisted it over one shoulder, then let it fall back around his face. *Los arcos* would have been the tall white arches that marked the entrance to the resort and marina.

"Did you go back to the boat for your wallet?"

He nodded. "I see him again. The man with the blue bag."

"What did the man do with the blue bag?" I asked. My cell phone sounded its peculiar tone from deep within the rucksack. I reached in and pressed the Mute button.

"He is . . . putting in the boat," Rafie said in a choked voice. "*La bolsa azul.* He put it on *Alcyone*. And he start the motor. *Y se fue.* He go away. Out of the port, very fast." Rafie began shivering again, teeth chattering. Zelda left the room and returned with a blanket. She draped it over her friend, and he huddled under the afghan and the blanket as if he were in a tent, two huge black eyes peering out the opening.

"The man that put the big blue bag on *Alcyone*. Did he see you when you went back to David's boat?"

"I do not think so. But later, when they find the boat and Tina is no there, *luego entendí lo que había visto.*"

Then I understood what I had seen.

Large tears rolled down Rafie's cheeks. Zelda produced a box of tissues and handed one to her friend. Sophia barked twice, licked Rafie's face, and resumed her pacing.

"What did you think you saw, Rafie?"

He choked and tried to speak. "*La señora . . . el cuerpo . . . dentro de la bolsa.*"

"You believed that Tina's body was in the blue sail bag?"

He nodded.

"But you didn't go to the sheriff."

He shook his head and struggled to breathe. "The day after they find *Alcyone*, I find this in my car." He unfolded his right hand, stared for a minute at the crumpled piece of paper, and then handed it to me. I opened it. The message was brief and explicit, written on white paper with a black felt marker. "Forget what you saw on Thursday night or you will die."

I stared at the death threat and took a deep breath. Rafie fumbled in his trouser pocket and brought out a wad of bills. "They leave this, too. For a, how do you say, *una mordida*? That is why David is so mad with me."

Una mordida. A bribe. Hush money.

"Even if I have to go back to Mexico, I have to tell you," he wept. "Even if *la migra* send me away. Because he will not stop. *El hombre muy flaco.* First Tina, then her brother. *No se puede aguantar más!*" Sophia leaped on the sofa and Rafie stroked her head.

In my peripheral vision, I picked up a motion at the doorway. I spun around, hand on the Beretta in my jacket pocket. But it was David Kean, white-faced and gaunt. He walked slowly into the room, sat down next to Rafie on the sofa, and put both arms around his lover. "Rafie, I am so sorry. I had no idea. And you will not be deported."

"Are you willing to talk to the sheriff now, Rafie?" I asked.

He nodded, weeping. I stood, picked up my rucksack, and left the room. Zelda followed me into the kitchen, and we stared at each other. "They need to be alone," I said.

She nodded. "So it was the Quinces. Do you think they killed Tina?"

"It would appear so. But I don't think that's his name." I reached for the cell phone, punched in the number of the sheriff's office. The sheriff was not in and I was connected to a Deputy Smith. I said I had information I wanted to give to the sheriff regarding the Tina Breckenridge disappearance and probable homicide.

"Sheriff Bishop is on medical leave. Can I help you?"

I asked for the undersheriff, who was in a meeting. I left a message asking that he call me.

I took a deep breath, dialed directory assistance for Island Hospital in Anacortes. I was referred to Patient Information. Kathryn Quince had been discharged that morning. I called directory assistance again and dialed the number for Canvas by Quince. The answering machine was not on and I hung up after seven rings. Either Katy was incommunicado or she'd disappeared down the same dark road as her husband. Whoever he was.

23

All the way out to Rouleau Road, the little gremlin sitting on my shoulder was telling me that going after Katy Quince was not what I had been hired to do, either by M. J. Carlyle or by Paul Breckenridge. I was no longer a law enforcement officer. Walking in on Katy and/or Danny Quince could be downright dangerous. Either of them could have discovered I was getting too close. They could well be the ones sending the anonymous E-mails. If they were running drugs, they'd be well armed.

The morning's sunlight had disappeared about noon, and the increasing overcast had produced an early twilight. A light drizzle was falling. I was driving too fast on Rouleau Road, overshot Meadow Road, and had to back up. At a curve in the lane, a doe and a fawn stood in the middle of the road. I braked hard, and the frightened creatures bolted into the bushes. Further on, a large brown-and-gray raccoon waddled along the side of the road and disappeared into the tall green grass.

There were no exterior lights at Canvas by Quince, and no lights or movement around the mobile home, but the workshop windows blazed with light. The only vehicle on the premises was a metallic green Ford pickup parked near the door of the workshop. I saw no sign of a second truck or the ill-fated motorcycle.

I shut off the Volvo headlights and motored slowly along the grassy lane past the entrance to Katy's place for several hundred yards, then turned off the engine and rolled down the window. I could hear the muted twang of a country and western guitar. It sounded like a Garth Brooks song Melissa had played incessantly the last time I'd seen her.

Glad that intuition had told me to carry the Beretta when I left *DragonSpray* after Zelda's call, I put the gun in my jacket pocket and got out of the car, every nerve on red alert. Stumbling twice over small, sharp rocks, I crept slowly down the lane and headed toward the shop, my shoes and pant legs soaked by the wet grass. I slowly circled the building, looking through the windows.

There was a muted crash, as if something had been thrown against a wall. I peered through the nearest window and saw Katy lurch across the room to the refrigerator, take out a can of Red Dog, and pop the cap. Her curly red hair was matted and hung stiffly around her large face. From the speakers, Garth Brooks gave one last riff to the guitar, and then the room was quiet. Katy's left arm lay in a white sling and a narrow bandage decorated her forehead. She took a swig of the beer and moved over to one of the filing cabinets that I remembered was labeled "Storage," the same files I had searched a few days ago. She leaned against the file cabinet momentarily, held the can of beer to her forehead, eyes closed. I stood motionless, watching. Katy began pulling files out of the drawers and throwing them on the floor. After several minutes she found what she was looking for. She backed away from the file cabinet, threw the file on the table, and opened it. The phone rang. She moved unsteadily across the room, out of my line of vision. I retraced my steps back to the side of the shop near the door and stood there for several minutes, peering through the partially open window. I heard Katy mur-

muring on the phone and was considering the feasibility of knocking on the door as soon as she finished the phone call when I heard her shout of rage.

"On Carrington?! With Cassi? *That goddamned SOB! I'll kill them both!*"

There was a pause. "I don't care, Debbie, I'm coming up. He promised. He swore he wouldn't see her again." Her voice was full of anguish.

Another pause. "Tomorrow. Just tell me how to get there." Katy had moved over to the worktable. She tucked the portable phone into the right side of her neck, reached for a pad of paper, and scribbled some words. "*Three* ferries? Shit! How can you guys live in the middle of fucking nowhere? Okay. I've got it. I'll call you when I get there. Can Pepper meet me at Whaletown?"

A long pause. "I don't give a *damn* about your fucking grow lights! I'll find another way to get to Carrington. And don't tell that asshole you called me."

So the Quinces, or whatever their names were, weren't just transporting drugs; they were growing them! Which, of course, meant B. C. Bud. I tried to remember where I'd heard of Whaletown.

Katy hung up the receiver without waiting for a reply and began to pound her fists on the table, head down. Sounds of her sobs filled the room for several minutes, then slowly diminished. She raised her head, sniffed, rubbed her wet eyes with her right hand. Unsteadily, her body braced against the table, she stood up. Her lips were set in a thin line, her eyes narrow. She walked laboriously to the back of the room, returned with a small dark blue canvas bag, and disappeared from sight behind the worktable. When she straightened up, she had a gun in her hand. She laid it on the table. She bent over again, brought up a box of ammunition, loaded the gun, checked the safety, put the weapon in the canvas bag. From a small cabinet near the computer workstation, she pulled out a

brown portfolio of maps, selected one, added it to the
canvas bag. She gave one last glance around the shop,
grabbed the canvas bag in her right hand, and headed
for the door. It was completely dark now. I flattened
myself against the wall of the shop, praying that she
wouldn't turn on the outside light.

The door creaked open, then closed with a vicious
slam. Katy limped toward the pickup, opened the driver's side, and climbed in. The engine started, then the
headlights and windshield wipers. The truck backed
away from the shop, made a U-turn, and fishtailed out
of the driveway.

By this time the light drizzle had turned to serious
rain. I stood by the door, wishing I'd thought to bring
a foul-weather jacket, watching the truck's headlights
bore tunnels of light in the darkness and rain along
Meadow Road. Katy Quince was off in hot pursuit of
someone, and it didn't take a lot of feminine intuition
to deduce that someone was her philandering husband, Danny.

A.k.a. the tall, thin man with the bulky blue sailbag.
I tried the shop door. It was unlocked. Judging by
the pile of crumpled Red Dog cans in the box against
the wall, the beer I saw her consume hadn't been her
first. I hoped there wasn't much traffic along Roche
Harbor Road tonight. The file folders that Katy had
pulled out of the cabinet lay on the floor. I stepped
over them and moved to the worktable. The file she'd
extracted from the cabinet and had been about to read
when the phone rang lay open. It was labeled "Space
Drifters" and contained a front-page article from the
Santa Cruz Sentinel dated February 8, 1993.

Meth Lab Busted: Rockers Arrested

Santa Cruz sheriff's deputies and state drug
task force officers raided a house on Oceanview
Lane Saturday and arrested three suspects for allegedly operating a suspected methamphetamine

lab. Taken into custody were people who were renting the property—Daniel Devine, 38, Russell Barker, 42, and Pepperdine Coswell, 36. Bail was set at $30,000 each. The three are facing state Violation of Uniform Controlled Substances Act charges. According to the Santa Cruz sheriff's office, the sheriff has been developing this case for nearly six months based on work by undercover agents and information from informants.

Inside the house on Oceanview Lane, the sheriff's deputies and the task force agents found chemicals, including lead acetate and mercuric acid, used to manufacture the white, crystalline substance. Because of the toxicity of the chemicals used in the manufacture of methamphetamine, members of the State Department of Ecology were on hand during the raid and supervised the removal of chemicals from the property. The chemicals and suspected methamphetamine residue were shipped to the state toxicology lab in Sacramento for testing.

Although a number of personal items were found in the house along with the drug paraphernalia and a small arsenal of weapons, sheriff's deputies reported it did not appear that anyone was living in the house at the time of the raid. The three arrested are members of a local band that call themselves the Marquis Space Drifters.

I read the article twice, and more of those slot machine cherries fell into place. Along with the newspaper clipping were several legal documents pertaining to the arrest, the last one being a dismissal of charges against Devine, Barker, and Coswell based on the fact that the search warrant had read "100 Oceanview Lane" instead of "1000." A prime witness had disappeared, and their lawyer had gotten them off on a technicality. The three had walked. No wonder Zelda hadn't been able to find anything on a Daniel Quince. I wondered why Katy had been looking for the file today. Was she planning to rat on her perfidious partner in crime?

In her haste, Katy had also forgotten the notes she'd scribbled on the yellow lined pad. I squinted to make out the words, which I interpreted as cryptic travel directions: "Tsawassen to Nanaimo. Campbell River Ferry to Quadra. Heriot Bay. Whaletown/Cortes. Carrington?"

Tsawassen, a suburb south of Vancouver, British Columbia, was the departure point for the huge white ferries that plied the Strait of Georgia between mainland British Columbia and Nanaimo. I'd never been in Campbell River, a small resort town on the northeast coast of Vancouver Island. Quadra and Cortes were islands in Desolation Sound. Heriot Bay and Carrington meant nothing to me. Whaletown sounded familiar, but I didn't know why.

I glanced at my watch. Eight-fifteen. Katy's comments to whomever she was talking to on the phone and her abrupt and angry departure from the shop would indicate immediate pursuit of her philandering spouse. The ferries were still on winter schedule, and the last ferry to the mainland had already left. Unless Katy was planning to charter a plane to Desolation Sound, she wouldn't be able to get off the island tonight.

I ran through the rain and wet grass and called Paul Breckenridge as soon as I was inside the Volvo. Stephan hadn't returned, Paul said, and no one had heard from him. I took a deep breath and gave him an encapsulated version of what Rafie had seen, which validated my earlier suspicions regarding Katy Quince's participation in Tina's disappearance and probable murder. There was a long silence.

"Those SOB's." His voice was low and ragged and full of grief. I knew at that moment he wouldn't agree with Jared's favorite adage that any truth was better than infinite doubt.

"They'll get them, Paul," I said without conviction. "Let me know if you hear from Stephan."

He didn't respond, and an instant later the line went dead.

I drove back to town, evaluating and reevaluating the information that had been piling up for the last two days. Information that suddenly took on form and substance within the context of Rafie Dominguez's report of what he had witnessed the night Tina disappeared. If I was reading all the signals right—Katy meeting a boat at midnight on Sucia Island the night before Tina disappeared, the list of names and phone numbers Parker Benjamin had E-mailed to Katy, the disgruntled insomniac Pleiades student who reported what she'd seen to Tina—then it was quite possible that Danny Devine and his partners in crime had simply fled from Santa Cruz and moved the basis of their operations north. And replaced the crystal meth lab with marijuana growing.

I coasted to a stop at the intersection on Tucker and Guard Streets, made a left turn and drove slowly downhill, past my office and the high school. The wet streets were deserted. At the intersection with Blair, I sat for several moments, listening to the whoosh whoosh of the windshield wipers. I was bone-tired. I pulled out my cell phone and called the sheriff's department again. The dispatcher said the undersheriff was unavailable and took my number once again. I had done all I could. Short of pursuing Katy Quince and her philandering husband into the wilds of British Columbia, my work was done.

Wasn't it?

I sat there in the dark street, thinking about Danny Devine. Despite my fatigue, I felt a slow rage building. He'd walked away from the meth lab charges in Santa

Cruz and moved his illegal drug operations north. He probably murdered Tina Breckenridge in cold blood, terrified Rafie Dominguez into silence, and possibly murdered M.J. Carlyle when M.J. found out about Katy peddling dope. And then closed up shop and headed north again. I dared not even contemplate that Stephan's disappearance was connected to Danny. When was someone going to stop him? For me, the case would never be closed until he was in custody. Then suddenly, the right neurons synapsed, and I remembered where I'd heard of Whaletown.

I grabbed the cell phone and dialed Jared's home number. No answer. I dialed the *Gazette* office, hoping he wasn't with Allison.

"Saperstein."

"Jared, Scotia. I need to talk to you."

"Come on by."

"See you in five."

Adrenaline suddenly flowing, I cruised past the theater and courthouse, turned left onto Spring Street, and drove slowly past the ferry loading area. There were three cars in line for the next ferry: the 6:00 A.M., or "red-eye," as the locals called it. The first vehicle was Katy Quince's metallic green Ford pickup. I drove past it, then turned left on Front. There was no one in the vehicle. I'd bet she was at George's. For several minutes I considered confronting her, making a citizen's arrest, and delivering her to the sheriff. But since I hadn't actually seen her commit a crime—and since what I really wanted was for her to lead me to Danny—I restrained myself and drove back up Spring Street to Blair. She wasn't going anywhere before morning.

Besides, I had another plan.

I coasted to a stop in front of Jared's office. He sat in a circle of light at the computer in the front window, balding head bent over the keyboard, pipe clenched firmly in his teeth.

"I was just thinking of you when you called," he said with a smile and a yawn. "I'm finishing an editorial on the handling of the Carlyle accident that's not going to make the sheriff very happy."

"The sheriff's on medical leave."

"I'm not surprised. He wasn't feeling well this morning. What's up?"

"I'd like to talk to your friend, the one who's writing a novel and lives in Whaletown."

"Ian Taylor? He doesn't live in Whaletown, but close enough. Why do you need him?"

"I think I know what happened to Tina Breckenridge. I talked to Rafie Dominguez, David Kean's partner. The night Tina disappeared, Rafie saw what was probably Tina's body being loaded aboard *Alcyone*. The guy he saw was Katy Quince's husband, whose name is actually Danny Devine. I'm also ninety-nine percent sure that the two are mixed up in some kind of drug running. Maybe even pot growing up in B.C. Danny's gone up to Desolation Sound, and Katy is right on his tail."

Jared gave a low whistle. "You've been busy. Sounds like I may as well put this story on hold. How about I close up here, you come over to the house, tell me what you have in mind, and we'll try to find Ian." He looked at me closely. "You've got a new haircut."

I nodded and watched him print out a draft of his editorial and shut down the computer.

A cold rain was still falling as we stepped out of the building. "Want to leave your car behind the office and drive with me?" Jared asked. "You could pick it up tomorrow."

"Thanks, but I've got to take the red-eye tomorrow. If you want to follow me, I could leave it at the port."

"Why not put it in line now?"

I shook my head again, too exhausted to explain why not.

*   *   *

We sat in Jared's worn, overstuffed chairs in front of the fireplace, feet on a shapeless old hassock. The wind was gusty and the logs crackled. Jared had poured two small glasses of Pernod, covered me with a soft fleece blanket, and put on a Keith Jarrett CD. I summarized Rafie's recital of what he saw the night Tina disappeared and what I had pieced together on Katy and Parker Benjamin. He read the file on Danny D and the Space Drifters that I'd filched from Canvas by Quince. And finally I explained, as much to myself as to Jared, why I had to go after Danny Devine.

"Why not turn your information over to the sheriff or the DEA or Border Patrol?"

"Even if I can get the sheriff's attention, which I haven't been able to do so far, the problem is Washington has capital punishment. The death penalty. Canada won't extradite to a state with the death penalty when the crime is murder unless a special written agreement is made with the extraditing state. By the time all that happens, Danny Devine will be in Argentina! Jared, I have to bring the guy back. From what you've told me, Desolation Sound is pretty rough and wild. I thought Ian might be able to give me some backup."

"I see. Sounds like an international kidnapping caper to me." Jared smiled into his glass and gently twirled the milky chartreuse liquid. "Which means Ian would love it. He was a hell-raiser thirty years ago and he probably hasn't changed. Let's call him."

Jared brought his portable phone from the kitchen, checked his address book, and dialed a number. I took another sip of the Pernod. My fatigue had disappeared. My disappointment over Nick's canceling our weekend seemed narcissistic at best. I wouldn't rest until I brought back Danny Devine to stand trial for the murder of Tina Breckenridge.

Jared handed me the phone. I identified myself and

told Ian as briefly as possible what I had in mind,
which was to go to Carrington Island and bring Danny
Devine back to Friday Harbor. And perhaps Katy
Quince as well. I didn't mention that Katy was armed
and bent on annihilating her husband.

Ian chuckled. "Jared did say you were a wild
woman. Well, Carrington Island is only about five
miles from Santiago, where I live," he said. "I know
the crew you're talking about. There's probably five
or six of them. I won't go into it now, but I've got my
own score to settle with those guys. However, you
should know that the scuttlebutt up here is that
they're well armed. There's at least one big dog, and
they've probably got booby traps and alarms. Most of
the serious growers do. It won't be easy to get in. But
I'll be glad to be your wilderness guide."

I hesitated. Short of having a professional law enforcement officer with me, I prefer to work alone.
Amateurs, however well meaning, can be dangerous.
"Ian, if you can just get me to Carrington or loan me
a boat, that would be enough."

"Don't want any amateurs getting in your way?"
There was a hint of amusement in his voice. "Well,
in case it's of interest to you, I did five years in the
Peace Corps in Ecuador and about the same amount
of time with Red Cross International. I'll defer to
your wishes, but unless you're planning to walk in
the front door of the compound on Carrington,
there's a big black mountain to climb over. Not to
mention the cougar."

Just what I needed. "Okay, you're deputized. This
is what I have in mind."

It took an hour to put together a detailed plan for
the invasion of Carrington Island and the retrieval of
one fugitive. Ian advised that I bring serious hiking
and rain gear. Ian said he would talk to a friend of
his and attempt to determine how many people were
involved in the grow operation at Carrington and sug-

gested not trying to bring a weapon, since the border was very tight right now. He had a Beretta Cougar .32 I could use. I agreed, wondering if Katy would get in trouble trying to tote her gun northward. He provided a phone and Fax number and detailed driving directions from Nanaimo to Campbell River. "I don't think you'll find any cell phone reception on Carrington, but the owner brought land lines over to Santiago. Let me give you the ferry schedule from Campbell River."

I grabbed a pen of Jared's from the table next to the chair.

"Here's the ferry schedule: If you make the 3:30 or the 4:15 ferry from Campbell River to Quadra, you'll be able to connect to the 5:05 from Heriot Bay to Whaletown. And if you miss the 5:05, I suggest a Molson draft at the Heriot Bay Inn while you wait for the next ferry, which is at 6:45. Call me when you get to Whaletown. I'll pick you up at Santiago Bay. Bon voyage."

I pressed the End button and smiled at Jared. I knew the whole idea was insane, but after talking with Ian, it almost seemed doable. Jared raised his glass in salute. "I'm a bit jealous, dear lady. I'd love to go along, but the knee I injured in Chiang Mai isn't getting any better. I don't think I'm up to climbing mountains and retrieving fugitives." He drained the glass. "Don't forget to pack a toothbrush. You won't find any shopping malls on Cortes Island."

"There's something else I probably won't find on Cortes Island," I said. "I've got to call Angela." The phone rang five times before she answered.

"It's Scotia. Sorry to call so late."

"What's up?" Her voice was sleepy.

"If you wanted someone unconscious or immobilized for three or four hours, and the someone possibly had consumed both cocaine and/or alcohol, what sort of knockout medicine would you use?"

"What are you up to?" she demanded, suddenly very much awake.

"Justice. Let me put it this way: if you were an ER physician and you had someone come in who had obviously been using drugs and alcohol and you had to do serious surgery, what anesthetic would you use and how long would it last?"

"Scotia, I'm going to tell you what you tell your clients. Let the sheriff handle whatever you've got planned."

"Please answer my question, Angela. And tell me where I can get some."

She was quiet for a minute, then said, "When do you need this Mickey Finn?"

"I'm leaving on the red-eye tomorrow."

"Most anesthetics have to be given by inhalation continuously. Are you talking short term sedation—a few minutes to a couple of hours—or longer?"

"At least a couple of hours."

"Typically, physicians use benzodiazepines like valium or ativan for sedation. They can be given orally or intramuscularly."

"Intramuscular would probably work best."

"I'm preparing a sea medicine bag to take to Alaska. I've also got some stuff stashed away. I'll catch up with you at the ferry."

The tall antique clock in the hallway chimed eleven times. I counted them and yawned and pulled the blanket closer around my shoulders, abhorring the thought of going out into the wet darkness.

Jared must have read my thoughts. "It's still raining hard. You're welcome to spend the night. And I'll be happy to awaken you at the crack of dawn."

I closed my eyes, sinking deeper into the chair. It had been a long, long day and the invitation was tempting.

"Wake me at four-thirty," I said. I would have to go back to *DragonSpray* and pack appropriate gear for fugitive hunting. The black pants and sexy sandals I'd packed in anticipation of my weekend with Nick just weren't going to make it over a big, black mountain.

PART 3

Here, said she
Is your card, the drowned Phoenician
Sailor

—T. S. Elliot

24

Jared awakened me at four-thirty on Thursday morning with what he called his contributions to justice: a thermos of hot coffee and two cheese sandwiches, Canadian Fisheries and Oceans chart number 3538 for Desolation Sound, and a book titled *Botany, Genetics and Marijuana*. The last item had a clipping from the *Vancouver Sun* tucked inside. He waited at the port building while I parked the Volvo in the ferry line and packed my big green seabag with warm clothes, hiking boots, and a dark-colored foul-weather jacket, then helped me tote it and the black rucksack over to the Volvo.

"Be very careful in the wilderness, my dear," he admonished with a farewell peck on my cheek. "It was always Holmes's belief that the lowest and vilest alleys in London did not present a more appalling record of sin than the smiling and beautiful countryside. And I'm sorry that all I had was cheese for the sandwiches. Your hair looks great, by the way."

I thanked him and promised to use extreme caution, eyeing Katy Quince's metallic green F-150 two lanes over and three cars in front of mine. I didn't see anyone in it, but she could be sleeping off last night's binge. It was 5:25. The ferry would be loading in fifteen minutes and there was no sign of Angela. I hastily reviewed the plan Ian and I had discussed the previous night and for no more than five seconds I wondered what I was getting myself into. I would have liked more background on my quarry. There was only one way to get it: I dialed Zelda's number at New Millennium and left a message asking her to conduct an urgent background check on Danny Devine and fax it to the number Ian had given me last night.

The ferry attendant motioned to the first line of cars to begin loading. Katy Quince's head popped up and the pickup was the first vehicle on the ferry. There was a tapping on the window; it was Angela. I rolled down the window and she handed me a small bag. "You give this intramuscularly. It's good for four hours. You can give two injections if you have to. It's safe even with alcohol and drugs. Read the instructions. And be careful."

I opened Angela's bag as soon as I was on the ferry. It contained a syringe and three ampules, and it all looked straightforward. I'd had emergency medical training when I was at the police academy and had practiced it on a number of occasions. I tucked the bag into my rucksack, reclined the seat, and prepared to catch up on the sleep I'd missed last night. Just before I dozed off, I realized I hadn't inquired as to the current status of Jared's romance with Allison Fisher. Or why Allison's name was on Jonathan Tyrell's guest list for Saturday's party, but Jared's wasn't.

Reluctant to risk a confrontation with the volatile, armed, and possibly still-inebriated canvas maker, I snoozed during most of the hour-and-a-half crossing from Friday Harbor to the mainland instead of going up to the passenger lounge. I also stayed in the Volvo on the B.C. ferry crossing from Tsawassen to Nanaimo, devoured a cheese sandwich, and read with interest the *Vancover Sun* clipping Jared had given me on the use of hydroponics for growing marijuana in B.C. When I disembarked in Nanaimo, I caught a glimpse of Katy's green truck again, way ahead of me.

I was glad the Volvo was nondescript, although if she
was as intent on revenge as she'd been last night, she
probably wasn't looking over her shoulder. I caught
up to her in the town of Courtenay when she stopped
at a McDonald's drive-through, and kept her in sight
all the rest of the trip up Island Highway 19A until I
got caught behind a truck hauling gravel on the outskirts of Campbell River.

The wind was kicking up whitecaps on Discovery
Passage, but large patches of blue sky were visible
among the high clouds. From the billboards on the
outskirts of town, I'd learned that Campbell River was
the self-designated Salmon Capital of the World and
had a population in excess of 18,000. The billboards
also advertised hotels, motels, banks, marinas, resorts,
white-water rafting, and whale-watching tours.

I drove into town on 19A, past the fishing pier and
marine supply stores, and cruised slowly by the entrance to the Quadra Island ferry terminal. There were
ten or so vehicles in line, and none was Katy's green
pickup. Where had she gone? She couldn't have gotten an earlier ferry. Perhaps she'd made a stop and
was taking the 4:15. I made a U-turn, drove down
Shopper's Row and back on Sixteenth Avenue to 19A,
searching for the metallic green truck. Nothing.

When I got back to the terminal at 3:45, the wind
had picked up and the patches of blue sky had disappeared. Katy's truck was three cars ahead of me, and
I breathed a sigh of relief. The ferry departed at 4:17,
and fourteen minutes later we docked at Quathiaski
Cove on the west side of Quadra Island. I stayed three
vehicles behind the F-150 all the way across Quadra to
Heriot Bay, where my surveillance began to unravel.

A long line of cars and trucks snaked down the hill
above the Heriot Bay Inn; the small white ferry from
Cortes was just approaching the dock as I came to a
stop on the top of the hill. As a veteran ferry rider, I
knew all the vehicles weren't going to get on. My only

hope was if I didn't get on, Katy wouldn't get on either.
Fifteen minutes later, I watched in increasing dismay
as we inched down the hill. Katy's truck and the vehicle
behind her were loaded, and the ferry attendant
stopped the tan Ford Suburban in front of me. I wasn't
going to get on, and there wasn't a damned thing I
could do about it! Now I would lose Katy! *Merde!* I
got out of the Volvo, locked it, and stomped over to
the Heriot Bay Inn to wait for the 6:45.

Two Molsons at the Heriot Bay Inn and a forty-five-
minute passage on the *Quadra Queen* and I arrived in
Whaletown in a more or less foul mood. I'd changed
American money for Canadian and called Zelda for
messages before I left the inn. She was into final preparations for the Gatsby party on Tyrell's yacht and
frantically attempting to replace the unfortunate Lindsey, who'd tripped over one of Henry's uncoiled dock
lines, fallen against the boat, and fractured several
ribs. Zelda wouldn't be in until Wednesday; she was
going with Jean Pierre and the Tyrells on a cruise to
North Pender Island after the party. I'd had a call
from Undersheriff Fountain, who had tried to reach
me on my cell phone, and one from Melissa. Nothing
from Nick. Yes, she'd done a fast check on Danny
Devine and had faxed it to Ian's number as requested.
Finally, she reported that according to the Friday Harbor grapevine, Allison Fisher had dumped Jared.
Something about her misinterpreting his interest in an
old estate she had the listing for on Orcas Island and
discovering that his finances weren't exactly what she
had hoped.
    I drove slowly off the ferry. There was a light drizzle
falling. The LCD screen on my cell phone announced,
"No service." I scanned both sides of the dirt road
for a telephone booth. There was none. I continued
up the hill to where the road forked, and came to a
stop. Two signs with arrows pointing to the right ad-

vertised the Arbutus Motel and the Lotus Restaurant. The arrow to the left announced the Whaletown Pub's Thursday night fish fry. A pub would have a public telephone.

I followed the dirt road, which meandered around several hairpin curves and intersected with yet another road with another Pub sign pointing downhill. At the bottom of the hill overlooking a small marina I found the two-story brown-shingled structure. The parking lot in front was full; several vehicles, mostly well-used trucks of one brand or another, had overflowed along the road. None was a metallic green Ford. The high decibels of a band playing a Van Morrison number wafted across the gravel parking lot.

There was no outside phone booth. I left the Volvo behind an ancient orange VW van that said CORTES PLUMBING AND HEATING, retrieved the notebook with Ian's number from my rucksack, locked up, and made my way across the parking lot. A sign that said THE PUB in undisciplined black letters was accompanied by a matching black arrow that pointed up the outside stairway. I followed the arrow and the decibels and the smell of frying fish and found myself inside a high-ceilinged barnlike room that smelled of wet clothes.

Fifty or sixty people occupied the room, most of them seated at tables for four or six. Nearly every table had a pitcher of beer or an open bottle of wine. The men outnumbered the women two to one, and all wore rough work clothes—heavy woolen sweaters, dark woolen jackets, worn cord trousers or blue jeans. And muddy work boots. Several men and women wore knitted wool caps pulled down over their ears. The caps reminded me of my grandmother's tea cozies. Immediately to my left was the kitchen, and taking up most of the entire back wall was a long, darkly varnished bar. Beyond the bar a crudely carved sign indicated WASHROOMS AND TELEPHONE. Several unsmiling faces turned to watch my progress through the crowded room. I found the telephone on the wall next to the women's room and dialed Ian's number. He answered on the first ring.

"Scotia MacKinnon. Wondered what happened to you. You make it to Whaletown?"

I had, I assured him, as far as I knew.

"And judging from the background noise, you found your way to the Pub."

"Correct again."

"You still want to invade Carrington tonight?"

I did, I said, if that was still possible. At the moment, I didn't know where Katy was, but I desperately wanted to get to Carrington Island before she administered frontier justice.

"Not particularly desirable," he said, "but possible. I can meet you at Santiago Bay in about an hour. Got a pencil and paper?"

I pulled the pen from the zippered pocket in the notebook and wrote down Ian's instructions for getting across the island to what sounded like the end of the world.

"Go back up the hill to the main road and turn left. At the first intersection, turn right on Santiago Bay Road. You'll dead-end at the bay. You can't miss it. We'll be waiting for you. Oh, yes," he added before I could inquire who the "we" was, "watch out for the oystermen." He chuckled and hung up.

I dialed the sheriff's number. Miracle of miracles, I was connected to Undersheriff Fountain.

"Jeff, Scotia MacKinnon. This may sound far-fetched, but I think I know what happened to Tina Breckenridge." I spoke rapidly, afraid of being interrupted. "I talked to Rafie Dominguez, David Kean's partner last night. The night Tina disappeared, Rafie saw a man loading what was probably Tina's body aboard *Alcyone*. The man he saw was Katy Quince's husband, whose name is actually Danny Devine. I don't know how this fits into M. J. Carlyle's death, but I'm ninety-nine percent sure Katy and Danny are mixed up in some kind of drug running and are connected to Parker Benjamin. And I'm seventy percent sure they're involved in a B. C. Bud grow operation."

There was a silence. "Well, that is a mouthful, Scotia, and I'd think it was far-fetched except for the fact that Parker Benjamin's attorney is trying to cut a deal and Parker has agreed to testify against Danny and Katy. And at eight o'clock this morning, David Kean and Rafie Dominguez were in my office. Rafie told me the same story he told you. I've just gotten a warrant to arrest both of the Quinces, but nobody seems to know where they are."

Fancy that.

"Katy Quince is somewhere on Cortes Island in Desolation Sound and Danny is allegedly holed up in a place called Carrington Island."

"Well, that changes things a bit. I can't go across the border to get them. We can try for extradition," he said doubtfully, "but that's a long, drawn-out procedure, particularly if they killed Tina."

I wondered how much I dared to tell him. "Jeff," I said slowly, "if Danny Devine, a.k.a. Danny Quince, were to show up in Friday Harbor in the next couple of days, would you arrest him without inquiring as to how he got there?"

"You mean, if somebody had observed him committing a crime and made a citizen's arrest and brought him in?"

"Ye-e-a-ah, something like that."

"Yes, ma'am, I certainly would arrest him."

"That's all I wanted to hear, Jeff," I said softly. "I'll be in touch."

I hung up the phone, tucked the pen and notebook in my jacket pocket, and headed for the only empty stool at the bar.

The tall blond bartender moved toward me. "Evening. What can I get you?"

"Hake Beck, please."

He put the green bottle and a pilsner glass in front of me. The dubious look he cast in my direction clearly indicated his mistrust of anyone who would waste her money on a non-alcoholic beverage. "You having dinner?"

I'd had only Jared's cheese sandwiches all day. I was suddenly ravenous. "Could I see a menu?"

"Everything's on the board." He motioned to the green chalkboard on the wall and moved down the bar to replenish the drinks of two women in black embroidered tea cozies.

When he returned, I ordered the halibut and chips, took a sip of the Hake Beck, and checked out the bar clientele in the mirror. The man to my immediate right had a very tanned and lived-in face and was fumbling in the pockets of his navy blue pea coat. He extracted several bills that he tossed on the bar along with some loose change. Then he gave me a look of withering disgust and departed. Before I could begin to fathom what I had done to offend the fellow, the barstool was reoccupied.

"Well, well, look who's here. Our San Juan Island rent-a-cop. Aren't you rather far afield?"

I glanced in the mirror at the woman at my side and tried to hide my surprise. It was Katy Quince, looking five years older than she had last night. She held a can of beer in her right hand, and a cigarette dangled from her lips. Her mop of red hair had been tucked under a frayed black Greek fisherman's cap. The white cast on her left arm sported a large brown stain. She must have arrived while I was on the phone with Ian. Or I had missed seeing her truck outside.

"Small world, I guess." I glanced at her cast. "Sorry to hear about your accident."

"Accident, my ass. Parker Benjamin checked that bike over for me last week. It was in A-1 one condition. The brakes were tampered with, pure and simple." She put the can of beer on the bar, took a long drag on the cigarette, and rested it in an ashtray. I wondered if she'd feel as confident of Parker's expertise if she knew he was ready to testify against her. At least it didn't appear that we were going to waste any time on small talk, which has never been my forté.

"Any idea who might have done it?" I watched her closely in the mirror.

"You bet your sweet ass I know who did it." She laughed mirthlessly, then began coughing, a thick cough from deep in her chest.

"Are you all right?"

"I may never be all right again. Danny D is the shithead that tampered with the brakes on the Ducati. After all I put up with from that SOB he tried to kill me."

I took another sip of my beer.

She took a long drag on the cigarette and stared moodily into the mirror.

"Danny your husband?"

"None other." Eyes narrowed, she finished the beer, and signaled the bartender for another.

"How do you know it was Danny?" I asked softly, not looking at her, terribly afraid she would stop talking.

She took a drag on the cigarette, blew out a plume of smoke, and watched it lazily ascend to the ceiling. "It all started in Santa Cruz. You ever meet somebody you just know is your long-lost soul mate and no matter what your friends tell you, you'd follow him to the ends of the earth?"

I nodded truthfully, thinking of Melissa's father, for whom I'd rearranged my entire life when I was nineteen. She continued, "That was me and Danny D the Space Drifter." She shook her head. "Little ol' country girl from Maine that takes everybody at face value. I divorced the nicest man I'll ever meet just because Danny D looked at me sideways. And how was I to know he was a snowbird with a two-hundred-dollar-a-day habit?"

The bartender delivered Katy's beer and my platter of halibut and chips, and slid a plastic bottle of ketchup and a plastic container of tartar sauce toward me. He tucked a small green rectangle of paper under the ketchup container.

"So why'd you leave Santa Cruz?" I asked idly, pouring ketchup on one side of the platter.

She popped the top on the beer, took a swig, and stared at me a long time in the mirror. Then she shrugged. "What the hell, I'm surprised you don't already know. The band rented a house and started cooking crystal meth. His ex turned him in."

"He do time?"

She shook her head, reached over with her right hand, and took one of my fries. "When it came time to testify, his ex had disappeared. At the time, I didn't think anything about it. Now I wonder." She took another fry from my plate and chewed it thoughtfully. "You know, his lawyer got him off on some technicality. Like the wrong address on the search warrant. He was just smart enough to know his time had run out in Santa Cruz, so we got married and headed north to Seattle. To start over. That's when Danny D, Drug Manufacturer, became Daniel Quince, Respectable Yacht Broker. And that was before I found out he's a womanizer and a pathological liar." She took a last drag on the cigarette, stubbed it out in the ashtray, hoisted the beer can and took a long swig. "Next stop was Friday Harbor. At the time, I thought it was a great idea. Nice pastoral island, no crime, no drugs, no easy women."

I almost choked on the "no easy women," but didn't want to interrupt her.

"When I think about it now," she continued, "I think Danny and the other two—Pepper and Russ— had their eyes on B.C. right from the beginning, and the San Juan Islands were very handy places for a staging area."

"Another meth lab in B.C.?"

"Nope." She laughed. "B. C. Bud, organic and hydroponic. Bumbleberry, Sweet Skunk, Black Mist. That wonderful stuff they pay three or four thousand dollars a pound for on the streets of Los Angeles." Her words had a slight slur to them.

"There are just the three partners?"

"Four," she corrected me. "Pepper recruited his cousin Elizabeth. She's a botanist. She takes care of the genetics and growing. Russ does the distribution in *Crying Angel*, and Pepper takes care of the trimming and packing."

Crying Angel. The gray boat the Pleiades student, Veronica, had seen at Sucia.

"And you were using Pleiades as a cover?"

She shrugged. "Danny started out doing the pickups himself and taking it directly over to the mainland brokers. Then all of a sudden he wanted to sell some in Friday Harbor, so he made a deal with Parker Benjamin. Parker said he had some rich clients on the island that would pay three hundred dollars an ounce. I told Danny he was crazy to get mixed up peddling to the bubblegum trade, but Danny's always looking to make a buck. Then he saw Tina's ad for a sailing instructor. Said she had a lily-white reputation and it would be duck soup for me to meet the boat from Carrington while I was doing a three- or four-day class. Long as I didn't cross the border, I didn't have to go through customs when I came back into Roche. Once it was on the island, Danny could run it over to Guemes or Camano or even to Seattle. Real easy, when you're a yacht broker." She looked at me slyly. "Of course, by now you've probably figured out what the yacht brokerage was for."

I blinked and almost burst out laughing. "Danny's laundering money!" Why hadn't I thought of it?

"Right-o. Dirty money coming in, a pretty yacht going out."

"After you rendezvoused with the delivery boat, how did you get the stuff unloaded?"

"Sometimes I'd call Danny on the cell when I left Sucia and I'd take the students into Reid Harbor or Prevost Harbor for a picnic. Danny would already be tied up at the dock. When they went up the hill to use the facilities, he'd unload it." She emptied the beer can and signaled the bartender, who pretended not to see her. It sounded like the harbors on Stuart Island were being used for more than romantic trysts.

"How did you get it to Parker?"

"Parker has a marine repair business. I'd call him when I rounded Turn Point, and he'd just bring his cart out to the dock at Roche, pick up the stuff, and be on his way while we were getting the boat put away."

"But Tina found out about it?"

She nodded and smiled grimly. "That bitch Veronica called her before she left and Miss Goody Two-shoes came roaring down to the boat. Said she was going to turn me in. I had to tell Danny. If Veronica had stayed in her bunk where she should have been, Tina would be snug in hers t'night."

"What happened to Tina?"

She made an ugly face, started to get off the barstool, lost her balance, and grabbed the bar for support. Katy Quince was a big girl, and for one long minute I thought she was going to fall into the lap of the burly, bearded man sitting next to her.

"Drowned. Jus' like the sheriff said." She grabbed the high back of her barstool and sat down again heavily, waving at the bartender. "But not down there, not at Sucia. Danny didn't want the body floating up. He met Pepper and they set the boat adrift and brought her body up here."

"Where up here?"

"Somewhere on Carrington Island. I didn't ask

where. Didn't care. She had it coming. I could have forgiven him everything but the women. He just can't keep his pants zipped. I'm gonna kill the bastard, I swear."

She yanked a sheet of paper from the breast pocket of her denim jacket and tossed it in my direction. It was an E-mail message.

Katy, I feel awful telling you this, but if it were me, I'd want to know. Danny brought Cassi up last night. He says they're moving in. Sorry, kiddo. Debbie.

"Who's Cassi?"

"Cassandra. His Seattle squeeze. Used to sing with the band in Santa Cruz. A camp-following slut from L.A. If he hadn't tampered with my bike, they'd both be history already."

So she'd been on her way to Carrington when she had the accident with the Ducati and landed in the hospital. Which explained the disorderly condition of the shop on my first clandestine visit. "When did you last see Danny?"

"Tuesday morning. It was World War III. I told him I'd tell everything if he ever saw that bitch again. He said he wasn't worried and took off. The reason the bastard wasn't worried was that he'd tampered with the brakes on the bike," she said bitterly. "And when he finds out that didn't work, he'll try something else. I'm too dangerous to him now. The E-mail is from Pepper's wife. She's on Carrington. Or was, until this morning. She and Pepper went over to Vancouver to check out the other grow operation there. Now I've got to find a water taxi or something."

Hooray for excursions to Vancouver. That meant there were two less on Carrington to contend with.

"Did Danny have anything to do with M.J.'s accident?"

She shrugged. "Wouldn't put it past him."

"What about Stephan?"

She stared at me, frowning. "Whadya mean?"

"Stephan Breckenridge, Tina's son. He's missing."

"Oh, God." She closed her eyes, swaying slightly from side to side. "Oh, no."

"Are you willing to testify against Danny?"

She made a grimace that could never pass for a smile and shook her head. "Sure I would, but I don't have to. Nobody has to. I'm going to kill 'im. Save the taxpayers a bundle of money." She climbed down from the barstool and lunged off toward the washroom, cradling her broken arm. It was eight-forty and I was due to meet Ian at nine o'clock. The big chap with the bushy beard sitting on the stool beyond Katy's had been eyeing me for the past ten minutes. Wondering if he was one of the oystermen Ian had warned about, I left a Canadian ten-dollar bill under the ketchup bottle and headed out to find Santiago Bay and whatever the night might hold.

25

It was almost dark when I got to the end of Santiago Bay Road, which dead-ended downhill onto a muddy beach. Or rather muddy tidal flats, to the right of which the Volvo headlights illuminated a white double-wide mobil home with a black pickup parked in front. I came to a stop at the top of the hill over-looking the bay. Smoke curled from the roof vent of the double-wide and a small blue skiff lay grounded in the mud. What now? Was this where Ian lived? Was the tiny blue skiff my transportation to Carrington Island? The rain had tapered off and a strong breeze off the water was whipping the fir trees into a frenzy. I pulled Jared's Desolation Sound chart from the seabag and turned on the overhead light. During the long two-hour ferry crossing from Tsawassen to Nanaimo I had tried to memorize the bays and inlets.

Cortes Island was larger than San Juan Island, bordered on the west by Sutil Channel and on the east by Lewis Channel. It had six bays or harbors. Santiago Bay lay on the east side of the island and Carrington Bay on the northwest. There were two islands in Carrington Bay—tiny Jane Island, which appeared to be surrounded by rocks, and the larger, more unprotected Carrington Island, which lay across the mouth of the bay. Ian had said it was five miles from Santiago Bay to Carrington. According to the soundings on the chart, the northwest side of Carrington appeared to be bordered by very deep water. The highest point on the island was 163 meters. A little over five hundred feet. Not as steep as I had imagined from Ian's description. A small, shallow cove lay on the southeast side. There was no indication of a road.

The perfect location for an illegal cash crop.

I turned out the lights, checked the bay with the binoculars, and made out the shapes of several work-type boats that were anchored a hundred yards or so off the beach. At the far end of the bay I spotted a small moving speck with running lights that slowly grew in size and materialized as a long, bargelike dark-colored powerboat with two people in it. The boat slowed and came to a stop where the water met the mud. It was towing a small inflatable.

A light came on that illuminated the long deck, and a tall bearded figure with a flashlight climbed out of the boat. He was wearing a yellow jacket, dark pants, and high black Wellingtons. He sloshed across several yards of shallow water, then began slogging his way through the mud. Was this Ian Taylor? The figure waved. As he approached the car, I made out a clean-shaven, weathered face, probably late fifties or early sixties, with a receding hairline and long salt-and-pepper hair. He was least six feet tall and wiry. His yellow foul-weather jacket had seen better days.

"Scotia. Sorry we're late." He slid into the front seat and extended his hand. It was strong and calloused. I returned the handshake, turned on the overhead light again, and gazed into smiling pale blue eyes.

"Thanks for meeting me," I said.

"I see you've been doing your homework." He gestured at the chart in my lap and reached into the pocket of his jacket. "By the way, this fax came through for you this afternoon. Is this your fugitive?"

The fax was a DataTech background report on Daniel Devine.

DataTech Confidential Report #1101901.
Daniel Patrick Devine
Aliases: Davy Daniel, Daniel Patrick

Date of Birth:	November 15, 1959
Place of Birth:	Los Angeles, CA
Height:	6'2"
Weight:	145 to 155 pounds
Build:	Slender
Hair:	Blond, blond-brown
Eyes:	Blue
Complexion:	Fair
Sex:	Male
Race:	White
Nationality:	American
Education:	Los Angeles Unified School District; Santa Barbara Community College
Marital Status:	1) To Phyllys M. Anderson, January 10, 1984; deceased 1990 2) To Callie Jean Urquhart, October 3, 1991; missing since 1995 3) To Kathryn Mary Quince, June 18, 1999
Occupation:	Musician, carpenter, salesman
FIT taxes due:	Subject is currently under investigation for tax fraud
Police record:	Charged in connection with armed robbery in Santa Monica, CA, 1993; acquitted Charged in connection with the manufacture of methamphetamines, Santa Cruz, CA 1995; case dismissed

| Scars and marks: | Has noticeable crescent scar above right cheekbone |
| Remarks: | None |

I read the report with increasing dismay and handed it to Ian. "That's the fugitive. As I told you, I believe he murdered a San Juan Island woman and is likely involved in drug smuggling. I think he's recently come north to Carrington Island, and I want to get him back to Friday Harbor to face the music. To be blunt about it, I mean to kidnap him."

He handed the report back. "Well, you've got your work cut out for you. They're not real fond of visitors over there. When some cruisers tried to anchor in the bay last week, a guy came out in a skiff and chased them off. Last night you and I discussed going in the back way, over the mountain. Morris and I talked about it some more today. It's a long way around, but it's still the best way."

"Who's Morris?"

He gestured toward the figure in the boat. "Good friend of mine. He's an oysterman. Morris has an oyster lease off the island, so he has a legitimate reason to go into the bay without arousing suspicion. Grew up here and knows these islands like the back of his hand. Used to be the RCMP on Quadra."

A Canadian cop. What the hell, the more the merrier. "What's an oyster lease consist of?"

"Just a lease with the Crown on waterfront land to pick oysters."

"So the oyster boat would be our cover?"

He nodded. "Morris grew up on Cortes. He says at low tide you can walk across on the tombolo between Jane Island and Carrington. We'll have a few hours before it starts covering again. We can drop you off on the tombolo and pick you up whenever you say or we can go in with you as your backup. It's your call."

I glanced out toward the long, flat vessel. We'd have wind and rough water between here and Carrington. That was a given. Then there could be dogs and alarms and booby traps. Cougars I hadn't counted on, but with deer around, they probably didn't bother humans. Katy said Tina Breckenridge's body had been brought to Carrington Island. If not buried, then cast into the cold, dark waters of Sutil Channel. Her husband deserved to know which, and he deserved the chance to claim the body, if possible. If I went in alone and failed—whether because of a broken leg on the hike down the mountain in the dark or because of a stray bullet or booby trap—Danny Devine would never face justice and Tina's death would go unavenged.

"I'd be honored to have you with me, Ian. And Morris, too."

"In that case, let's get started. Morris knows this old trail that goes over the mountain. I told him what you have in mind. You go over the details with him on our way to Carrington. When we get to the compound, it's your project and we'll do what you say. However, I have a friend with a float plane. Another American ex-pat who's been complaining how boring life is up here. He's standing by in case you want to do a bit of, shall we say, evacuation. He was a helicopter pilot in 'Nam. By the way, are you carrying?"

"No. I followed your advice. Didn't want to deal with a petty bureaucrat at the border. I don't exactly have a legitimate purpose for being here."

He reached into the right pocket of the foul-weather jacket and handed me a Beretta Cougar .32 automatic. "Morris and I have our own. Did you bring something to slow down your drug dealer and make him more amenable to being escorted south?"

"I did. All we have to do is get close enough to administer it with a needle." I checked the chamber on the Beretta. It was loaded. Ian reached in his pocket. "Here's an extra clip of ammo. Hopefully you won't need it."

I slipped the weapon and the extra clip into my jacket pocket. "Where shall I leave the car?"

"You can park it up the hill." He gestured behind me toward the crest of a hill, where I'd seen a dark green minivan and a rusted-out white truck. "Nobody'll bother it. Just lock it up and we'll retrieve it tomorrow. Or whenever."

The "whenever" bothered me, but I grabbed my foul-weather jacket from the backseat, put it on, and stashed the binoculars and the chart back in the rucksack. Ian took the seabag and rucksack from me and waited while I parked the Volvo and joined him at the bottom of the hill. He stared at my hiking boots, and I suddenly realized there was no dock—I was going to have to wade through the water to get to the boat.

"Forgot to bring you a pair of Wellies," he muttered, wiping the rain out of his eyes. "Oh, well, Morris can carry you. Wait here." He headed across the mud with long strides.

I stared dubiously after him as he waded to the boat, hoisted my gear aboard, and consulted with the tall, bulky figure at the wheel. They exchanged a few words, then Ian took the wheel and Morris jumped off the wallowing boat and came across the barnacle-encrusted rocks that littered the muddy beach. Involuntarily, I moved back a step.

Morris was at least six-four and probably weighed 250 pounds, although his plaid wool jacket may have added some bulk. A black watch cap only partly covered the masses of dark hair and beard. He was a dead ringer for Charles Manson.

And like Ian, he was wearing his Wellies.

Morris gave me a gap-toothed grin, scooped me up,

walked through the water as if I were a six-year-old and we were crossing a child's wading pool, and deposited me in the boat, which was named the *Sutil Maiden*. There were no amenities on the open boat except a steering wheel. I grabbed at one of the gunwales for balance and donned the dirty orange PFD that Ian handed me. The vessel was sturdier than it had appeared at a distance, and it sported a large black Mercury engine with a "45" stenciled on the top. The wind and falling tide had pushed the bow of the boat closer to the beach, a problem that Morris remedied with one push of a long pole.

Gondolier, Northwest style.

The boat ride from Santiago Bay was cold and windy, but thankfully without rain. The rising moon was white above the high, scudding clouds. Ian drove the boat and Morris listened intently while I reviewed the plan I'd proposed to Ian on the phone the previous night—a plan that was based on my training at the police academy for apprehending a fugitive on the run. I'd completed the course just before donning the uniform of a San Diego patrol officer, and I had put it to the test only once, when I was in the Harbor Patrol unit. The plan took into account the fact that I didn't want any of us to be recognized. Both men grinned when I pulled out ski masks. I showed them how to use the two-way radios, and Morris immediately appointed himself radio officer.

When I finished, Morris gave me another grin and recounted how he and his brother, also an R.C.M.P., had tracked down and arrested a nest of biker drug dealers over on Quadra ten years ago. "Of course, we were in our own territory and had a writ for their arrest. We hit 'em about three A.M., after they'd had an all-night beer bust. They were so fuzzy-headed they couldn't even remember where they'd stashed their guns. Easiest arrests I ever made. Probably the most entertaining, too, with all the mamas running around in the buff.''

Morris guffawed at the memory, and I breathed a sigh of relief as we rounded the furthest point on Cortes and moved slowly into the narrow, protected channel of Carrington Bay. Even in the dark I could see that the island was covered in dense stands of what would be fir and cedar. On the southeast side, facing Carrington Bay, the island became flatter, leveling off to a broad, boulder-studded sand-and-gravel beach and rapidly shoaling water. A dock and a ramp had been constructed in the cove. The dock and the area on both sides were illuminated by a searchlight. Thousands of oysters, more oysters than I had ever seen in my entire life, were clinging to stones and rock outcroppings. A small powerboat that looked like a Grady-White was tied up at the dock, but there was no sign of the larger powerboat that Katy's discontented student had spied—the one Danny's compadres had used to bring the marijuana south to the San Juans and the mainland. The *Crying Angel*.

"The compound's up the hill from there. You can't see it 'cause the trees are so thick." Morris nodded toward the area above the dock. "They may have some kind of alarm system around the perimeter, though trip lines and booby traps get kind of dicey when you have deer around. There's a tiny spring-fed lake up at the top. We used to come over here and camp when I was in high school. I'd bet these bozos don't even know the trail and the lake are there. And on a night like this, they're probably stoned out of their minds."

The tombolo, the thin sandbar that lay between Jane Islet and Carrington Island, was dry. Morris anchored the *Sutil Maiden* on the northeast side of Jane and used the inflatable to get us to the tombolo. Ian and Morris exchanged their Wellies for sturdy hiking boots. I shouldered my rucksack, and we walked single file along the narrow strip of sand over to Carrington, picking our way over moss-covered stones and boulders, carrying our red inflatable dinghy with a long line to tie to a tree on the Carrington side, where we could retrieve it after the tide started coming in.

Morris glanced back at the inflatable bouncing on the waves below us. He smiled, snapped on a flashlight, pulled the hood of his jacket up over his flowing hair, and began climbing what looked like a vertical trail. I pulled out my own flashlight and followed Morris. Ian brought up the rear. The rain had begun to fall again.

The trail climbed steadily, twisting around huge trees, often blocked by downfall. There was no wind here, but the rain never let up. Ian and Morris were tall enough to scramble over the huge trees that had come down, but most of the time I had to crawl underneath, and soon my jeans were soaking. Twice I tripped over small rocks or tree roots and went sprawling. After what seemed like hours, every muscle screaming, I stumbled out of the trees behind Morris onto a high moss-covered plateau. Morris focused his flashlight below, and I saw the tiny lake surrounded by boulders.

"We're going to circle the lake," he said, "we'll climb over the hill on the other side and come down behind their compound. We can't use the flashlights on the other side of the hill. They're off the grid, so there may be a generator running."

I thought about Katy and wondered how she would attempt her assault on the island. If she managed to hire a water taxi or otherwise persuade the big fisherman at the bar or someone else to transport her, and if she came in the front way, there was a strong possibility she would end up like Tina. Missing and presumed dead. I shivered and slogged on after Morris, whose stride was twice the length of mine. On the opposite side of the lake I looked at the trail Morris was headed up and cursed silently, shaking my head. It made the one we had just climbed seem like child's play.

"Having second thoughts?" Ian inquired from behind me.

I was, but I wasn't ready to admit it. My legs ached from my ankles to my hips, and my back hurt. I was out of shape and the Bikram yoga apparently hadn't toned the right muscles for mountain climbing. I could probably make it up the mountain, but I wasn't yet ready to think about the subsequent descent in rain and pitch-blackness. And I wondered where the cougar hung out. I assumed he would be as nocturnal as his more domesticated feline cousins.

"Just girding myself for the climb," I said, and continued putting one foot ahead of the other, reminding myself that a walk of a thousand miles begins with the first step.

An hour later we huddled together on the hillside and stared down at the compound surrounded by trees, silent and ethereal in the mist. There were four structures, beyond which I could glimpse through the trees the dock we'd seen when we passed the cove. If I'd been building the compound, I'd have put the sheds in a clearing, so intruders would be easily visible. On the other hand, probably the trio was more intimidated by the possibility of helicopter surveillance, which would account for the buildings nestling under the trees, a layout that made our approach easier.

Several minutes passed. Nothing moved. I touched the backlight button on my watch. Twelve-thirty. The rain had ceased and the moon was making a second attempt to escape from the clouds. We had not been attacked by the cougar, I'd survived the plunge down the mountain and fallen only three times, and all my bones appeared to be unfractured. I was cold and soaked to the skin from my waist down. I scanned the four buildings, searching for some clue that might indicate the presence of the miscreant who was the cause of my pain and discomfort.

There were no gardens that I could see. Two of the structures were long and barnlike and appeared to be windowless, while the other two were more traditional houses. One was dark, one showed a small interior light. The only sound was the loud hum of a generator, coming from a smaller building between the barnlike buildings. I guessed that the barns were for growing the prizewinning cannabis and that the other buildings were residences for the group.

"I'd like to check out the grow sheds first," I whispered, nodding toward the two barns. "If anyone's up, it's likely they're working there. We don't want any surprises when we go in for Danny."

"Morris is a wizard with electricity," Ian whispered back. "Want him to check for alarms?"

I nodded. The oysterman was turning out to be worth his weight in gold. Morris grinned, donned the ski mask, moved downhill, and melted into the darkness. The wind soughed through the branches around us, and the moon lit up the clearing. From somewhere up the mountain, I heard a quick, sharp cry, then silence. I checked my watch. Five minutes passed. Then ten, then fifteen. I was troubled by an endless list of unanswered questions, suddenly overwhelmed with what I was attempting to do. The most worrisome problem was that we didn't have a clear idea of how many people were in the compound. Another ten minutes passed, and there was a sudden separation of a tall black figure from black shadows. Morris was back, holding up two thumbs.

"Three alarms and probably eight motion detectors, and they're all useless right now," he reported. "Didn't find any booby traps or any sign of a dog." I wanted to kiss him.

"I'm going down and check the dock," I whispered, pulling on my own mask. "I want to make sure no more boats have come in." I squatted on the ground and pulled out the two-way radios. I checked my radio and took the Beretta from my jacket. I began picking my way down the trail, far more adept than I'd been several hours ago at maneuvering through the thick salal and avoiding the foot-grabbing vines and tree roots. I circled the compound along the edge of the hill and stood near the path that led to the ramp and dock. The ramp was steeply canted from the low tide, and I couldn't see the dock from where I stood. The moon was still out and I hesitated, not wanting to move into the light. A branch broke behind me and a figure moved in the thick bushes.

Merde!

I whirled around, taking the safety off the Beretta. Another branch broke to the other side of me and my legs turned to rubber.

There were two of them!

I moved back a step, heart thudding, and panned with the Beretta. Something leaped through the salal and came to a stop almost at my feet. I stared at the tiny spotted fawn that was immediately joined by its mother and almost laughed aloud with relief.

I stood motionless. The doe and I stared at each other for several long moments, then she nudged the fawn gently and they both trotted back toward the compound. No booby traps were set off, and I sent up a fervent prayer, for them and for myself, that the cougar was on the far side of the mountain.

The moon was gone again, and I moved to the top of the ramp. No new boats had arrived at the dock since we'd passed it several hours ago. Only the Grady-White bounced against its dock fenders in the waves and swell. Which allowed me to make several assumptions: The first was that the lucrative enterprise consisted of only the three former rockers, the cousin who was the botanist, and their various partners or spouses, which made a total of eight if all were in residence. If Katy's friend Deb and her husband had gone to Vancouver to check out the grow operation there, the number went down to six. Since *Crying Angel* was not at the dock, that might mean one of the partners was off on a delivery. That would leave two plus Danny and his camp-following slut, Cassandra. We were outnumbered, but four gave us far better odds than eight, particularly with darkness and the element of surprise on our side.

Twenty minutes had passed since I left Ian and Morris. When I returned to our overlook, Ian was frowning and scanning the compound. "Nobody moving around," he said. "Everything is dark and quiet."

I gave them my revised estimate of how many people might be in the compound. I wanted them to cover me, but I wanted to check out the sheds and the houses myself. Enough people had already died or disappeared in this case. And we still didn't know for sure if there were dogs. They were to stand watch at the edge of the clearing.

I stood outside the door to the first shed, Beretta in hand. Silence was everywhere. No crack of light came from under the door. I touched the door handle. To my surprise, it turned. For a minute I held it there, then slowly, slowly inched the door open. No howling hounds appeared. I stepped inside and scanned the room. The tall, leafy plants were growing on four large tables with raised edges. There was a muted thrum in the room that seemed to be coming from the sodium lights that were moving slowly back and forth over all except one of the tables. At the end of each table was a large fan that appeared to be washing air over the plants. There was only one door in the room, a closet behind which I found a CO_2 canister and a large electrical panel on one wall. The plants—thirty to a table—were lush, and each one had a long cluster of buds. Now I understood where the funds for Katy and Danny's new house were coming from. I exited the first shed, carefully closing the door, and moved on to the second.

It was a carbon copy of the first, with the addition of a long sealed room that I assumed was the trimming and manicuring room.

The rain was coming down again. I motioned to Ian and Morris, and we moved silently over to the smaller house that was dark. I would go in and check it out first. If I found Danny, I'd signal them with the vibrator on the radio so they could keep the girlfriend quiet while I used the sedative Angela had provided. I pulled Angela's little bag from my rucksack, extracted the syringe, plunged it into the ampule, and capped the needle. I carefully put both in my right hand jacket pocket. In the left pocket I put the handcuffs I'd brought.

I circled the house, grateful for the sound of the rain to cover any inadvertent noises I might make. All the windows were closed and locked, which left only the front or back door. The back door lock looked vulnerable to my lock picks and it was, although it took me so long I started sweating even though the temperature couldn't have been more than fifty degrees. The door opened into a mudroom cum laundry room that was filled with muddy boots and what looked like piles of sorted dirty laundry. It had the kind of silence that pervades an empty house, and in two minutes I had checked the messy kitchen, its sink filled with dirty dishes, the small living room, and the two empty bedrooms, and was outside again.

"Empty," I whispered. "He's got to be over there." I nodded toward the second house, which was built in an L shape. "Same M.O. as before."

Whether Danny was more paranoid than his partners, or whether the second house had been planned to be more attackproof, both the front and back doors had deadbolts. I flattened myself against the outside of the house and inched my way to the first window, which, judging by what looked like a digital stove clock, was probably the kitchen. Also locked. Ditto the windows for the long room with open drapes that overlooked the cove. That left the bedrooms or bathrooms, which appeared to be in a separate wing of the house. Ten minutes later, I found what I was looking for: a small bathroom window at the back of the house that was unlocked, unscreened, and open. I stood under the high window, trying to figure out how to get up to it. I almost screamed when Morris's tall figure appeared soundlessly at my side.

He made a stirrup of his hands, and two minutes later I was through the window. I dropped with a small thud into the empty bathroom and stood silently. There was no sound. I moved cautiously down the hall to the kitchen, which smelled of onions and fried meat. I wiped the rain off my face and focused the flashlight on the countertops, which were stacked with dirty dishes, dirty glasses, and an empty Jack Daniel's bottle. Near the sink I found a Ziploc bag with white powder, a spoon, several burnt matches, and what looked like a bag of M&M's.

I moved back into the hallway and silently unlocked the front door, then followed the hallway into the bedroom wing. The first two bedrooms I checked were empty, although both had unmade beds. I found Danny, snoring softly in the king-size bed in the room at the end of the hall. Or, by process of elimination, I decided it must be Danny, since he and the female curled up by his side were the only people in the house. Or in the compound, apparently. I stood in the hallway, staring at the two sleeping figures whose faces were illuminated in the light from the digital clock radio on Danny's side of the bed. The light also illuminated a snub-nosed revolver lying on the bedside table. I snatched the weapon and pressed the vibrator button on my two-way radio. I turned back toward the hallway and saw both my masked accomplices there, with weapons ready. I handed the revolver to Morris, took the safety off the Beretta, laid it against Danny's temple, and shone the flashlight in his face.

"Hey, scumbag, wake up," Ian shouted.

This was the man who had killed Tina and stuffed her body in a sail bag. It would have given me great pleasure to have done the shouting myself, but I didn't want Danny to hear a woman's voice. The crescent scar above his cheekbone mentioned in the DataTech report was clearly illuminated.

"What the fuck?" He started to leap up, then realized that the gun against his temple and the two others aimed at his head were real, not part of a bad dream. He lay back on the pillow, eyes narrowed, and his howls of rage filled the house. "None of you are gonna live to get out of here!" Hate streamed from his deepset eyes, and I felt goose bumps rise all over my body.

"Make one move, Danny, and we'll blow you away," Morris growled, per my previous instructions. "And you can scream your head off. There's no one around to hear you."

I transferred the Beretta to my left hand, keeping an eye on the girlfriend cowering under the sheet, staring at us with swollen, half-open eyes, her teeth chattering in fear. I reached into my pocket for Angela's syringe and nodded to Morris and Ian, who moved in closer. They each pinned an arm while I pocketed the Beretta, pulled the ampule off the syringe, and made a fast jab at Danny's shoulder. Slowly his eyes began to droop and I breathed a shallow sigh of relief. The sedative was fast-acting. As his head rolled to one side, Morris pulled the sheet aside, tossed the tall, thin, comatose figure clad in striped pajamas over his shoulder, and headed for the hallway. As he did, I heard the faraway buzz of a motorboat. It was either the couple coming back from Vancouver or *Crying Angel* returning from a delivery.

Ian hesitated. "Go," I urged in a frantic whisper. "Go! I'll be right behind you." The girlfriend sat up in bed in a naked and tousled stupor, a Marilyn Monroe look-alike. She opened her mouth but only the tiniest of screams came out. I could have used the sedative on her, too, but I didn't know how long Danny might be unconscious. I might need the other ampules for him. So I tapped her jaw smartly with my fist and watched as she toppled back on the pillow, closed her eyes, and slowly slithered down in the big bed.

I pocketed the syringe and raced out of the house after Ian and Morris. Ian was just outside the door, and the buzz of the large motor was much closer, already in Carrington Bay. Morris was a huge, dark, barely discernible figure in the hard rain, moving steadily away from the compound with his unwieldy burden, headed for the rocky shore that we would have to traverse in order to get back to the red inflatable tied to the tree. Ian was waiting for me, and I ran after Morris, praying I wouldn't stumble on a rock or a twist an ankle on a salal vine. By the time we got to the shore, the returning boat was approaching the dock. The fact that there was no light on the dock was sure to alarm the arrivals. I figured we had no more than ten minutes maximum before they found the comatose blonde and Morris's handiwork with the electrical circuits.

We were running along the beach now. There was more mud than sand, and I stumbled twice over small rocks. I would have fallen if Ian hadn't grabbed my arm. My lungs were on fire and not even the adrenaline that had been flowing for the past hour could help me. Ahead of us, Morris disappeared around the curve of the island. It couldn't be much further, I told myself, but it seemed like hours before I realized that Morris had put our fugitive down on the beach and was pulling in the long line of the dinghy, which slowly floated over the shallow water.

Morris dumped the unconscious Danny into the front end of the inflatable and we all crowded in after him. I glanced back at the island and saw it suddenly burst into light behind the hill. I held my breath as Ian rowed the inflatable over what had earlier been the beach on the tombolo, and then I saw the dark, shadowy shape of the *Sutil Maiden* drifting slowly around the anchor she rode in the steady rain.

Morris climbed quickly aboard, the motor turned over immediately, and we hoisted Danny to the flat deck and strapped him onto the litter that Morris just happened to have on board. Ian gave me a high five, and Morris released a deep chuckle as he smoothly shifted into high speed and we headed back to Santiago Island.

26

I stared at the framed sepia drawing of a reclining nude on the gray-white wall in front of me and struggled for some hint in my surroundings that would tell me where I was. The comforter under my chin was white, and virtually everything in the small bedroom was white. Sunlight flooded through the window to my left, a window that framed tall stands of madrona and Douglas fir trees. I stretched one leg and then both legs and recoiled at the stiff muscles. And then the events of last night came back.

The excruciating hike over the mountain in the rain. The mouth-drying search through the compound. The chaotic apprehension of Tina's killer and the final dash out of the compound and along the rocky beach with the sedated prisoner as the powerboat approached. The arrival at the long dock on Santiago Island and Ian's call to his pilot friend to arrange for a float plane pickup just after dawn for our "sick friend."

Danny had slept peacefully until nearly daylight. We were all exhausted and soaked from head to toe. Morris lugged my seabag up from the boat and we took turns showering and downing cups of hot chocolate that seemed to appear as if by magic on the kitchen counter. Fifteen minutes past daylight, the De Havilland Beaver was alongside the dock. Encouraged by another injection, Danny was sleeping like a baby. We helped the pilot and copilot, both looking like bit players in a movie featuring Balkan mercenaries, load the sleeper aboard the plane for his nonstop flight to Friday Harbor.

As the plane lifted off into a pale pink and mauve sunrise, I made a quick call to the San Juan County Sheriff's Department and was patched through to Jeffrey Fountain's home phone. The undersheriff, now acting sheriff, promised to be on hand to greet the float plane when it landed. I leaned back in the chair at the desk Ian used for his writing and rubbed my aching head. My nose was dripping, and I was sure the mother of all sore throats was moving in.

But there was one more call to make.

It was too early to call Meredith Martin at the customs office, so I called directory assistance and reached her at home. Her voice was brisk. Even though she sounded like she'd been up for hours, I apologized for calling so early.

"Not a problem. Hold on while I get my coffee." I listened to a faint news broadcast in the background and considered the favor I was going to ask her. I liked to think that Meredith and I had become good friends; on the other hand, Meredith was very conscientious about her job. Oh, well, all she could say was no. "I've been on the phone for an hour," she said. "You probably read that we got the big drug runner I've been pursuing."

"The Canadian fishing trawler that was in Juan de Fuca with a cargo of cocaine?"

"That's the one. They must think we're deaf, dumb and blind." I heard her take a sip of coffee. "Is this a social call or otherwise?"

"Otherwise. I'm up in B.C."

"On vacation or on a case?"

"On vacation," I lied. I hesitated for a couple of seconds, then plunged in, choosing my words carefully so that if the fit hit the shan, Meredith would be innocent of any wrongdoing.

"I'm staying with a friend in Desolation Sound. A neighbor of his is ill and we've medevaced him by charter float plane to Friday Harbor. Should be arriving in about two hours. Would you have time to make sure his customs clearance is expedited? The pilot and copilot will be returning directly to Canada. The passenger's name is Devine. There will be someone there to pick him up and see that he gets immediate attention."

"Devine," she said. "Let me write that down. Yeah, I think I can manage that. By the way, this guy's not drunk and disorderly, is he?"

"Drunk and disorderly? No, not at all. A . . . a paramedic gave him a sedative." I wasn't lying this time; my police academy training virtually qualified me to be a paramedic. "Why do you ask?"

"I just got a call a few minutes ago from Canadian customs. Let's see. They said a woman from Friday Harbor got drunk and disorderly in a bar on Cortes Island last night. Is that anywhere near where you are?"

"Not too far away. What happened to her?"

"They called the RCMP and she resisted arrest, so they put her in jail overnight. She'll have a hearing this morning and is due back here this afternoon. We're going to be waiting for her when she arrives. Her name's Katy Quince. You know her?"

"Katy Quince? I think I've heard the name before. You might also let Jeff Fountain know she's coming."

"Will do," she said briskly. "And I'll take care of your Mr. Devine. I've got another call coming in. Let's have a drink when you get back. I need to talk to you about raising girls."

I sat back, let the tension run out of my body, and was about to fall asleep in the chair when Ian appeared and led me across a small bridge to the guest-house. The last thought I had before falling into the deep, dark, bottomless chasm of sleep was that I'd had no opportunity to ask Danny where Tina's body was buried. I would have to trust that it would come out in Jeffrey's interrogation.

"Ready for some Santiago Bay French Toast?" It was Ian peering around the bedroom door of the small guesthouse—barefoot, but with his hair neatly combed, wearing clean blue jeans and a faded, shape-less wine-colored sweatshirt that said VANCOUVER ROWING CLUB. A large golden retriever stood by his side, tail wagging, red tongue hanging out.

"Absolutely," I said, sitting up. "I'm starving."

"We'll see you over in the main house when you're ready. Jared called a bit ago and would like to hear from you."

I showered again, letting the hot water soak into my bruised body, and lathered on the fragrant herbal shampoo I found in the guest bathroom. The black sweater and faded blue jeans in the seabag were mi-raculously dry. Ecstatic over the pleasure of soft, dry socks, I mused that a number of large and small des-tinies had been rearranged when Nick had backed out of our weekend date.

Kismet. Or karma. Or something.

I sat in the flowered chintz love seat in the tiny main room of the guesthouse that overlooked the upper end of Santiago Bay and dried my hair with my portable mini-dryer. The windows faced across the dark blue water to a thickly forested mountain of Douglas fir and cedar trees. Further up the shore to the north I spied a small house on the beach. I wondered if that was the cabin Ian moved to when the estate owners came up for their annual two weeks. I checked my cell phone for messages and got a No Service message. Oh, well.

In the main house, three glasses of what looked like

reshly squeezed orange juice sat on the refectory
able in the dining area. I sniffed the brewed coffee.
an was behind the large island in the kitchen, putting
riangular pieces of egg-soaked bread in a sizzling fry-
ng pan. "French toast'll be ready in five minutes.
Help yourself to the coffee."

I filled a cobalt-blue stoneware mug with coffee that
melled even better than Zelda's and added milk.

"Feel free to use the phone on my desk if you need
o check messages," Ian said. "It's a land line." I
lanced at him and wondered if he was telepathic,
hen dialed the number of my cell phone that I had
n my pocket. Which was just as convoluted as it
ounded. There was one message; it was from Paul
Breckenridge, left early that morning. Stephan had
urfaced; he had hung out with Parker Benjamin for
wo days, then made his way to Seattle and eventually
o his great-aunt's house in Ballard. Paul was getting
eady to leave for Alaska, and Stephan had refused
o come back home. "I don't know what to do with
tim. Maybe you could call me on Monday. I don't
hink there's any use in spending more money on
Tina." His recorded voice sounded listless and de-
eated. I saved the message and wondered if he would
ome to Carrington to get Tina's body before he re-
urned to Alaska.

I took my coffee cup and walked across the polished
hardwood floor and down into the sunken living room,
which had the same view as the guesthouse. Except
hat here walls of glass framed a view of mini-islands
and Tolkien-like snow-covered mountains shrouded in
mist. The Coast Range and the Silverthrone Glacier,
recalled from my perusal of Jared's chart. The house
was built on a rocky outcropping. Below and to the
eft, the top of a reef was visible, a convenient perch
or a gathering of brown and gray feathered cousins
of Jonathan Livingston.

I heard steps behind me. I turned, expecting to find

the boyish, gap-toothed smile of my courtly Charle
Manson look-alike. But it was not the burly Morri
who was standing behind me. I stared—and stared
again, openmouthed.

"I don't think you two have met," Ian said. "Scotia
MacKinnon, Tina Breckenridge."

I continued to stare, still openmouthed, at the slen
der, dark-haired woman whose likeness I had seen
only in two photos. They could never do justice to her
incredible violet eyes. She was wearing a V-neck white
T-shirt under faded blue denim overalls. Her hair was
longer than in the photos, her face thinner and more
serious. There were several scratches across her fore
head and a long, healing cut above one cheekbone. I
tried to speak, but no words came out. I tried again
"But how? And when? And why didn't you—?" I
stopped, overwhelmed.

Ian moved over to Tina and put an arm around her
shoulders. "I scraped her off the reef out here in a
big storm. Good thing she was such a good sailor and
was wearing her PFD. Anyway, the toast is done. Let's
eat and she'll tell you how and where and when."

"I think I knew something was going on with Katy
way back last year." Tina poured thick maple syrup
on her French toast and spread it with her fork. Her
hands were small, with long slender fingers and short
oval nails. The only ring she was wearing was a small
cameo pinkie ring on her right hand. "Little things
kept happening that would get filed away in the back
of my head and never connected together. Like running into Parker Benjamin a couple of times when I
went down to *Alcyone* for the debriefing with the students. And finding a dent in *Alcyone*'s gel coat that
Katy couldn't explain." She paused, cut a small piece
of the golden-brown French toast and ate it. "Probably I didn't piece it all together because I was having
a hard time keeping up with Stephan. He got a Minor

in Possession last fall and was really hard to handle. And there were some other problems. Personal stuff." She thoughtfully cut another piece of the toast. I recalled what Jonathan Tyrell had said about her not wanting to live with Paul anymore. About her wanting him, Jonathan, to divorce his wife. "And then that Thursday, I got the phone call from the woman in the heavy-weather class. I think she was from the East Coast."

"Veronica Walker?"

She nodded and looked surprised. "I think that was her name. I never actually spoke to her. She left me a message that morning. About seeing a gray power-boat at Sucia and Katy yelling at her. I thought about it all morning. In the afternoon, I recalled something Lily had heard from Sean: that Parker Benjamin was selling dope. I was at the garage in town, waiting for my car to be done, when I suddenly remembered the times I'd seen Parker on the docks right after Katy had brought the boat in. The pieces all fit together. I tried to call Veronica back, but I got her voice mail. And stupid me, instead of calling the sheriff, I went roaring right down to the boat and confronted Katy. The students had already left. I told Katy in no uncertain terms that she was done, to get her gear off the boat and never come back."

"What happened then?"

"She said something obscene, gathered up her bag, and flounced away up the dock. I locked up the boat and went back to the parking lot and drove home. Stephan wasn't there. We'd had a big argument that morning. He hated it when I called other parents to check on him, so I just called Lily. She thought he might be with Sean, but she wasn't sure. She and Mac were going out. I had a glass of wine and was fixing some supper. The last thing I remember was hearing the door open, and then something hit me hard on the side of the head. When I came to I was tied up in what turned out to be one of *Alcyone*'s sail bags. I could barely breathe, and my head was bleeding." She paused again, finished off the French toast, and took a sip of coffee.

"You were on *Alcyone* at that point?"

She nodded. "I figured out later that the original plan was for Danny to motor *Alcyone* out to deep water, dump me overboard, meet up with *Crying Angel* and set *Alcyone* adrift. Then Danny and Pepper—I found out his name when we got up here— would head north. No body, no crime, no suspects."

"When did they revise the plan?"

"When we got to the rendezvous spot, Danny changed his mind. Said he didn't want a body floating up right away, so he talked Pepper into taking me north and getting rid of me up here. Danny wanted to shoot me then and there, so I wouldn't be a bother on the way. Pepper said no, he didn't want me bleeding all over the boat and having to explain a dead body if they got boarded by the Coast Guard. He was adamant and threatened Danny. Something about somebody named Callie Jean, who disappeared in Santa Cruz."

"So they headed for Carrington," I said. "And would imagine there were no border stops."

"No border stops," she said with a little smile. "Just a fast trip up the strait and around Cortes to their little hideout. Pepper wanted to knock me out and dump me overboard right before they got to Carrington. I guess the waters out here are five or six hundred feet deep." She shuddered.

"Eleven and twelve hundred in some places," I a put in.

"Danny's plan was to shoot me and bury me o Carrington where I'd never be found." She took deep breath and put one slender hand on her throa Her fork clattered to her plate.

"I've never been so frightened in my life."

"How did you escape?" I asked.

"A storm was coming in the afternoon when we arrived. Katy and Pepper's wife were furious that they'd brought me back. Pepper's wife started crying and saying there was going to be a manhunt and they'd all go to jail. Then everybody started drinking and Danny said he wasn't going to dig a grave in the rain, so he tied me up with a promise to end my misery the next day. Then they all got stoned. About three in the morning, I managed to get loose. I'll never know how." She held out her wrists and I saw the crisscrossed red scars, still flaming red. She stared at them and shook her head, unable to continue.

Ian reached across the table and put his hand over hers. "And then she found her way down to the dock, stole one of their inflatables, and headed out. Now you know what I meant about the score I had to settle with those scumbags." There was a long silence in the room. The dog got up from his futon and approached Tina, snuggling under her arm. The phone rang and Ian got up to answer it.

"It was a god-awful night," Tina continued. "Pouring rain, huge waves, freezing cold. All I had on was the sweats I'd been wearing when Danny grabbed me from home. I didn't know where I was or where to go. It was a nightmare." She shivered and closed her eyes. "But anyplace was better than that awful island. There were two PFD's on the Grady-White, but I couldn't find any keys and I was terrified to go back to the house and look for them. So I took the inflatable. It had a little two-and-a-half-horsepower Nissan that was fine for a while, but as soon as I got out of the bay and into the channel, the seas got bigger and bigger. I couldn't see anything. I must have driven the inflatable right onto the reef out here. It flipped over, and I don't remember anything else until Ian found me."

Ian hung up the phone and returned to the table.

"I always have my coffee in that alcove there," he said, pointing to the corner window. "There's usually some mergansers hanging about and lots of gulls. When I looked through the glasses and saw her that morning, I thought I'd discovered some exotic new form of wildfowl."

"And nobody ever came looking for you?" I asked, incredulous. If Danny had taken so much trouble to bring her north, why did he let her go so easily?

"Oh, they most certainly did," Ian said with a chuckle "But as soon as she told me her story, I threw the tattered PFD in the bay. And that afternoon, we saw both the *Crying Angel* and the Grady-White out searching. They even tied up at the dock down here and came knocking at the door. There were two of them. The tall one said his wife had been caught out in the storm in her boat and he was desperate to find her. Put on a really good act. When I went over to Cortes to get the mail the next day, the couple in the double-wide told me they'd found both the inflatable and the PFD and notified the Coast Guard." He shrugged and drained his coffee cup. "There were some helicopters flying over for a couple of days. The Grady-White cruised up and down for about a week, and then that was it."

Tina had twice escaped a watery death and twice been given up for drowned. It gave me goose bumps.

"And you never let anyone know."

She avoided my eyes and stared into her empty coffee cup. "I let Peg know. Peg O'Reilly. She's Stephan's godmother, and she promised to keep an eye on him for me."

Which explained Peg's exhortation that I let sleeping dogs lie.

"She told me M.J. had hired you and you were looking for me. I think she even . . . sent you an E-mail or something."

So Peg was the anonymous E-mail sender! "She

sent me three E-mails! And each one got more threatening. Peg would make a good terrorist. What's the significance of her address: *pacific1875?*"

"Peg's great uncle was lost in a shipwreck off the coast back in the nineteenth century. The vessel he was on was the *Pacific*. Peg thinks it's a great address."

"By the way," Ian said, "that phone call was from Morris. His sister is a waitress at the Pub. Seems as if somebody from Friday Harbor by the name of Katy got drunk and disorderly last night and attacked a poor oysterman."

Tina smiled.

"You didn't hear it from me," I said, "but I understand there's going to be a welcoming committee waiting for Katy when she gets back."

The phone rang again. This time it was Jared, for me.

"Congratulations," he said. "You accomplished your mission. Where'd you find those two flyboys? They're a real piece of work!"

"Danny's back?"

"He's back. Locked up in the jail. You know," he said, his voice half teasing, half serious, "you could have called me when you called Jeff. We don't have big stories like this one every day of the week. Is Katy coming back? The sheriff is going to need her testimony to hold the bastard."

"Oh, God, Jared, I'm sorry. I forgot to call. After all night on a wet mountain, my brain was mush. I don't think I'd make a great bounty hunter." I glanced into the kitchen. Tina was stacking our breakfast dishes, and Ian's arm was around her waist. I started to tell Jared that Tina was alive and well, but now was not the time, particularly since I didn't know if Tina was planning to go back. "I believe Katy will be back, although not necessarily voluntarily. In fact, I've heard rumors that she may be showing up in Friday

Harbor sometime today. Check with Meredith Martin. Maybe you can get a photo of her arrival. Oh, yes, the flyboys are friends of Ian's."

"I might have known. Call me when you get back."

It was almost noon. I wanted to go home. My job was done. I had found Tina and I had found her kidnapper and would-be murderer. Rafie had already given his statement, and I hoped that both Tina and Katy would also testify. But as I moved toward the couple now standing in front of the big windows in the living room, innumerable unanswered questions nagged at me: Why had Tina never gotten in touch with her husband or son? Why had she let them think she was dead? If she went back, would she try to resume her liaison with Jonathan Tyrell? Or divulge to Jonathan that Stephan was his son? Or tell Paul? Had Danny had a hand in M.J.'s death? And, most important, if Tina didn't want Paul to know where she was now, was I going to tell him?

27

I arrived back in Friday Harbor on Saturday night after a twelve-hour trip from Santiago. I'd wanted to come back the day before, but given the three ferries whose various schedules had to be synchronized, there was no way.

On Saturday morning Ian ferried Tina and me over to the beach at the head of the bay where I'd left the Volvo, and then he followed us in his rusted-out white truck to the ferry terminal. Friday's sunshine had disappeared and the sky was overcast. There was a long embrace between Ian and Tina before we boarded the ferry for Quadra Island. Ian and I exchanged firm handshakes, and I expressed sincere words of gratitude for his and Morris's participation in Thursday night's pursuit.

"Morris had the time of his life," Ian said, laughing. "His wife insisted he get out of law enforcement, but there's nothing he likes better than a good chase. I hope your prisoner gets life imprisonment for what he did to Tina, but it's not likely. I'll see you both in Friday Harbor." Ian gave Tina another quick hug, climbed into his truck, and was gone.

Once on Quadra, we drove in silence the ten miles or so to Quathiaski Cove and were second in line for the ferry to Campbell River. While we waited, Tina left the car and made a phone call. The traffic was

light in Campbell River and somewhere between there
and Courtenay, Tina began talking. Her emotional
and fragmented meanderings and outbursts answered
most of my nagging questions.

"I know you want to know why I didn't tell Paul
and Stephan where I was," she began in a semi-angry,
semi-defensive tone.

"I'm sure you must have had your reasons."

"I would have . . . eventually. I just needed some
time." She stared out the window, then continued.
"The week before they kidnapped me was one of the
worst of my life. Stephan was totally out of control,
he actually threatened me with a knife. All because I
said I didn't want him hanging out with Parker Benjamin and his friends. My own son!"

"Raising a teenager is an endless challenge," I murmured. "And you have to make up the rules as you
go along." Compared to Tina, I'd been lucky with
Melissa, because I'd had Albert to help through the
really hellish years. And there's no doubt that disci-
pline commands more respect when it comes from a
male.

"It's worse because Stephan was home-schooled.
He's such an innocent, he's easily led astray. When I
had to take a stand with him, his father either wasn't
around or wouldn't back me up. And on top of it all,
Paul was going to bring his mother over from Sedro
Wooley to live with us and then take off for Alaska.
I thought I was going to go crazy!"

I murmured a sympathetic response, and Tina was
silent for a while. South of Courtenay, the traffic grew
heavier. A light rain began to fall, and I concentrated
on staying in the correct lane to get around Nanaimo.
North and south of Malahat, the highway wound along
the Strait of Georgia, past rustic motels and waterside
restaurants. I mused on how nice it would be to spend
time up there with Nick. Not just a long weekend,
which was all we ever seemed to get, but to take off

on *DragonSpray* and explore the whole inside passage. Or even a car trip. We could drive over the mountains to the west coast of Vancouver Island, walk the wide sand beach, and watch the huge breakers rolling in. But who knew if or when I'd see him again. He'd only left one message since our brief conversation on Thursday. Did Cathy move back into the condo with him so he could "keep an eye on her"? Suppose she decided to move to Seattle permanently? The mere thought made me nauseous.

"In a strange way, the whole kidnapping incident gave me some breathing space." Tina was speaking again, more slowly now. "I didn't have to make up my mind to do anything; it was all done for me. I was so angry at both Paul and Stephan, I didn't even care if they thought I was dead. Served them right! They didn't appreciate me when I was there." She paused, then added, "You haven't mentioned him, but I know about M.J. falling off the cliff. It was really awful, and I thought about going back when it happened. But M.J. is dead. I can't do anything for him."

"I don't know if Peg O'Reilly knew, or if she told you," I said. "Stephan left home on Wednesday, and Paul didn't know where he was until yesterday. I believe they had an argument about Stephan going to Alaska with Paul."

She caught her breath. "Peg didn't tell me. Is he back home?"

"He's in Seattle, with your aunt. He says he's not coming back to the island."

"Aunt Patsy is a treasure. She took us in when my mom divorced my dad. We didn't have anywhere else to go." She was quiet for a long time after that. By five o'clock we were approaching Victoria and I made a left turn on McKenzie, which would allow me to bypass downtown Victoria at rush hour.

Thirty minutes later we were in Sidney and I pulled into the ferry line, creeping past the U.S. Customs shed. When queried as to the purpose of our visit to Canada Tina and I had both replied "vacation"—without going into any details about her extraordinary departure—then moved on to buy our ticket to Friday Harbor and join the lines of cars that were already loading onto the ferry.

I didn't know when I would see Tina Breckenridge again, and what she did with her life was none of my business. I had no idea if she was ever going to tell Paul that Stephan was not his son. But since she was very much alive, there was no need for me to have the small wooden box of mementos that Stephan had brought to my office.

"I have a personal item of yours, Tina, that Stephan gave to me for safekeeping. I'd like to get it back to you. If you're going to be in town for a while, perhaps you could come by my office."

She turned and stared at me and gave a great sigh. "It's the stuff that was in the safe-deposit box, isn't it? Stephan knows, then? About Jonathan and me?"

I nodded. "Jonathan was one of the people I talked to when I was trying to find an explanation for your disappearance."

"Did you tell him about Stephan?"

I shook my head.

"I'd like to get the box back," she said. "Could I pick it up tomorrow? I know it's Sunday, but I was thinking of going down to Seattle tomorrow night."

"Come by the office about noon. I'll meet you there."

"Thanks."

"Are you going to let Jonathan know you're back?" It was none of my business, but I asked anyway.

"Is he still around?"

I thought about the surprise party Zelda was arranging for Helen Tyrell on Saturday night. And the plans for an Alaska cruise. "He's anchored at Roche Harbor."

"I'm going to tell him about Stephan. But I don't want anything to do with him anymore. That's one of the things I got clear on while I was at Santiago. I was trying to hold on to something that happened a long time ago." She closed her eyes and tears slid down her face. "I really don't belong in his life." She wiped away the tears with her sleeve. "But I am going to leave Paul . . . and . . . and get a divorce. I never thought I could do it. It was so awful when my parents divorced. But I can't pretend anymore."

"Ian appears to be very fond of you," I said. The ferry attendant motioned and we drove onto the ferry.

"He is. The people that own the house he caretakes are coming up in a few weeks and he's going to come down to Seattle. He says he's been hiding from the world long enough. He wants to see me. Who knows? Something good might happen. And if Aunt Patsy will have both of us, I think I'll move down to Ballard until Stephan graduates. I can always do the sailing school from Seattle." She opened the car door. "Let's go upstairs. I need to find a restroom."

We arrived in Friday Harbor at seven-thirty. Tina and I sat in silence for the thirty minutes it took to get past the overly conscientious Customs agent. Fortunately for Tina, the agent didn't ask for identification. Peg O'Reilly was waiting for Tina in front of the ice cream parlor. It was almost nine o'clock by the time I parked the Volvo in the lot, loaded my gear in the dock cart, and dragged my weary body down to G-73 and *DragonSpray*'s cozy cabin.

The docks were deserted, and only Calico was waiting when I climbed aboard my floating home. *Pumpkin Seed* was dark. I recalled my last telephone conversation with Zelda: Lindsey had tripped over one of Henry's dock lines and broken something. I hope Zelda had located, bribed, or otherwise coerced a replacement serving wench for Jonathan Tyrell's Gatsby party.

My answering machine's digital window announced four messages. I listened to them only to be sure there were no new crises: Melissa, reiterating her intention to visit me in Friday Harbor; Jewel Moon, querulously reminding me I hadn't returned her call; Nick, asking where I was. And finally, a garbled message from Zelda about Abigail going out to American Camp and taking a photograph of Mac MacGregor's truck. All would have to wait until the morrow, even Nick's. I couldn't have spoken a complete sentence if my life depended on it.

I opened a can of Whiskas mixed grill for Calico, washed my tired and grubby face, and struggled into my flannel pj's. Ten seconds later I was asleep, and for the remainder of the night, I clawed and stumbled my way up a dark, wet mountain, relentlessly pursued by a huge golden cougar.

I awoke at nine o'clock on Sunday morning, deeply regretting that I'd promised to meet Tina at the office. Neither my body nor my mind wanted to face the world, not even after a long, hot shower. The day was bright with spring sunshine, though, and I dressed in clean blue jeans and my favorite St. Ann's Bay sweatshirt and locked up *DragonSpray*. Calico leaped to the cabin top and settled in for her morning sunbath. The curtains were drawn on *Pumpkin Seed*, and neither Henry nor Lindsey appeared. At the Bakery, I picked up a latté and a cinnamon roll and sauntered slowly up the hill, praying I wouldn't run into anyone I know until my psyche had returned to normal. The last thing I was prepared for was the pandemonium I encountered when I arrived at the Olde Gazette Building.

New Millennium reverberated with the overture from *The Marriage of Figaro* while Dakota and his winsome poodle companion Sophia played tug-of-war with what, when I had last been in the office, was a recognizable red fleece futon. I spied the stiff backbone and the long white plait that belonged to Abigail Leedle, ensconced on a tall stool at the worktable near the supply closet. She was sorting through a mountainous pile of black-and-white photos.

Zelda, attired in oversize blue denim overalls, a flowered pink shirt, and magenta zoris, was on the phone. Her hairstyle could only be described as windblown. "I don't give a rat's ass what time *Maia* is supposed to weigh anchor," she snapped. "I want my bags back here before you leave." She slammed down the phone and whirled to face me with a large grin.

"I'm not going to Alaska," she announced over the din.

"Why not?" I inquired, zigzagging my way around a number of boxes and tugging canines toward the coffee and the mail cubbies. I retrieved three pink message slips and a large manila envelope from my cubby. The only clean coffee cup was a blue one that said, DIVERS DO IT DEEPER.

"Because Jean Pierre treated me like the hired help and spent the whole evening coming on to some blond twit in fuck-me shoes and a red dress cut down to her navel. Besides, I got seasick."

"Sitting at the dock?!"

"They took *Maia* out for a midnight cruise in Haro Strait and I barfed for two hours."

"Sounds like you've made a wise decision. Did the celebration go all right otherwise?"

She shrugged. "Mostly. Except the guest of honor didn't show."

I stared at her. "Helen Tyrell?"

She nodded. "Called about eleven o'clock and said she'd missed the float plane from Seattle."

"That must have put a damper on the festivities."

"I'm not sure anyone noticed. It was pretty weird,

people just eating and drinking and drifting around from stateroom to stateroom. I don't think half of them even knew who Jonathan was."

So Daisy had not shown and Gatsby was alone in his crowd of guests on the classic old yacht. The parallel was ironically obvious.

"By the way," I asked, "to what do we owe the honor of this visit from darling Sophia?" I braced myself against the onslaught of her large curly white body as she fishtailed away from Dakota and into the back of my knees.

"Rafie and David are leaving for Cancún tomorrow. And then they're going to P.V. to spend some time with Rafie's father, who he hasn't seen in thirty years. So Shel and I are watching Sophia."

"You and Shel?"

"Yeah. He's off work for a month, and I'm staying at his aunt's place at the Cape till I find a new place to house-sit. And, boss?"

"Yes?"

"I want you to know that I'm going to go on with the events arranging, but I still want to do my graphics stuff and your computer research."

Why I felt relieved that this emotional hurricane would continue to be around, I'm not sure, but I did. Abigail climbed down from her stool, carried a tall stack of photos to Zelda's desk, and exhaled deeply.

"Morning, Scotia."

"Morning, Abigail. Nice to see you back in the world."

"Yes, well, we won, you know. The catalog miscreants left, the whole kit and caboodle, on the red-eye on Friday."

"How did that come about?"

"Guess they just decided this wasn't the photographic paradise they hoped for," she said in a silky voice. "Edie the Ogre was heard blathering about scenes from *Deliverance*. But the photographer will still have to come back and face charges."

"Soliciting favors from the commissioner's niece? Or was it his daughter?"

"Niece." She dumped the stack of photos on Zelda's desk. "I've got to have these scanned and get the .tif files to my editor Monday. Is that doable?"

Zelda nodded. "Not a problem."

"Good. I'm going home, then. I want to enjoy my new carpet. Don't forget to tell Scotia about Mac." I watched our infamous ex-con gather up the remainder of the photos and stomp out the door.

"New carpet? Mac MacGregor? What have I missed?"

"Have a seat, boss. This is a biggie." She smiled a Cheshire cat smile, crossed one leg over the other, and leaned back. "You remember that Abigail got arrested on Friday morning. The same day that M.J. fell to his death."

"Okay. I wasn't keeping track, but if you say so."

"The reason she got so mad that day and lit into the On the Edge crew was that she had been at the redoubt before dawn, all set up for a perfect shot of the foxes when the sun came up. She was just sitting in the long grass when this truck pulls up and parks and these three big guys come tromping down the path. They even knocked over her tripod and broke it. Apparently they didn't see her. They were carrying something, and she thought it was the On the Edge crew, so she took a photo of the men and of their truck. She was going to file a complaint with the Park Service because no one is supposed to be in the park before daylight."

"What about her?"

"She's got a special permit from the ranger. He's her grandson."

"I see. Where are we going with this?" I was tired and impatient and still ached all over.

"She couldn't get her tripod set up again, so she gave up and trucked all her stuff back to the car and was about to leave when the vans from On the Edge pulled up. Edie was with them, and she let her dog loose and it took off across the prairie toward the fox burrows. Abigail got into it with Edie, who called the sheriff, and the rest is history." Zelda paused for effect. "Now comes the good stuff. Abby didn't get the roll of film developed until this last Thursday. When she saw what she had, she took the photos to the acting sheriff and guess whose truck was out at American Camp before daylight the day M.J.'s body was found?"

The light came on, very brightly. "Mac MacGregor's?!"

"Very good. And guess who was with him?"

"His two buddies from the Hunting Club."

"Right again. Jeff Fountain was already watching the trio after one of them was overserved at George's earlier in the week and was bragging as to how Mac had taught M.J. some manners. So he brought Kenny and Al in and had a persuasive chat with them. I think it was Kenny who finally admitted that they trailed M.J. out to Eagle Cove when he met with Edie, and then followed him back to town and beat him up. And when M.J. tried some fancy karate kicks, Mac hit him with a hammer he had in the truck."

Edie was right. It was a scene from *Deliverance*.

"And the next morning they had to get rid of the body," I said.

She nodded. "When the acting sheriff got a search warrant, he went out to Mac's place and searched the truck. Mac hadn't even bothered to get rid of the hammer. The blood on it matched M.J.'s perfectly. Mac's hearing is Monday."

I was speechless—although given Mac's history, it should not have been a surprise. Meredith and Joy had both been right. Unless Mac hired a very clever attorney, it sounded like Lily wouldn't have to wait until Sean graduated for some peace of mind.

"Pretty bizarre, eh?"

"Unbelievable. Now tell me about the carpet."

"Oh, the carpet. Well, the reason Abby didn't mind getting arrested was that she was having the house recarpeted and she wanted a place to stay."

New Millennium's phone rang. I fought back a hysterical giggle and climbed the stairs, my calf muscles objecting with every step.

I unlocked the door, turned on the lights and heat, and hung up my jacket, feeling that perhaps the planets had begun revolving around the sun at a slightly different angle while I was away. I stared at the pink message slips that were mostly a repeat of the ones I'd listened to last night. Curiously, I felt no compunction to call Nick, but I wondered if Jared had an update on my "sick friend" from Carrington. One of his editors answered: Jared was talking with the undersheriff, did I want to hold? I did. I leaned back in my chair, propped my feet on the desk, and watched the maple leaves outside the window gently undulating in the morning breeze. Across the street, a group of raucous young women in white shorts and Friday Harbor High School sweatshirts were about to board a big yellow school bus.

"Scotia, you're back! Just talked to Jeff Fountain. Says it's the funniest case he's ever done. Danny D was denying everything and screaming about being kidnapped by three men in ski masks and suing for false arrest when who arrives at the sheriff's office, escorted by Meredith Martin, but Katy Quince. She thinks her hubby is still up on Carrington and has this long tale of kidnapping and murder and drug dealing. While Jeff is taking *her* statement, he gets a call from Tina Breckenridge, who's on her way back. With you, as it turns out. And you, my dear, orchestrated the whole thing." He began to laugh. "I think it's going to take Jeff a week to sort it all out. Meanwhile, our front-page story will sell some newspapers this Friday!''

He wanted to get together with me, but was leaving the next day to go down to San Francisco for the annual gathering of the Baker Street Irregulars, a dedicated group of Sherlock Holmes buffs. We agreed to meet for a drink after work. I glanced back at the message slips and idly read the one from my Bikram yoga instructor advising that the classes were being rescheduled for four in the afternoon. I made an executive decision that I had subjected myself to a sufficient amount of physical torture for the month and threw the message slip away. From below, Mozart was replaced by Verdi. Zelda shouted at the dogs, then I heard the door open downstairs. I wondered if it was the arrival of Zelda's gear from *Maia* since Tina wasn't due to arrive for another hour, I turned to the computer and was about to go on-line when I heard quick footsteps on the stairs.

"Mom? Aren't you even going to say hello?"

I whirled around and stared at Melissa, her golden-brown eyes shining, blond hair shorter than it had ever been, smiling an anxious smile.

"Melissa!" I stood up and hugged her. "What are you doing here?"

"I kept calling and you were never in and didn't return my calls. You're not still angry with me for going to Mendocino, are you?"

"I am not angry with you, Melissa. You're old enough to live your own life."

"I'm glad." She folded her long, lanky body into the wicker chair by the desk and looked me over. "Great haircut, Mom. You look just like Meg Ryan."

I laughed. "In my dreams, sweetie. So what brings you to Friday Harbor?"

"I just finished finals, and a friend of mine and her

parents were going to Victoria, so I hitched a ride and got off the ferry here."

"How did the finals go?"

"I did okay except for calculus. I just wasn't ready for the exam. My instructor was really nice. He's going to give me an Incomplete and I can redo the final next semester."

"What are your plans for the summer? I understand they're hiring out at Roche Harbor."

"I don't think so, Mom. Last week I met this really cool girl from Colorado. She says I can work as a wrangler on her dad's guest ranch starting in about two weeks. What do you think?"

"Sounds fascinating," I said. My intercom buzzed. It was Zelda, who usually just shouted up the stairs. "You have a delivery from the Secret Garden," she informed me. "He's going to bring it up. I'm on the phone with Shel."

The stairs creaked and a gangly young man in trousers that were about to succumb to gravity brought in a long silver-white box.

"Hi," he said. "I'm Sean. Mom's had this order for about two days and wanted you to have it."

"Thanks, Sean." I stared at the box. Sean cast a wistful glance at Melissa and backed out of the room.

"Aren't you going to open it?" Melissa asked.

I pulled off the cover. There were a dozen of them, deep red and long-stemmed. I touched one of the moist petals. Melissa stared, openmouthed. "Wow! Red roses! Do you have an admirer or what?" She reached for the card and read it aloud: "Profuse apologies. Can I make it up to you with a week on the north shore of Oahu? Please call me. Love, Nick."

"Hawaii. Is that cool! Are you going to go?"

Before I could answer, the phone rang and I absentmindedly pressed the speaker phone button. It was Jared.

"Scotia, I'm about to make reservations in San Francisco for the Baker Street reunion. I thought might drive down, take the road along the coast Would you like to go with me?"

Melissa began laughing. "Well, Mom? What are you going to do?"

Sharon Duncan

DEATH ON A CASUAL FRIDAY
A Scotia MacKinnon Mystery

Meet Scotia MacKinnon, a tough, sexy ex-cop living on San
Juan Island and juggling a boyfriend, a complicated family
life, a sleuthing career—and the murder of a female client.

"You'll love this snappy mystery debut."

—Dorothy Cannell

"Scotia MacKinnon is tough, clever, interesting,
and believable."

—Carolyn Hart

0-451-20398-4

To order call: 1-800-788-6262